Tools of Ignorance: Lisa's Story

Book Two in the Clarksonville Series

Barbara L. Clanton

Regal Crest
Young Adult Books

Port Arthur, Texas

Copyright © 2010 by Barbara L. Clanton

All rights reserved. No part of this publication may be reproduced, transmitted in any form or by any means, electronic or mechanical, including photocopy, recording, or any information storage and retrieval system, without permission in writing from the publisher. The characters, incidents and dialogue herein are fictional and any resemblance to actual events or persons, living or dead, is purely coincidental.

ISBN 978-1-935053-40-8
1-935053-40-X

First Printing 2010

9 8 7 6 5 4 3 2 1

Cover design by Donna Pawlowski

Published by:

Regal Crest Enterprises, LLC
4700 Highway 365, Suite A, PMB 210
Port Arthur, Texas 77642

Find us on the World Wide Web at
http://www.regalcrest.biz

Printed in the United States of America

Acknowledgments

Thanks once again to the great folks at Regal Crest—Cathy LeNoir, Mary Phillips, J. Robin Whitley, and Donna Pawlowski. Collectively, we make a great team. Thanks also to my awesome beta readers Sheri Milburn, Vicky Snyder, and Diana Schnitzer for catching inconsistencies, subtleties, and rough spots. Thanks, as always, to my folks Paul and JoAnne Clanton, my "in-laws" Mamie and Joe Weathers, my brothers John and Paul and their respective families for remaining supportive of my writing. And thanks, finally, to my shelter, Jackie Weathers, who is my sanctuary in a very noisy world.

Dedication

For Jackie Weathers
who continually reminds me not to sweat the small stuff,
but who's always by my side for the big stuff.

Chapter One

Just a Catcher

LISA BROWN PICKED up the phone in her room and hesitated. Her fingers hovered over the keypad. With a deep breath for courage, she punched in the memorized phone number.

"Oh, my God," Lisa fell back against the pillows on her bed. Why was asking Marlee to hang out so freakin' difficult?

"Hello?"

"Marlee? It's Lisa." *Duh, state the obvious.*

"Lisa Brown, world's greatest catcher. What's up?"

Lisa smiled at her pitcher's praise. "That's what I was going to ask you. Some of us from the team are going to the Roxy tonight. They finally changed the movie. And, we'll probably get some ice cream at Stewart's after." She held her hand over the mouthpiece and blew out a sigh. She pulled her long dark braid over her shoulder and twirled the end.

"Sounds like fun. But Bobby's coming over and we're...well, actually, I don't know what we're doing, but he's coming over, and we're doing something. Sorry."

Lisa knew that Marlee had a boyfriend, but Lisa also knew it was only a matter of time before Marlee dumped the boyfriend and looked at her as more than just a catcher. Lisa had really good gaydar, and Marlee shot Lisa's gaydar to maximum ping.

Lisa tried to hide the disappointment in her voice when she said, "Okay. That's cool." She wasn't sure what else to say, but added, "Just figured I'd try. Maybe next time, eh?"

"Maybe we can play catch tomorrow. I gotta work on my stride for that stupid rise ball. I'll call you, okay?"

Lisa smiled. All was not lost. "All right. Cool. I'll talk to you tomorrow. See ya." She leaned forward to hang up the phone and blew out a sigh of relief as she fell back into the pillows. She only needed one more month's allowance to finally afford a cell phone, so by mid-May she could call Marlee with complete privacy.

The door to Lisa's bedroom slowly squeaked open.

"Weesa?" Bridget, Lisa's three-year old sister, peeked in.

"Yes, Sweetpea?"

"Ki come in?"

"Of course you can. It's your room, too." Lisa sat up and patted her bed in invitation.

Bridget ran past her own bed and leaped onto Lisa's. "Did you finish your 'portent phone call?"

Lisa smiled at her baby sister. "I did, but my friend doesn't want to hang out with me today."

"You can hang down with me if you want," Bridget offered and patted Lisa's hand. "Okay?"

Lisa tried not to laugh at her youngest sister's furrowed brow. "I would love to hang *down* with you anytime, Sweetpea. In fact, you and I and Lynnie and Lawrence Jr. are going to hang down all afternoon at the playground. Mama has a customer today."

Bridget looked at her big sister wide-eyed. "Ki ride my bike?"

"Course you can. A bike ride will make it twice as fun, eh?"

"Okay, but I want my hair in a braid wike yours. Mama says she'll cut my hair off if I tangle it again."

Lisa laughed. "Okay, one braid coming up. Go get your brush."

Bridget leaped off the bed and scurried to her dresser. She grabbed the brush and ran back.

"Turn around."

Lisa began the arduous process of combing out her sister's tangle of curls. A recent bubble gum incident had forced their mom to cut out the tangles along with the gum. Bridget had cried for days, but since their mother cut and styled hair to make extra income for the family, Lisa knew it must have been the only way to fix it.

"Weesa?"

"Yes?"

"How come your friend doesn't wike you?"

Lisa grunted. "Oh, she does, I think, but she's busy today. But you know what?"

"What?"

"Don't ever fall in love. It'll tear your heart up."

"That would hurt."

Lisa took a deep breath and said, "Yeah, Tara broke my heart big time, but you know what else?"

"What?"

"I still have lots of friends. Like Marlee and Julie."

"Julie's nice. She's brown."

"Yeah, that's true. Julie's skin is a lot darker than ours." Lisa chuckled. "But don't worry. I have a lot of friends who are happy to hang out with me."

"Friends are fun 'cept when they break your stuff."

"Geez, you're right about that."

Lisa's mother knocked on the open bedroom door just as Lisa finished her sister's braid. "C'mon, Sweetpea. Let's leave Lisa alone for another hour. She's has to do her homework."

"Thanks, Mom."

Her mother smiled and then ushered the three year old out of the room. "Thank you for taking them to the playground while I do

Mrs. Winfred."

"Another perm?"

"Unfortunately, but she pays cash, so I'm not complaining. And since your father's got that big roofing job at the library, he'll be gone all day and can't fuss about the smell. Oh, if Lynnie gives you a hard time about going to the playground, tell her she can sit on the bench and read her book."

"Okay."

Her mother started to back out and close the door, but Lisa blurted, "Mom, can I go to Marlee's tomorrow? To play catch?"

"After church? Sure."

"Geez, Mom. Of course after church."

"Okay, we'll drop you off on the way home. Bring your softball stuff and a change of clothes with you."

Lisa didn't have a chance to answer because Bridget ran back into the room and blurted. "Weesa, don't get your heart tord up, today."

Too late, Lisa thought. "Okay, I won't."

Lisa's mother smiled, but raised an inquisitive eyebrow. Lisa shrugged and grinned sheepishly.

As soon as the door closed, Lisa pulled her geometry textbook from her backpack and leaned back against her pillow.

She read the first homework problem out loud. "Prove that the diagonal of a parallelogram creates two congruent triangles." She drew the diagram in her notebook and tapped the pencil on the paper. She knew it was an easy proof, but she couldn't focus. With a sigh she slammed the book shut and tossed it on the bottom of her bed. The notebook followed. "Who cares if two triangles are congruent?" she mumbled. She wasn't in the right frame of mind for geometry. She'd ask Julie how to do it later when they went to the movies.

Lisa opened the drawer on her bedside stand. She reached way in the back and pulled out her journal. Tucked inside was her favorite extra fine blue gel pen, just where she'd left it. She uncapped the pen and began writing.

<u>Tara: The Good Things</u>
1. Tara was my first and only girlfriend.
2. Tara's hot.
3. Tara didn't care that I'm a five foot nine sequoia.
4. Tara's the first girl I ever kissed. (And only!)

Lisa had met Tara at the State Univeristy New York Rockville softball camp downstate in Cayuga County the summer before. Lisa had just finished ninth grade. She hugged the journal to her chest as she remembered.

The drive to the camp in Cayuga County was long–about three and a half hours. She hugged her mother goodbye in the parking lot in the Rockville College campus and instant homesickness squeezed her chest before her mother had even gotten back in the family minivan. Lisa had never been away from her family before. With three siblings under the age of ten, she knew she should have been happy to have a week away from that madness, but she couldn't help missing her family immediately.

She watched her mother drive away, tears hazing her vision. She jumped when one of the older girls said, "Catcher, huh?"

Lisa nodded and wiped at her tears. When she could finally see clearly, she looked up into the most perfect pair of hazel eyes she'd ever seen.

"Let me help you with your gear." The older girl picked up the bag of catcher's equipment.

Lisa's breath caught in her throat for a second until she remembered her manners. "Oh, thanks."

"I'm Tara." The older girl smiled and stuck out her hand.

Lisa grabbed the offered hand. "Thanks. I don't, uh; I don't know where I'm supposed to go."

"Here, let me see your registration form."

Lisa reached into the back pocket of her shorts and handed Tara the rumpled form. While Tara looked it over, Lisa took in Tara's tanned skin and perfect shoulder length brown hair. Lisa suddenly felt giant and awkward in front of this hot girl.

"Oh, cool," Tara said. "You're in my dorm. Coach Greer's our resident supervisor. She's a pushover."

Lisa walked side by side with Tara and couldn't help but register the girl's strong gait and confident manner. *This cute girl would probably die if she knew I was checking her out,* Lisa thought. Up until that point Lisa had only come out to one person—herself. No one else on the planet knew she was gay. She hadn't had the nerve to tell anybody.

Tara looked at Lisa and smiled again. "I'm from Long Island. Brookhaven. Where are you from?"

"Oh, the North Country. Clarksonville."

"Nope, sorry. Never heard of it." Tara smiled at Lisa with her eyes, and Lisa felt something stir inside her chest. "Rockville's as far upstate as I've ever been." She laughed. "But, then again, everything north of the Bronx is upstate to me."

"We're all apple pickers to you guys, eh?"

Tara stopped walking and laughed. "That's freakin' funny, Lisa. Nope, I'm gonna call you apple picker. That's your new name." They headed into the dormitory lobby. "And you apple pickers probably think that all Long Islanders are hoodlums, right?"

Lisa took a few steps away from Tara and asked, "*Are* you a hoodlum?"

Tara narrowed her eyes. "Maybe I am, apple picker, maybe I am."

Lisa settled in fairly quickly with Tara's help. The next day after dinner, Tara asked Lisa to go with her to get a bag of softballs from the equipment shed for Coach Greer. Lisa willingly followed Tara toward the shed on the far end of the practice fields. In only a day and a half, Lisa had willingly done anything Tara wanted her to do. She couldn't help it.

"Hey, I want to show you something." Tara veered off the path and into the stand of trees bordering the field.

"What is it?"

"You'll see, c'mon."

The trees grew thicker, and the trail grew darker the further they got into the woods. After a while, Lisa couldn't see the practice fields anymore.

"Shouldn't we be getting those softballs for Coach Greer?"

"Yeah, yeah, but I want to show you this first. Here it is." Tara pointed to a barely discernable cement structure almost completely hidden by vines and dead leaves. If Tara hadn't pointed it out, Lisa might not have seen it.

"C'mere. I want to show you inside," Tara said.

"Inside?"

"Yeah, it used to be an old shooting range. I bet if we looked hard enough we could find some old bullets, but come inside here first." Tara grabbed Lisa's hand and led her to the open doorway about fifty feet down.

Tara didn't let go of her hand as they walked. Lisa's heart raced the entire way. She let herself be led through the metal doorway and was disappointed when Tara released her hand.

A concrete tunnel about six feet wide and just as high went off into the pitch black darkness. She couldn't tell how far the tunnel went. Without flashlights it was hard to see much past the open door. The empty beer cans and stale smell of urine weren't very appealing, so Lisa headed back toward the doorway.

"Kind of cool, huh?" Tara followed Lisa out.

"Kind of stinky, eh?"

Tara stepped closer to Lisa. "You apple pickers are so cute, *eh*?"

"Are you making fun of me, hoodlum?" Lisa didn't back up even though Tara moved dangerously close, closer than she should have.

Tara took another step and put her right hand on Lisa's hip. The smile faded from her eyes, and she said softly, "Stop me if this isn't okay."

Lisa's heart thumped hard against her chest. She gulped but made no move to stop the older girl.

Tara put her left hand on Lisa's other hip and pulled her closer. Lisa whimpered when their bodies touched. Tara leaned in closer still. The only things in Lisa's world at that moment were Tara's lips, inches away. Tara closed the distance, and their lips met.

Lisa drank in the sweet, sweet taste of the beautiful hoodlum from Long Island. She threw her arms around Tara's neck. Meanwhile, Tara slid her hands slowly up and down Lisa's back. Lisa moaned.

Tara pulled away slightly. "Like it, don't ya, apple picker?" Tara kissed Lisa's neck and started to lift up Lisa's T-shirt.

Lisa pulled back. "No, no." She pulled the T-shirt back down.

"Too much?"

Lisa nodded. "You're the first girl I ever kissed."

Tara's eyes lit up. "I'm your first? Really?" Tara sounded proud.

Lisa nodded and felt herself blush even more.

"Okay, we'll go slower."

Lisa wanted Tara to kiss her again. Tara must have read her mind and obliged.

Lisa closed her journal for a moment and sighed at the memory. Their first kiss had been so sweet, but the week had been so short. Tara must have known how short, because she invited Lisa to her dorm room that same night.

Alone in Tara's room after lights out, Lisa let Tara have her way with the T-shirt. She had trembled so much that she was sure Tara was going to laugh at her.

"I'm not going to bite you," Tara said after easing Lisa's shirt off. "Unless you want me to, that is."

Lisa would have laughed, but Tara fell to her knees and started kissing her bare stomach.

Lisa sighed and stopped the memory in mid-stomach. There was no point in it. She reopened her journal and hesitated, not sure she wanted to dredge up this part of her past with Tara.

<u>Tara: The Not-So-Good Things</u>
1. Brookhaven, Long Island is four hundred miles away.
2. Tara graduates in June and won't be at camp this summer.

Lisa pressed hard against the paper when she wrote the next two items.

3. I got Tara's "Dear Jane" letter today.
4. Tara is a hoodlum.

She slammed her journal shut and then threw it and the pen across the room. Tara hadn't even bothered to call to break up with her. She'd written a letter. She buried her face into her pillow. Maybe Marlee would turn out differently. Despite her best efforts, she couldn't stop the tears from flowing.

Chapter Two

The Kagillion Dollar Question

REVEREND OWENS PREACHED, but Lisa didn't hear. Marlee had called just before they left for church and invited her over to play catch. It was all Lisa could think about. Bridget squirmed next to her in the pew. On church days, her father was in charge of Lynnie, her mom was in charge of Lawrence Jr., and she was in charge of Bridget.

Her mother shot her a glance as if to say, "Get that child under control."

Lisa nodded and pulled Bridget onto her lap. Bridget protested at first, but then Lisa produced a small picture book about kittens from her purse, and Bridget settled down a bit. Lisa went back to ignoring Reverend Owens and thinking about Marlee.

Marlee had to be gay. How could she not be? At camp, Tara taught Lisa all about gaydar. She'd made Lisa guess who was and who wasn't gay, and Lisa had been right every single time. Actually, they fought over whether Brandy, the shortstop from Elmira, was gay. Lisa said yes. Tara said no. Lisa supposed they'd never know who was right, but despite that one disagreement, Lisa discovered that her gaydar was fully operational. Tara told her the best clues were short hair and comfortable shoes, but Lisa had laughed then, because she herself had long hair and wore heels to church just about every Sunday. Marlee, though, fit the bill with her short-cropped blond hair and perpetual sneakers.

Lisa sighed. Reverend Owens needed to wrap things up soon, or she would get as squirmy as Bridget. She couldn't wait until Marlee got a look at her in her dress and heels. She'd worn the dress with the blue and white flowered print, the one that clung nicely and showed off her curves. The dress was modest enough for church, but barely. She'd wanted to show a little more cleavage, but her mother would have sent her right back inside to change. With her two-inch heels, Lisa would tower over Marlee's five foot six. Two inches were her limit, though, because otherwise she'd turn into the Empire State Building.

Bridget squirmed again and threw the kitten book on the floor, apparently done with it. Lisa squeezed her sister gently to send a silent message to settle down. She leaned down and picked up the book. Why did Reverend Owens have to pick that day, of all days, to be so long-winded? Lisa cheered silently when he finally held out both hands toward the congregation and said, "Go with love."

"Go wit wuv," Bridget echoed loudly and the people sitting near them laughed.

Lisa smiled at the people around them, but at the same moment thought, *Nah, love sucks.* She laughed at herself. *Yeah, right. That's why you can't wait to get your hands on Marlee.* She stood up with a sigh. "C'mon, Sweetpea. Let's go shake hands with Reverend Owens."

"Weesa?" Bridget reached for Lisa's outstretched hand.

"Yes?"

"Don't get your heart tord up."

Lisa cringed. She had to watch what she said around her all-ears littlest sister. "Okay, I won't. I promise." *Tara took care of that yesterday.*

LISA SLID OPEN the side door to the Brown family minivan and walked to the rear. She pulled out her softball bag.

"Bye, you guys," she called from the back. Her sister Lynnie didn't look up from her book, but her brother Lawrence Jr. turned around, waved his transformer action figure at her, and said "Bye."

Her father looked her way and said, "Have fun, Lisa Bear."

"Papa! C'mon, I'm sixteen."

Her father laughed. "What? I can't call my first-born by her pet name anymore?"

Lisa rolled her eyes for his benefit and said, "Geez, okay. If you have to."

"Call when you want us to pick you up. I'd love to stay and play catch with you and Marlee, but Mama's got me under the knife this afternoon."

"Oh, Larry." Lisa's mother smacked her husband on the knee.

"What? You do." Her father's thinning brown hair was a bit disheveled, and Lisa knew her mother was going to give him a haircut later that day.

"Bye Weesa! Member what I said, 'kay?"

Lisa nodded and gave her littlest sister a thumbs-up which was enthusiastically returned. She closed the rear door and then slid the side door shut.

Lisa slung her softball bag over her shoulder and picked her way up the long gravel driveway, a harrowing task in heels. She thought it funny that her father called her his first-born. They both knew she wasn't. Her real father, well, she preferred to think of him as her biological father, didn't have the nerve to stay with her mother when she got pregnant during their senior year of high school. Luckily, though, Lisa's grandparents were very supportive. When Lisa was six years old, Lawrence Brown, the man she now called Papa, entered their lives.

Lisa didn't even know her bio dad's name. When she turned

eighteen, her mother promised to tell her everything. At age thirteen, Lisa snuck into her parents' bedroom to look through her mother's high school yearbooks. She tried to pick out her bio dad from the photographs, but nobody really stood out. After a few months she stopped trying.

Lisa almost made it all the way up Marlee's driveway when the side door to the kitchen opened.

"Wow." Marlee held open the screen door. "You clean up well."

So do you. Marlee looked so cute with her short blond hair and perfect blue eyes. Lisa felt herself blush. She couldn't help grinning. "Oh, this is just one of my church dresses."

Marlee smiled. "I'd never be caught dead in a dress."

I know, Lisa thought, her gaydar happily pinging away.

Marlee held the door open for Lisa to enter. The McAllisters always used the side door that opened into their large country kitchen. The Brown family kitchen, by contrast, was modern day mayhem. Four kids and two grownups in one small house tended to do that. Marlee didn't talk about it too much, but her father had passed away when she was in middle school. Lisa always felt kind of sad for Marlee in that regard, because even though Lisa's bio dad chose not to be a part of her life, at least she had a stepfather who treated her like his own.

Lisa set her softball bag on the kitchen table and unzipped it. She pulled out a P&C grocery sack with some practice clothes. "Where can I change?"

"Oh, follow me." Marlee led the way down a narrow hallway off the kitchen. "Here." She pointed to an open bathroom door.

"Okay, I'll just be a minute."

Lisa's hands shook as she changed clothes. She scolded herself. She was there to play catch. That was it. Nothing was going to happen. Marlee wasn't going to pull her into the garage or take her up to her bedroom and seduce her like Tara had. Lisa groaned. No, she wouldn't think about Tara. Tara could stay in Long Island with the rest of her hoodlums.

Lisa shoved her clothes into the grocery sack knowing she should have at least folded her dress, but she couldn't wait. She adjusted the sports bra under her Rockville softball camp T-shirt and shrugged on her Clarksonville sweatshirt.

"That was fast," Marlee said from the kitchen.

"Anything to get out of that dress, eh?"

"Hey, do you want something to drink?" Marlee opened a cupboard and pulled out a glass.

"Nah, maybe later after we've worked up a sweat."

"Sounds good." Marlee yelled up the stairs, "Mom? Lisa and I are going to play catch outside, okay?"

"Okay." She peeked down the stairs and said, "Hello, Lisa. How are you?"

"Fine thanks. How are you?"

"Good, except for all this housework." She laughed. "You girls have fun. I'll be changing sheets and doing laundry if you need me."

"Okay, Mom." Marlee headed toward the door. "I'll help you fold later, okay?"

"Sounds good."

Outside, they stretched their muscles on the side lawn near the big oak tree. A truck tire swung to and fro in the mid-April breeze.

"Bridget and Lawrence Jr. would love this tire swing." Lisa stretched her throwing arm behind her head one last time.

"You should bring them over some day to use it. I haven't used it since..."

Marlee didn't finish her sentence. She was probably thinking about her father, so Lisa quickly changed the subject. "So what did you end up doing with Bobby yesterday?"

"Oh, uh," Marlee hesitated, "we just hung out. Nothing special." Marlee ran a hand through her hair.

Lisa could tell that Marlee wasn't telling the whole truth, but she didn't press it. "Hey, let's work on that rise ball of yours. You almost took out that East Valley left fielder on Tuesday, you know."

"I know." Marlee rolled her eyes, but then a fleeting expression crossed her face.

Lisa wasn't sure how to interpret the look, so she said, "I can't believe we lost. I mean, are we ever going to beat East Valley?"

"I predict we're going to kick some East Valley Panther butt next time we play them."

"Oh, yeah? How are we going to do that? We play them on their field next time. And their field looks like Yankee Stadium."

"More like Citifield, if you don't mind." Marlee looked offended, but Lisa knew she was kidding.

"Oh, that's right. You're a Mets fan, aren't you?" Lisa took her mitt off and reached for her chest protector from her softball bag.

"Yeah, and you're Yankees, right?"

Lisa nodded and playfully narrowed her eyes. "I think we have to tell Coach Spears that this, uh, pitching and catching thing isn't going to work out for us anymore."

Marlee laughed. "Oh, man, can you imagine? Hey, Coach Spears, Lisa and I have to break up because Mets and Yankees fans can't see eye to eye on anything."

Lisa almost choked when Marlee said, "break up." Lisa felt her cheeks getting hot, so she turned away. She put the chest protector over her head.

"Let me help you with your shinnies." Marlee kneeled down to strap on the right shin guard while Lisa adjusted the chest protector. Lisa tried to act calm and cool while Marlee reached behind her leg to fasten the straps, but she couldn't get her knees to stop shaking. She prayed Marlee didn't notice.

"I'll—" Lisa choked on the word, cleared her throat, and tried again. "I'll do the other one. Thanks. Oh, hey," Lisa tried to find more neutral ground, "Julie, Johnna, Kerry, and I went to see Ellen Page's movie last night."

"How was it?" Marlee pulled a softball out of the bag.

"It was really good, but you have to see it for yourself. I'd definitely go again." *Way to be obvious, dorkhead.* Lisa cringed, but desperate times called for desperate measures.

Marlee tossed Lisa the ball. "Yeah, my mom wants to see it, too."

Wrong answer, Marlee, totally wrong answer. Lisa sighed. "That's cool." *But not really.*

"Yeah, maybe Jeri'll want to go, too."

"Sounds like fun," Lisa said with as much enthusiasm as she could muster.

They threw the ball back and forth overhand for a few minutes to warm up their arms.

"Let me know when you're ready to pitch," Lisa said.

"I'm ready. I'll keep the bag of balls by me because I'm sure I'll throw most of them over your head."

Lisa laughed and moved behind the home plate that Marlee had put in on the side lawn near the garage. Coach Spears had given Marlee an old home plate and pitching rubber the year before, so they could practice at Marlee's house any time. Lisa remained standing while Marlee stood about twenty feet away and flicked the ball to her with her wrist only. After a few minutes of wrist work, Marlee backed up to the pitching rubber forty feet away.

"Okay, Marlee. Let's loosen up with meatball fastballs right down the middle of the plate."

Lisa squatted down and flashed the sign for fastball by closing the fist on her right hand and then flicking her index finger toward the ground. Lisa felt self-conscious having Marlee stare right at her crotch for the signs, but this was softball and that's the way it was.

Marlee's first pitch landed in the dirt. Lisa blocked the ball with her shin guards. "Geez, Marlee, don't take me out on the first pitch."

"Sorry." Marlee grinned.

Marlee's next few pitches were nice and fat in the strike zone. Once Lisa felt Marlee was warmed up enough, she said, "Okay, let's work the ladder."

Marlee nodded.

Lisa flashed the fastball sign and positioned her mitt low and inside nearest a right-handed batter. The ladder had three 'rungs' to it—knee height, waist height, and chest height. After working Marlee through a few knee-height pitches, Lisa worked up the rungs of the invisible ladder by positioning her mitt at waist height for a few pitches and then finally at chest height. She then shifted to the outside of the plate and worked Marlee back through the three rungs, but in reverse order.

Smack! Marlee's pitch popped into Lisa's mitt at the desired spot.

"Nice." Lisa stood up. "Where was all of this on Tuesday?" She walked toward Marlee, so she could stretch her legs a bit.

"I know. I can't believe Susie hit a grand slam off of me."

She knows her name. This isn't good. Lisa's gaydar went on high alert. "Do you know her?"

"Oh, no. No," Marlee stumbled and ran her fingers through her short hair.

Lisa's gaydar had gone off big time on Tuesday when the cute East Valley left fielder got up to bat, so maybe, just maybe, Marlee was crossing over to the lavender ladies club. Lisa decided to push it.

"Did you see that blonde second baseman of theirs? Wasn't she pretty?"

"Yeah, she was." The relief on Marlee's face at the change of subject was obvious, and Lisa began to worry that this Susie person might be her competition.

"That second baseman doesn't really look like a softball player, you know? She looks more like a cheerleader or something." Lisa's stomach had done a flip-flop when the pretty blonde spoke to her during their last game.

"Yeah, she does look like a cheerleader."

"Hey, no law says you can't be both, right? A cheerleader and a softball player?"

"Yeah, really." Marlee smiled and then rolled her eyes. "Man, that whole East Valley team is good. Christy Loveland's an awesome pitcher."

"Do you have rise ball envy?"

Marlee burst out laughing. "I don't know. I just might."

Lisa headed back to her catcher's spot, "Hey, you and I both know that great pitching will beat good pitching, so let's work on that rise ball of yours and make you great."

"No pressure there, Lisa." Marlee set up on her pitching rubber. "Okay, let's do this."

"Supersonic back spin, Marlee. Make this thing defy gravity. Let the spin do the work." Lisa squatted down. "Oh, and remember what Coach said about your stride length? Long and aggressive to keep your weight back. Okay?"

"Yeah, yeah. I got it."

Lisa flashed the sign for rise ball and positioned her mitt in the middle of the strike zone. Marlee's pitched sailed right over Lisa's head and smashed into the garage. "Marlee, you used your shoulder to muscle that ball to me. Coach Spears said the spin is the key to the rise. C'mon, try again. Keep your weight back."

Marlee and Lisa worked on Marlee's rise ball until all the balls from the bag had successfully hit the garage.

"Lisa, I'm worn out. Let's call it a day, okay? We'll work on this at practice tomorrow"

"Okay. We made a lot of progress, though."

Marlee frowned.

"No, really. We did." They walked side-by-side to the garage and picked up the balls. Lisa was disappointed that their session was over, but knew it had to end sometime. "We need to work on that screwball of yours, too."

"Oh, yeah. We'll have to do that during practice, too, I guess." Marlee put the last ball in the bag. "Hey, let me ask my mom if I can drive you home."

Lisa's heart did a flip. Would they finally be alone?

"I could use the practice driving."

Lisa's heart sank. Oh, yeah. Marlee only had her permit, and Marlee's mom would be in the car as the licensed driver.

"Thanks," Lisa said. "That'd be great."

Lisa took off her gear while Marlee ran into the house to ask her mother. *Geez, Marlee, how can I tell you I want to be alone with you? That I want to run my fingers through your hair like you do when you're nervous? How can I tell you these things if we're never alone? But what the hell would I do if I ever got you alone?*

That was the kagillion dollar question.

Chapter Three

Bring It On

LISA SAT IN the backseat of Jeri D'Amico's brand new Mustang, ecstatic that Marlee invited her to go with them to East Valley to see a softball game. Apparently Jeri and Marlee had been hanging out with the East Valley team recently.

In one short week, several amazing things had happened for Lisa. For one thing, Marlee finally broke up with her boyfriend. He broke up with her, actually, but the result was the same. The next great thing was that their softball team beat Northwood on Tuesday and then beat Racquette that afternoon, giving them a winning record. Well, to be fair, beating both Northwood and Racquette wasn't that amazing because they weren't very good. Marlee's pitching overwhelmed most of the batters on both teams, but the third and most awesome thing was that Marlee asked her to go with them to East Valley. She and Marlee, oh, and Jeri, too, were going to watch a game and then go to an East Valley player's house afterward to hang out.

Lisa tried to stretch her long legs in the cramped backseat, but couldn't quite do it. Oh, well, she'd have to suck it up for the forty-five minute trip. She was with Marlee, after all, so it was okay.

Marlee sat in the front seat and confided in Jeri and Lisa about her now ex-boyfriend Bobby. "Did you know that I could never get him to understand the infield fly rule? I mean he's a jock, so how can he not understand a simple rule like that?"

Lisa didn't dare say anything, but the infield fly rule was far from simple. There had to be less than two outs, a force play at third or at home, and the ball had to be catchable. Bobby didn't even play baseball, just football, so he might not know the rule.

"And how come all he wanted to do was go to Lake Birch?" Marlee said.

"Lake Birch?" Lisa wondered out loud.

"Sometimes guys can be in an awful hurry," Jeri said. "You know what I mean?"

"Oh." Lisa hadn't ever let herself think about Marlee and Bobby that way. It didn't matter, though. They had broken up.

Of course, neither Jeri nor Marlee knew that Tara had broken up with Lisa just the week before. Her heart still hurt, but she had pretty much known the break up was inevitable. Tara lived downstate, four-hundred miles away, and the only connection they had after camp was through phone calls, emails, cards, and letters. Apparently that wasn't quite enough for Tara anymore because Tara hadn't returned any of Lisa's calls for almost a month. Maybe the relationship was doomed from the beginning, anyway. Lisa sighed and tried to push Tara out of her mind.

"We're gonna move on and be just fine," Jeri said to Marlee.

"Yeah, me, too," Lisa blurted before she could stop herself.

Jeri glanced over her shoulder at Lisa in the back seat, her long black curls swaying as she did. "Move on from whom, girl? Who've you gone out with?"

"Oh, uh...Nobody. I guess I just got caught up in the moment." Lisa sighed but was sure neither Jeri nor Marlee heard it over the roar of the Mustang's engine.

"You're weird, Lisa," Jeri teased.

"So they say."

The conversation went back to Marlee's breakup, but Lisa was relieved when they finally reached Sandstoner Fields, the East Valley Panthers' home field. Jeri dropped them off on the East Valley side of the field and drove off to park at the far end of the lot. Lisa zipped up her ski jacket to keep out the late-April cold. She pulled her braid free and jammed her hands in her pockets as they walked toward the East Valley bleachers.

As soon as they reached the fence, Lisa could tell that Marlee was distracted. They stood near the East Valley dugout and out of the corner of her eye, she watched Marlee search the field for someone.

The East Valley second baseman popped out of the dugout and yelled to Marlee, "Hey, Pitcher." The uber cute blonde stepped closer and said again, "Hey, Pitcher."

"Hey, Second Base," Marlee said. "What's up? This is Lisa. She's my catcher."

"Hey, Catcher. Nice to meet you officially." The girl stuck two fingers through the fence. Lisa grasped the pretty blonde's fingers firmly in handshake. She didn't mean to, but she got caught in the girl's intense blue-gray eyes and held on to her fingers longer than she should have. She pulled her hand away and felt her cheeks flush. The cute second baseman must not have noticed because she said, "Heard you guys beat Northwood on Tuesday. Think we stand a chance?"

Since Marlee looked preoccupied, Lisa answered the question. "Of course you're going to win. And you know it, too." The girl didn't seem to mind that Marlee was off in space, so Lisa teased, "Geez, you have Loveland pitching, so gimme a break."

"Well, yeah, there's that." The second baseman smiled, and Lisa became mesmerized by her beautifully smooth skin, her perfectly applied eye liner, and silky blond hair. Lisa's gaydar pinged ever so slightly. She tried to make her mouth move, so she could ask the girl her name, but couldn't get it to cooperate.

"Sam, c'mon!" the East Valley shortstop yelled over. "Coach

wants us on the field."

Her name is Sam, Lisa thought. *Samantha maybe?*

Sam looked apologetic. "Oops, infield warmup." Sam waved to Lisa and trotted out to her position at second base.

Lisa thought it strange that Sam waved only to her and not to Marlee, but then again, Lisa's stomach had done that flippy thing when Sam walked over, so maybe it was okay. She felt a little guilty about being attracted to Sam, a virtual stranger, with Marlee standing right there.

Lisa watched Sam field a grounder at second base. The immaculately groomed infield and outfield really did remind her of Yankee Stadium. East Valley would probably end up going to States again like they did practically every year. The Clarksonville Cougars had come in second place the year before, and Lisa remembered Coach Spears wondering out loud if her Cougars would ever be able to push the East Valley Panthers off their lofty mountain.

Sam fielded her grounders cleanly and was quick turning the double play. Their whole infield was good, but their pitcher, Christy Loveland, was phenomenal. She was probably the best pitcher in the entire New York State North Country. Marlee would disagree, of course, but Lisa knew better. Christy threw a lot of different pitches, and she threw all of them well. Even though Marlee was getting better all the time, she still hadn't gotten a handle on her rise ball and hadn't even begun to master the screwball. After the game they were going to hang out at Christy's house. Lisa thought it was weird to even consider hanging out with the team that always beat them, but she didn't care. Marlee was there. And with a small smile, she remembered that Sam might be there, too.

Susie, the East Valley left fielder, walked over and said, "*Dios mio*. There is way too much Cougar blue here today." Susie's dark skin and long auburn hair made her look exotic. She was kind of hot, actually, and Lisa's gaydar went off again big time. She wasn't sure, but thought maybe Susie was Puerto Rican or something. The "*Dios mio*" was a big clue. Susie looked at both Marlee and Lisa and said, "Hey, Cougars," as if she could care less that they existed.

Lisa knew the girl was teasing and smiled at her. "Hey."

Marlee, on the other hand, said, "Hey, Panther," with the same indifferent tone Susie had used.

Marlee didn't introduce Lisa to Susie and talked to Susie as if Lisa wasn't even there. Lisa felt a stab of jealousy and was relieved when Susie ran out for her own warmup.

Jeri got back from parking the car, and they found seats on the home team side of the bleachers. The game started, and Lisa decided that she'd probably overreacted. Marlee was just being nice to the East Valley left-fielder, just like Sam had been nice to her. No big deal. Still, she had nagging doubts, especially when all attempts at conversation with Marlee during the game were futile.

The East Valley team beat Northwood easily, but unfortunately, sitting was not the same as playing, and Lisa shivered in the cold night air.

When they got back in the car, Jeri put the heater on full blast. Before heading out to Christy Loveland's house, they drove to Stewart's, so Jeri could get cigarettes. Once they got to Christy's house, they had to park down the street because a kagillion cars were parked in front of the house already. Lisa had just about thawed out in Jeri's car, but started shivering again when she got out of the car.

The Loveland's two-story house was so big it looked like it had at least five bedrooms. Lisa couldn't wait to get her own house with at least three upstairs bedrooms far away from the madness of the kitchen and family room. She wanted a fenced in yard for kids and pets and barbeques and everything.

Jeri knocked on the heavy oak door, but when no one answered, they let themselves in. The elegant sunken living room and framed art on the walls took Lisa's breath away. She knew people lived in luxury like that, but she'd never seen it.

Someone yelled from another room, and Lisa followed Jeri and Marlee into a room filled with East Valley softball players gathered around a ping-pong table. The left fielder named Susie was just about to lose a ping pong game to Christy. Christy stopped the game and had them write their names on slips of paper to get in on the ping-pong tournament.

They wrote their names down and sat on a bench underneath a window. Just as they sat down, Christy sent a hard smash past Susie to win the match. Looking dejected, Susie came over and sat on the floor next to Marlee. Lisa's chest tightened when Susie oh-so-casually leaned her shoulder against Marlee's leg. When Marlee's name was called for the next ping-pong game, Lisa cheered inside because Susie wouldn't be able to touch Marlee anymore.

Lisa cheered inside again when the uber-cute Sam stood up as Marlee's opponent. Sam had changed from her red and black softball uniform into a low-cut mint green blouse and white Capri pants. Her gold necklace had some kind of charm on it which brought Lisa's eye directly down to Sam's generous cleavage. Lisa swallowed hard. She couldn't take her eyes off the pretty blonde from East Valley, and when the girl pulled her hair back into a ponytail, Lisa almost whimpered because she had imagined running her fingers through it.

Lisa took a deep breath and let out a sigh. What was the matter with her? She had spent the last month or so pining for Marlee, but now Sam was stirring her up in ways that only Tara had done before.

Sam scored three quick points and practically had to show Marlee which end of the paddle to hold. Lisa laughed along with the girls from East Valley, but she also felt bad for Marlee. It was inevitable, but Marlee lost to Sam fairly quickly and sat back down next to Susie. Sam went to the white board and wrote her name in the winner's bracket. She then pulled two more names out of the hat.

"Mary?" Sam called, and a girl with brown shoulder length hair and bangs stood up and reached for Sam's discarded red paddle. Sam called, "Lisa?" and looked right at Lisa.

Lisa pointed to herself and asked, "Me?"

Sam nodded.

Lisa headed to the table and picked up the blue paddle. Out of the corner of her eye, she saw Susie and Marlee leaning close talking. Jeri and Christy got up to leave, and Lisa wondered how long Jeri and Christy had been friends.

Lisa smiled and shook hands with Mary after Sam introduced them.

"Okay, girls," Sam said, "we play to a score of twenty-one. The winner must be ahead by two. We want a good clean fight here. No kidney punches. Okay?"

"Okay. Bring it on, Mary." Lisa tapped the table with her paddle.

Mary served the ball, but Lisa completely missed it because she saw Susie and Marlee stand up to leave. She laughed out loud and tapped the table with her paddle. "Okay, Mary. I dare you to do that again."

"Anytime," Mary said with a laugh. She served the ball again, and even though Susie led Marlee out of the room, Lisa stayed focused enough to return the serve.

On the outside, Lisa played ping-pong and made it look as if she were enjoying herself with some new friends, which she kind of was, but on the inside, she was desperate to know what Marlee and Susie were doing in the other room. Maybe they were just talking about softball. Marlee was the one, after all, who had invited her to go with them to East Valley. Maybe Marlee was too shy about coming out to her. That must be it. Maybe Marlee wanted to gather up her courage, and that's why she had left the room for a while. *Pfft, yeah, right. In some alternate universe maybe.*

Lisa kept up pretty well with Mary and after a while was only losing by a score of 12-15. It was Lisa's turn to serve, but she hesitated when she saw movement outside the window. Marlee and Susie walked together in the dark backyard.

Lisa served the ball over the net, and Mary returned it cleanly. Thinking about Marlee alone in the dark with Susie, Lisa smashed the ball over the net for a point.

"Yeah!" Lisa shouted and punched a fist in the air. The other girls cheered her impressive smash.

"Easy, there, tiger," Mary said. "Don't kill your first opponent. It wouldn't look good."

"Sorry," Lisa said, but it had felt good. Lisa snuck another peek outside the window, a peek she instantly regretted. She watched in horror as Susie grabbed Marlee's hand and led her across the yard behind a shed. Marlee's betrayal was immediate and deep. White-hot anger boiled in Lisa's gut. She tore her gaze away from the window and took a deep breath willing herself not to throw the ping-pong paddle through the window toward Marlee.

Sam put her hand on Lisa's forearm. "Are you okay? You look like somebody just stole home plate on you." Sam's expression of concern made Lisa realize that she probably looked as traumatized as she felt.

Lisa laughed, even though she had nothing to laugh about. She took a deep breath and looked Sam in the eye. "Yeah, yeah, yeah, I'm okay. Whatever." Lisa rapped the table twice with her paddle and glared at her opponent. "Okay, Mary, bring it on."

Chapter Four

Don't Look Back

LISA SLID THE top drawer to her bedside stand open and pulled out her journal. The blue gel pen fell out into her lap. She picked it up and peeked at Bridget. Her little sister looked peaceful in her Dora the Explorer pajamas, her chest rising and falling slowly in sleep.

Lisa uncapped the pen and opened to the next empty page.

> Friday, April 27
>
> We lost to Clarksonville County Community College today. Geez! They are soooooooo good! I don't know why Coach Spears wanted us to play them. I think she's friends with the CCCC coach. My gaydar went off for their coach, but then again my gaydar goes off all the time lately. It even goes off for Coach Spears, but I'll probably never know if she's family or not. Maybe when I'm a real grownup, I'll bump into Coach Spears at a gay bar in Syracuse or Montreal or somewhere. Ha! That would be hilarious. Her gray hair would fall completely out. Geez, what am I thinking? She's too old to be clubbing!

Lisa chuckled at the thought of meeting her softball coach at a gay bar. Tara told her how she used a fake ID to get into the gay bars on Long Island, and apparently there were a lot of them on Long Island. Lisa didn't know of any in the North Country. It wasn't like she could use the family computer in the living room to search for one. She had no clue how to get a fake ID, either. She tapped her pen on the journal page with a frown. Even if she did figure out how to get a fake ID, she wasn't sure she'd feel comfortable using it. She went back to her journal.

> Anyway, we played a good game against CCCC, even though we lost. I saw the pitches really well today, too. Their pitcher had a really, really, really good change-up. Yeah, I struck out on it, but just the first time! She didn't get me again. I got two singles and went two for three. Yeah, I only got up to bat three times, because nobody else could hit! Grrr! Well, Johnna and Marlee got hits at least, but I don't want to think about Marlee right now. Jeri's our leadoff batter, and she struck out every single time! Lead off batters are

supposed to get on base! Argh! Julie struck out a couple of times, too. Julie and I are getting really good in the weight room. I'm glad she picked weight lifting for our fitness unit in PE so I wouldn't be the only girl. All the other girls picked jazzercise or some other stupid thing, but Julie and I want to be strong. Except I think I scared her yesterday. I kind of scared myself, too, actually.

Lisa chewed on the blunt end of her gel pen remembering her stupidity in the weight lifting class the day before.

JULIE WHITE STOOD with her hands on her hips and said, "Brown Girl, you're crazy." Since Lisa's last name was Brown, Julie called her 'Brown Girl' in fun, and since Julie's last name was White, Lisa reciprocated by calling her 'White Girl.' It was their private joke with each other.

Lisa didn't look at her friend as she put ten more pounds on each end of the bar.

"Lisa, you're going to hurt yourself," Julie pleaded.

"C'mon, White Girl. Are you chicken? Let's do this before Mr. Mullins sees us."

Julie shook her head as if she didn't want to be part of it, but stood behind the bench by Lisa's head. She put her hands around the heavy metal bar, without touching it, and waited. Lisa took a deep breath, and let it out. She wrapped her middle fingers around the bar a little more than shoulder width apart and then gripped it firmly with both hands. She pushed the 130 pounds up off the rack and held it with her arms extended. *Holy Jesus, that's heavy.* She picked a spot on the weight room ceiling, so she'd know where to aim once she pressed the weight back up. She slowly lowered the bar to her chest.

This one's for you, Marlee, for breaking my heart. "Unghhh," she grunted and pressed the weight back up slowly.

"I'm right here, Lisa." Julie leaned over the rack, ready to grab the bar if necessary.

Lisa almost lost her concentration when she pressed the weights to their full height. It was so heavy.

"I'm right here, Lisa," Julie said again, but Lisa barely heard her.

This next one's for you, Susie, for stealing my girlfriend. Lisa lowered the weight, felt it brush her chest, and pressed it back up immediately. "Unghhh!" she grunted even louder, sure she'd attract Mr. Mullins attention with that repetition.

"That's two, Lisa," Julie said.

Lisa lowered the bar for a third rep.

"Push it now, Brown Girl, push it!"

Lisa thought about Susie holding Marlee's hand in the backyard and used that to fuel the third repetition. She brought the weight back down, aware that Mr. Mullins and a few of the guys in the class had surrounded her and Julie. She couldn't stop now. She had at least one more in her.

What did you and Susie do behind that shed, Marlee? Lisa practically threw the weights up over her head.

"Nice one, Lisa," one of the guys in the class encouraged.

"You got one more in you, Brown Girl. C'mon," Julie pushed.

Lisa considered racking the bar, but lowered it instead when she remembered the look on Marlee's face after she and Susie came back into Christy's house. It was so freakin' obvious something had happened between them that Marlee could have been wearing a neon sign.

"Ahhh!" Lisa yelled and heaved the weights toward the ceiling. Her classmates cheered and clapped for her, but she didn't take any satisfaction in it. She let Julie guide the weights back on the rack.

Lisa sat up, and the guys surrounding her clapped her on the back and told her how awesome she was. Weight lifters, Lisa had come to realize, were competitive, but they recognized individual accomplishment when they saw it.

"Great job, Lisa," Mr. Mullins said. "One hundred and thirty pounds. I never would have thunk it." He shook his head and pointed to one of her classmates. "Marcus weighs one thirty. You just bench pressed Marcus." Marcus Ranley was a sophomore whose surfer blond hair made him look more like a California beach boy than a North Country weight lifter. Mr. Mullins waited until the boys had gone back to their own workouts before saying, "Honestly, I don't think half the boys in this school can do five reps at one thirty."

Lisa smiled.

"But, hey, next time? Ask one of the senior guys to spot you."

"Okay, sorry. Next time I will."

Once Coach Mullins was out of earshot, Lisa smiled sheepishly. "Sorry, Julie. I didn't mean to get you in trouble."

Marcus slid back over and said, "Damn, Lisa. One thirty. That's pretty good for a girl."

Lisa knew by his grin that he was teasing, so she wrinkled her nose at him and scowled. "Thanks. I think."

Marcus laughed and smiled at Julie, "How much do you bench, Julie?"

It was a little hard to tell with Julie's dark brown skin, but Lisa was sure she was blushing. With Marcus, it was way easier, because his lily-white skin had turned red all the way to the roots of his blond hair. Lisa busied herself putting the weights back, so she could give them some privacy.

Lisa stopped chewing on the pen and tapped her journal with it.

She laughed and murmured, "I guess I'm not the only one with secrets." She turned back to her journal and wrote.

> Yeah, so I benched 130 yesterday, and I was sore for today's game. I'll be even sorer for sure tomorrow for our makeup game against Southbridge. (Oh, we got snowed out with them on Tuesday. Bummer.) Back to the rotten part of my life. I gotta figure out a way to accept the fact that Marlee will NEVER EVER like me the way I want her to. I've got twelve more hours to come up with something so I can keep my sanity (even though Julie thinks I've already lost it! Ha-ha). But, damn, when Marlee came back into Christy's house last Friday night, I knew she'd kissed Susie! Or worse! I don't even want to think about THAT! I was so mad. Some of the girls moved the coffee table out of the living room and put on some club music. It was too loud, but I didn't care because I was trying hard not to think about Marlee and Susie anyway. Sam asked me to dance, so I did to make Marlee jealous, but she didn't even notice me. Whatever. Sam's a good dancer, though, and I think she even flirted with me a little. My gaydar's malfunctioning around her, so I don't know. She's so pretty. She could be in magazines. She's blond, too. Maybe I have a thing for blondes now. Ha-ha. She's probably straight, so I shouldn't get all hot and bothered by her. I already had my heart stomped on twice in two weeks, so I'm lying low from now on. Besides, even if Sam isn't straight, what would such a femmy girl want with me, the amazon who can bench 130 pounds?
>
> Damn. I digressed. I was writing about Marlee who didn't even look at me while I danced with Sam. I can hold my own on a dance floor, too, you know! Oh, great, who am I talking to? I'm tired. Really, really tired! I need to close up now and go to sleep. Big makeup game against Southbridge tomorrow. We only have one league loss so far. Go Cougars!

Lisa yawned and tucked the gel pen back into her journal. She hid the book in the back of the top drawer and turned off the light. She closed her eyes hoping sleep would come quickly, so she could stop thinking about Marlee and Tara.

LISA ROLLED THE ball toward the pitcher's circle after Marlee struck out the Southbridge batter for the third out in the middle of the fifth inning. Even though the Cougars were up by four runs, Marlee was wildly unfocussed and sloppy. She had even walked five batters, which was unheard of in the McAllister-Brown battery. To top it all off, Marlee had a no-hitter going and didn't even realize it.

Lisa pulled Marlee aside and asked her what was going on. Why was she so out of it?

"Chill out Lisa. I'm cool."

Far from it! Lisa grabbed Marlee's uniform sleeve as she started to walk back to the Cougars' bench. Marlee whirled back around blinking as the bright sunshine hit her face. She pulled her hat lower.

"Marlee, you pulled that one on me in the East Valley game. I'm on to you." Lisa pointed a finger in her face. *And I know about your little girlfriend, too.*

Marlee must have read her thoughts, because her eyes flew open wide as if assessing how much Lisa knew.

"When you're on," Lisa said, "I can feel your focus, right on me. When you're off, like now, I can tell you're scattered. Where is your mind?" *As if I didn't know.*

Marlee tried to dodge the question by asking if Coach Spears had sent Lisa over, which she hadn't, of course. Lisa pressed the issue. "Geez, Marlee, what is going on with you?"

Marlee mumbled something lame about being distracted, and Lisa roared, "I know!" She implored Marlee to get herself together. "You are such a better pitcher than that!" Lisa walked off in a huff and kicked a stray batting helmet that was in her way. Her teammates scattered.

Lisa fumed. She was angry because Marlee and Susie had obviously hooked up, but she was angrier still because softball was the only thing she had left with Marlee, and now Marlee was mucking that up. She wanted to tell Marlee she had the no-hitter going, but Lisa knew softball etiquette. You never talked about no-hitters or perfect games when a pitcher was in the middle of one. Lisa sat on the rickety bench trying to calm down, and noticed Susie walking up from the parking lot. Everything became crystal clear. *Ah,* Lisa thought, *that's it. You're new girlfriend was late.*

Julie walked over to where Lisa stood steaming. "Brown Girl, are you okay?" She nodded her head toward Marlee.

Lisa rubbed her forehead. Her pectoral muscles protested the small movement. "She doesn't even know she has a no-hitter going."

"Shh!" Julie warned.

"Oh, she can't hear me. She's not even here today. She hasn't shaken off any of my signals. She usually shakes off five every inning."

Paula, the Cougar batter at the plate, flew out to the left fielder, and Julie headed to the on-deck circle.

Jeri stepped into the batter's box and Lisa yelled, "Get a hit Jeri. Julie'll move you over." To Julie she said, "Hey, you still going bowling with us tonight?"

"Yeah. I don't have any other plans." Julie rolled her eyes and took a practice swing.

"Marcus hasn't asked you out yet?"

"Shh!" Julie looked around wide-eyed. "No one knows, but you. And, no, he hasn't. Not yet." She grinned.

Jeri grounded out to the second baseman to end the fifth inning, so Julie took off her batting helmet and tossed it near her bag on the ground. Lisa picked up her face mask, and they walked toward home plate together.

"So," Lisa said with a grin, "you could always ask him out. Eh, White Girl?"

"Whatever." Julie turned her back and trotted toward first base.

"Geez," Lisa mumbled as she squatted for Marlee's first warm up pitch, "everybody's got love trouble today."

"How's that, catcher?" the umpire asked.

"Oh, nothing." Lisa laughed. "Just mumbling to myself."

The umpire laughed. "You're too young to be senile."

Lisa relaxed an inch when Marlee struck out the side to end the Southbridge half of the sixth inning. They were three Southbridge outs away from Marlee's first ever no-hitter, but the Cougars had to get up to bat first.

Lisa walked to her softball bag behind the team bench and took off her chest protector. She wiped her brow. Despite the chill in the air, she was sweating. She leaned over and unhooked both sets of shin guards and let them fall where she stood.

If all went well this would be the last inning the Cougars had to bat. Julie led off the bottom of the sixth inning and fouled off a few pitches before ultimately popping up to the Southbridge shortstop.

Marlee stepped into the batter's box next, and Lisa moved into the on-deck circle for a few practice swings. Marlee swung at the first pitch and hit a long fly ball to left field, but the Southbridge left fielder made an awesome over the shoulder catch and robbed her of an extra base hit.

"C'mon, Lisa," Marlee said as Lisa moved toward the batter's box, "pick me up. We can't go down one, two, three."

Lisa nodded. Once Marlee passed by her, she saw Marlee smile at Susie. The way Susie's face lit up made Lisa's stomach clench. She dug her heels into the batter's box and waited for her pitch.

"Ball one," the umpire said as the pitch flew inside.

Lisa tried not to let her smile show. The pitcher was going to work her inside then out. Sure enough, Lisa saw the catcher set up on the outside of the plate. The pitch came in right where Lisa expected it, and she exploded, chest muscles screaming. The ball screamed down the right field line. Lisa took off for first base, and Kerry, the first base coach, sent her to second. Lisa didn't let up around second because she'd seen the ball skip past the right fielder and roll to the fence. Coach Spears waved her arm in a circle. Green light. Lisa turned on the afterburners, rounded third, and flew home. Johnna stood on deck and put her hands way up in the air telling Lisa not to slide. Lisa pounded the plate with her right foot and pumped a fist in the air.

Julie and the rest of the team mobbed her after her in-the-park solo homerun. "Way to go, Brown Girl!" Julie said.

"Nice hitting, Lisa." Marlee patted her on the back.

"Thanks." Lisa looked away quickly.

Johnna hit a soft line drive to the Southbridge pitcher to end the bottom of the sixth inning. Lisa took another second to catch her breath before strapping on her gear. *No rest for the weary,* she thought. She was grateful that Marlee didn't help her get dressed. It was better that way for now. Lisa needed a little distance.

Lisa called for a fastball, curveball, fastball combination which successfully struck out the first Southbridge batter. The next batter jumped on the first pitch, but hit a soft grounder to Johnna at shortstop. Julie handled Johnna's throw easily for the second out of the inning.

"One more, Marlee," Lisa called. "You can do it." The Southbridge shortstop dug her heels in the batter's box. Lisa saw the look of determination on the girl's face and knew not to take her lightly. She was a good hitter. Lisa flashed the sign for fastball. If they could get this first strike, then they could play with other pitches, like Marlee's drop or curve. Marlee threw the requested pitch with good speed, but the batter got a good bead on it and smacked the ball to center field. Lisa's heart leaped into her throat for a second until she realized that the ball was sailing right toward Jeri in center field. Lisa trotted toward Marlee to congratulate her on her no-hitter, when the the unthinkable happened. Jeri pulled her hat low, held her glove in the air to block the sun, but it didn't seem to help. The ball flew over her head for a base hit.

"Dammit," Lisa mumbled under her breath and ran back to guard home plate. Marlee didn't seem too upset about losing her no hitter, probably because she didn't even know she'd had one going, but Jeri pounded her glove on her thigh after throwing the ball back in. Jeri must have felt awful. The only thing Lisa could do was get back behind the plate. The next batter struck out for the last out of the game giving Marlee a one-hitter.

After the high-five line, Jeri was nowhere to be seen until Marlee finally looked into the outfield. Jeri sat in center field with her head in her hands, obviously upset about blowing the pop up. Marlee ran out to get her. When they came back in from the outfield, Lisa pretended to focus on putting her gear away, but instead watched Marlee greet Susie. Her heart dropped. The looks on their faces totally gave away the fact that they had hooked up. Lisa forced herself to calmly place her gear in her bag. Even though they had won the game, Lisa had lost Marlee.

Jeri plopped on the bench next to her. "Are you and Julie still going out tonight?"

"Yeah, you want to come?"

"Why not?" Jeri stood up and picked up her bag. "Do you need a ride home?"

Lisa was surprised that Jeri offered to take her home. Maybe Marlee was pulling away from Jeri, too.

"Sure. Thanks," Lisa said. "Let me tell Julie, okay?" She was going to get a ride home from Julie's parents, but it made more sense for Jeri to drive her home since it was on her way.

As Lisa and Jeri headed toward the parking lot, Lisa muttered to herself under her breath, "Don't look back. Don't look back."

Chapter Five

Dark Cloud

TWO WEEKS AFTER winning that stupid Southbridge game, but losing Marlee, Lisa sat on her bed trying to do her geometry homework. She was trying to pass the time until Jeri picked her up.

Lisa put her pencil down and thought about the game against East Valley the night before. The game had been tied 0-0 and had to go into extra innings. Christy seemed really pissed about something, but Lisa didn't know what. Marlee stepped into the batter's box. As soon as the pitch left Christy's hand, Lisa knew instantly that it was going to hit Marlee. And it did. Right in the head. Marlee fell back and landed hard on her shoulder. Her bat lay still by her side, and she started groaning. Lisa ran to her fallen friend, but didn't know what to do. Coach Spears took charge and told somebody to call 911.

After Marlee and her mother were loaded up into the ambulance, Jeri called the team together. "You guys? We have to win this for Marlee." The teammates put their hands together in the middle of the circle and yelled, "Marlee!"

THE PHONE RANG making Lisa jump. Her pencil flew off her geometry book onto the floor. She grabbed the receiver from her bedside stand, grateful for the interruption.

"Hello?" Lisa said into the phone.

"Lisa?"

"Yeah. Who's this?" It didn't sound like anybody she knew.

"It's Sam. From East Valley."

Lisa sat up taller on the bed. Her heart started pumping faster. "Oh, hi."

"Thanks for giving me your phone number last night," Sam said.

"Oh, no problem. You're calling about Marlee, right?" *And maybe to talk to me, too? Maybe?*

"How's she doing?"

"Okay, I think. Coach Spears called this morning and said Marlee has a mild concussion and slight shoulder sprain. Something like that. Jeri's coming by to pick me up in a few minutes to go over there."

"It sucks that you guys were playing us when it happened."

Lisa smiled. "It could have happened against anybody, I guess." *Even though Christy probably beaned her on purpose, but that's a conversation for another day.*

"Maybe. Hey, do you think me and Susie could come out there to visit Marlee, too?"

"Today?"

"Yeah."

"Why not? Oh, I should call her mother first, though." Lisa prayed Mrs. McAllister would say yes.

"Cool. Call me right back okay?"

Lisa could have sworn she heard Sam smile on the other end of the line. "Sure. Give me your number. We don't have caller ID."

Lisa wrote the number down and then hung up. She called Marlee's mother who hesitated for the briefest of moments, but then okayed the two extra visitors saying it might cheer Marlee up. Lisa's second phone conversation with Sam was even shorter than the first because Sam said she had to hang up, call Susie, and then get ready. Lisa wasn't sure what there was to get ready for, since they were just coming to Clarksonville see an injured friend.

After hanging up with Sam, Lisa tried unsuccessfully to finish the geometry proof she'd been struggling with. She heard a car outside, so she slammed her book shut, tossed it aside, and leaped off her bed. She ran to the living room to look out the front window.

"Mom, Jeri's here," Lisa called. "I'm going."

"Okay, hang on a minute," her mother called from the master bedroom. Lisa smiled when her mother said, "Sweetpea, let's go say goodbye to Lisa. She's going to her friend Marlee's house, remember?"

"Mahwee?"

"Marlee got hurt in Lisa's game last night. She hurt her head."

Bridget exploded out of the master bedroom and threw a hug around Lisa's waist. "Is your friend, okay? Mama said she gotted hurt. She needs a bike hemmet. I get mine." Bridget turned to run toward the garage, brown curls flopping every which way, but Lisa scooped her up before she got very far.

"Hold on, Sweetpea. Marlee already has a helmet, but I'll make sure she uses it every time she gets up to bat, okay?" *Too bad it didn't work against Christy last night.* "Your helmet would be too small, anyway, eh?"

"Okay." Bridget squirmed out of Lisa's arms.

"Bye, Mom." Lisa gave her mother a hug. She opened the front door. "I won't stay too long. Mrs. McAllister doesn't want us to tire her out."

"Okay. Tell Marlee the whole Brown clan sends their good wishes. Oh, and tell Jeri thanks for being your taxi."

"I will." She squatted down and held her arms open for another hug from her baby sister. "You be a good girl, okay? Mama has some customers today, so don't bother her. If you need something, ask Lynnie."

"'Kay, Weesa." Bridget pulled out of the hug. "Bye."

Lisa stepped onto the front landing and waved to Jeri who had started to walk toward the front door. Lisa closed the door behind her and took a deep breath of the heady aroma from her mother's lilacs.

"Hey, Jeri."

"Hey." Jeri spun on her heels, and together they headed toward the Mustang.

"Thanks for picking me up." Lisa opened the passenger door and plopped down on the seat. She was glad not to have to fold herself in the back.

"No problem." Jeri started the car and drove off. "I can't believe what happened last night. I mean, it looked like Christy threw that pitch at Marlee on purpose."

"And what the hell did Marlee ever do to her?" *Except maybe steal her best friend away, kind of like Susie's doing to Jeri.*

Jeri snorted. "I think Marlee was pitching better, and Christy didn't like it. Maybe she wanted to take out her competition."

"That's pretty low if you ask me." Lisa wondered how anybody could sink to that level. She looked out the car window and watched the cows as the mustang whizzed by. She looked back at Jeri. "I hope Marlee's up for company."

"Her mom said she'd wake her up when we got there."

"Sam and Susie are coming over, too."

Jeri was quiet for a minute. "They are?"

"Yeah, Sam called me this morning."

"Sam has your phone number?" Jeri looked at her with raised eyebrows.

"Yeah, she asked me for it after the game. She wanted to call about Marlee."

"That's cool." Jeri sighed. "Girl, I can't believe I got in a fight with Marlee yesterday. So what if she wanted to go to Susie's house without us after the game? I was so selfish. But, God, when she got hit by Christy's pitch right in the head and fell…"

Lisa felt bad for Jeri because in the three weeks since Susie had come to the make-up game against Southbridge, Marlee had been distant to everyone. Lisa was pretty sure she knew why, but apparently Jeri didn't. For her part, Lisa decided to accept Marlee and Susie hooking up and just move on. Sam's phone call that morning helped her see that there might actually be life after Marlee and Tara.

Lisa tapped the arm rest and smiled as she thought about Sam.

"What?" Jeri said.

Lisa looked over. "What?"

"You smiled. What were you thinking about?" Jeri flicked on her signal to turn into Marlee's driveway.

Lisa's brain went into overdrive searching for something believable. "Oh, I was thinking about the next time we play East Valley. Marlee should throw a fastball at Christy's head, knock her out, and send her to the hospital to make it even."

"You are evil, Lisa."

"I know, right?" *Phew,* Lisa sighed mentally, *close call.*

"But there's one hole in your nefarious plan."

"What's that?"

"Christy's the flex player. She doesn't bat." Jeri turned off the engine. "Marlee'll just have to hit a line drive at her in the pitcher's circle."

"Ooh, even better." They walked up to the kitchen door. "You're more devious than I am."

Jeri grinned as they got out of the car. After greeting Marlee's mother, they headed up the stairs to Marlee's bedroom. Lisa wasn't sure what they'd see when they opened Marlee's bedroom door, but as soon as they entered the room, Marlee asked, "Did we win?"

Lisa burst out laughing and almost toppled over Jeri trying to get into the bedroom. Marlee's room was small, especially with the huge green recliner taking up all the space at the foot of Marlee's bed, but the room was also bright and sunny.

"Oh, she's okay." Jeri glanced at Lisa. "And we were worried."

Lisa looked at Marlee, and her heart clenched. Marlee looked so pale and vulnerable. That's what having a concussion looked like, she supposed.

Lisa sat on the recliner, but Jeri remained standing. Jeri told Marlee how Christy got thrown out of the game right after mowing Marlee down. Obviously, the umpire knew Christy had done it on purpose.

"Then East Valley put in their back up pitcher," Jeri said. "I forgot her name."

"Mary something-or-other," Lisa said. Mary, ironically, was the girl Lisa had played ping-pong against at Christy's the one time she had gone out there. "But then I was up to bat with Kerry on first base."

Jeri took up the tale describing Lisa's awesome triple into the left-center field gap that scored Kerry. As it turned out, Kerry scored the games only run, and the Cougars won 1-0.

Marlee asked a few questions about the game, but Lisa could tell that she was in some pain.

"So," Jeri asked, "are you okay? What did the doctor say?"

"I have a mild concussion, nothing serious, and my shoulder is only slightly sprained." Despite looking exhausted, Marlee sounded upbeat. "And, and this really sucks, I can't play ball for at least a week, maybe more."

"Oh, my God!" Lisa slammed the foot rest of the recliner back in place. "A week?" Lisa bemoaned the fact that they had two games coming up, and their chances of keeping the same overall win-loss record as East Valley was becoming seriously compromised.

"But listen," Lisa said, "before I forget. Sam called me this morning. She seemed so eager, and your mom said it was okay. She and Susie are coming by today."

Lisa hid a smile behind her hand when Marlee's face brightened. Through the open window she heard a car pull up the gravel driveway. She hurried to look out the window. "Ooh, I see Sam. I'll go down and meet them." She didn't wait for a response, ran out of the bedroom, made it as far as the stairs, and scurried back to close Marlee's bedroom door. She then flew down the stairs to the kitchen.

She slowed down long enough to greet Marlee's mother again. "Sam and Susie are here. I'm going to let them in, okay?"

"That's fine. How's Marlee doing?" Marlee's mother took a sip of coffee.

Lisa opened the inside storm door and glanced out through the screen door. "She seems tired, but she's in good spirits considering."

"I'm glad she has such good friends." Marlee's mother smiled, but Lisa could tell she was worried.

Lisa opened the screen door. Her breath caught when Sam stepped out of the car. Sam's blond hair was loose, a few strands splayed in front of her shoulders. She wore tight white jeans and a salmon colored silk shirt that was tied at the waist with a matching scarf. Susie looked nice, too, with her own tight jeans and white tank top. The dark green button up shirt she wore over it did nothing to hide her strong body.

Sam waved.

Lisa waved back. "Hey ho, Panthers," she called as they walked up. Lisa's heart started beating faster. *Marlee never ever made me feel like this when I looked at her. Never.*

"Hey, Lisa," Sam said.

"Hey," Lisa said again and held the screen door open for them to pass through.

"Let me introduce you." Lisa turned toward Marlee's mother. "Mrs. McAllister, this is Susie, and this is Sam. They're the friends from East Valley I called you about this morning."

"Ah, yes," Marlee's mother said. "It's nice to see you again Susie."

"Nice to see you again, too, Mrs. M."

"And it's nice to meet you Sam. That is such a pretty blouse."

"Oh, thanks." A tinge of red colored Sam's cheeks. "Thanks for letting us come by."

"No problem. Go on up stairs. Marlee's expecting you."

"Thanks." Lisa led the way up the stairs. She looked back over her shoulder and said softly, "Weird game last night, eh?"

"Yeah," Susie said, but didn't elaborate. She was looking intently at Marlee's closed bedroom door.

"It sucks that Marlee got hurt," Sam whispered back.

Lisa nodded in agreement and opened the door to let Sam and

Susie go in first.

Marlee relayed her injuries to her new set of visitors, and then after a few minutes Lisa sensed that Marlee wanted to be alone with Susie.

"Listen, we're gonna wait downstairs. Hope you're feeling better, Marlee." She nodded toward the door and said to Jeri and Sam, "Let's go outside, eh?"

They said quick goodbyes, and Lisa let Sam and Jeri precede her. She closed the door firmly behind her giving Marlee and Susie privacy.

They made their way out of the kitchen and onto the gravel driveway. Lisa blurted to Sam, "So, do you like bowling?"

Sam laughed. "Sure, bring it on." She leaned against the front of Susie's compact Toyota.

Jeri leaned against her Mustang and lit a cigarette. Lisa wanted desperately to lean next to Sam, but didn't want to dis Jeri, so she stood between the two cars facing them, hands in her pockets.

"Marlee looks tired, doesn't she?" Jeri said.

Lisa nodded. "She should be tired. She was pitching an awesome game—"

"She freakin' struck me out three times." Sam grinned and held up three fingers.

Jeri and Lisa laughed. Lisa wagged a finger at Sam. "You should have listened to me when I called those pitches."

Jeri raised an eyebrow in question.

"Oh, she teased me last night," Sam said. "Every time I got up to bat, she'd tell me what pitch Marlee was going to throw." She turned toward Lisa. "I couldn't tell if you were trying to trick me or not. I mean, I thought maybe you'd tell me fastball and then she'd throw that stupid rise ball."

"I said you could trust me." Lisa smiled suggestively hoping Jeri wouldn't notice.

"I'll have to remember that." Sam smiled back. "And, uh, now that our teams have beaten each other once, we'll probably end up tied at the end of the season."

"I don't know about that." Jeri said. "Christy knocked out our best pitcher."

Sam took a deep breath. "I know," she said softly. "I'm not sure what to think about that. I tell you what, though, if Christy did it on purpose, then she just lost me as a friend. I can't stand dirty players."

"Here, here," Lisa said. "Just win or lose, but play fair and square, right?" Sensing the mood needed lightening, Lisa said, "So, when can I beat you at bowling?"

Before Sam could answer, Susie stormed out of the house. The screen door slammed behind her, and she barreled toward her car. Lisa backed up a step.

Susie barked to Sam, "Let's go."

Sam, wide eyed, hurried toward the passenger door. She shrugged and shot Lisa a look that said, "I'm clueless."

Lisa had no idea what was going on, either. "Call me, okay?"

Sam nodded. "Bye, Jeri." She scurried into the car.

"See ya, girl. See ya, Susie." Jeri crushed out her cigarette and pushed off the car.

Susie nodded once, gunned the engine, and slammed the car in reverse. Sam scrambled to put her seatbelt on.

Jeri shook her head. "What the hell was that all about?"

Lisa felt as confused as Jeri looked. "I have no idea."

"Should we go back up?" Jeri took a step toward the house.

Lisa shook her head. "Marlee's exhausted."

"You're right. I'll call her later." Jeri opened the driver's side door and got in.

Lisa got in the passenger side. "That's probably the best thing." Lisa wasn't sure what had happened between Susie and Marlee, but judging by the look on Susie's face, maybe Marlee had broken up with her. Maybe Marlee was so pissed at Christy that she took it out on Susie. *And I should be happy about that because now the door's wide open for me, but...*

Lisa strangely didn't feel tempted by the notion that Marlee might be available again. Sam had started to take up some major space in Lisa's brain.

Jeri seemed lost in thought, so the ride home from Marlee's was rather quiet.

When Jeri pulled up in front of the house, Lisa opened the door and got out. "Thanks again. See you on Monday?"

"Yeah, see ya." Jeri drove off.

Before Lisa had a chance to get all the way to the front door, the screen door burst open, and Bridget ran out. "Give me a ride, Weesa."

"Okay, Sweetpea. What do you want? Tree trunk, fireman, or back-scratcher?"

"Fighman, fighman!"

Lisa laughed. "Okay, get ready." She scooped up her little sister by the waist and threw her over her shoulder in a fireman's carry. Bridget's feet dangled in front. Lawrence Jr., her six-year old brother, stood inside behind the closed screened door.

"Excuse me, sir," Lisa said. "Have you seen my little sister, Bridget? About this high?" She used her free hand to indicate a short person.

Lawrence Jr. giggled. "She's right behind you."

Lisa turned all the way around. "Where? I don't see her." Bridget giggled behind her.

"There," he said with another giggle and pointed.

Lisa spun in the opposite direction. "Lawrence Jr., I don't see her.

Why are you lying to me?"

Lawrence Jr. opened the front door to let them in.

Lisa put Bridget down.

"Here I am." Bridget hugged her big sister.

"Oh, geez. I thought you ran off to join the circus." Lisa heard her mother on the phone in the master bedroom. "Oops," she whispered. "Mama's on the phone, so let's be quiet."

Her mother said low into the phone, "Billy, I don't—Okay, sorry. William. I don't think it's a good idea right now. You agreed to wait until—No. No, I don't."

Lisa walked by the open doorway on the way to her room. Her mother saw her and said, "Billy, I can't talk about this right now. No, I have to go." She hung up the phone and looked at her daughter. "How's Marlee?"

"She's fine." Lisa gestured toward the telephone. "Is everything okay?"

"Yes, yes." Her mother waved in dismissal at the phone. "Don't worry about that."

Lisa wanted to ask her mother who she had been talking to, but Lawrence Jr. tugged on her shirt. "Can we go to the playground? Mama said she's had enough of us."

Lisa stifled a laugh. "Sure, give me a second to get ready, okay? In about five minutes?"

"Okay."

The phone rang, and her mother sighed again. Lisa wondered if it was that same Billy person calling back. She headed toward her bedroom to let her mother answer the phone in private.

"Lisa?" Lisa's mother called out. "It's for you."

"For me? Who is it?"

Her mother shook her head.

Lisa took the cordless phone and said to Bridget, "Go play transformers with Lawrence Jr. for a minute." She put the phone to her ear and said, "Hello?"

"Lisa?"

"Sam?" Lisa went to her bedroom and closed the door.

"Yeah, it's me. We're at a parking area on C.R. 62."

"Are you okay?" Lisa sat on the edge of her bed.

"Me? I'm fine. Susie's out walking. She's crying her eyes out, and I have no idea why. She won't talk to me. She kept banging the steering wheel and then she pulled into this parking area."

"She was pretty upset when you guys left."

"I know. Oh, crap, she's coming back. Hey, can I come over later?"

"Later?"

"Yeah. In about an hour? When Susie drops me off, I'll jump in my car and turn right back around."

You will? "Uh, yeah, sure. Yeah."

"Quick give me your address. I'll use my GPS."

Lisa rattled off her address, and Sam repeated it twice. "Crap, I gotta go." She hung up.

Lisa flopped back onto her pillows. Sam was coming all the way back from East Valley just to see her. Maybe Marlee getting hurt wasn't such a dark cloud after all.

Chapter Six

Second is Way Better

LISA PUSHED BRIDGET on the swings while Lawrence Jr. climbed on the monkey bars. Lynnie sat on a bench by herself reading a novel about magic cats. Lisa whirled her head at the sound of a car. The driver was a middle-aged woman, not Sam. She wished she knew what Sam's car looked like, because it had been over an hour since Sam called. Luckily Lisa could see both the road and her house from the playground, so she wouldn't miss her.

"Higher," Bridget squealed, and Lisa obliged by giving her sister a bigger shove.

"Me, too. Me, too." Lawrence Jr. hopped on the swing next to Bridget.

"You guys are going to wear me out." She alternately pushed Lawrence Jr. and then Bridget.

Another car drove by. Lisa's heart jumped when she saw Sam in a red convertible with the top down. Lisa waved, and Sam pointed to the playground indicating she'd meet her there.

"Hey," Lawrence Jr. said, "keep pushing."

"Sorry." Lisa pushed him again.

The convertible pulled up to the playground, and Lisa grabbed the chains of Bridget's swing and pulled her to a full stop.

"Hey guys, my friend Sam is here. Let's go say hi."

Lawrence Jr. leaped off the swing at maximum height. "Oof," he grunted when he landed on his rear end.

"Lawrence Jr.," Lisa scolded. She helped Bridget off the swing and ran over to him. "Are you all right?"

"I'm okay." He sprung to his feet. "I timed it wrong."

"I'll say," Sam said, and Lisa jumped. "Sorry. I didn't mean to scare you."

Lisa put a hand to her heart. "That's okay. Dealing with these guys, I'm usually ready for anything." Lisa almost melted in the light of Sam's blue-gray eyes, her long blond hair loose over her shoulders.

"These are relations, I presume?"

Lisa laughed. "Yes." She brushed Lawrence Jr. off. "You guys, this is my friend Sam." She leaned closer and whispered, "Is that short for Samantha?"

Sam nodded.

Lisa tapped her brother on the head. "This is Lawrence Jr."

"Please to meet you, sir." Sam stuck out her hand, but just as he was about to grab it, she pulled it away and said, "Too slow. What d'ya know?"

Lawrence Jr. giggled. "Do it again. Do it again."

Sam put her hand out and yanked it back just as Lawrence Jr. was about to grab it.

"Me, too." Bridget pushed Lawrence Jr. out of the way.

"Okay." Sam put her hand out. Bridget reached for it, but Sam pulled it away at the last second. Sam laughed and turned to Lisa. "And who is this?"

"This is Bridget." Lisa put both hands on Bridget's shoulders. "Bridget, say hi to Sam."

"Hi, Sam." Bridget put her hand out for another shake. This time Sam shook Bridget's hand and arm vigorously causing Bridget to giggle.

"C'mon," Lisa said, "they'll have you at this all day if we don't go now."

"Okay. How far is your house?"

Lisa pointed. "Fifth one on the left."

"I think we can fit the four of us in the Sebring."

"How about five?"

"Five?" Sam raised an eyebrow.

Lisa nodded and pointed to Lynnie sitting on the bench thoroughly engrossed in her book.

Sam nodded. "Five it is."

"C'mon Lynnie," Lisa yelled over. "We're going home."

Lynnie didn't move.

"Lynnie, c'mon. My friend is here, and we have to go."

Once again Lynnie didn't acknowledge Lisa's existence, so Lisa walked over letting her shadow fall across the book.

"What?" Lynnie snapped and looked up at her sister. "I'm reading. Mama said I could."

"I know, but my friend is here, and we have to go."

"So?"

Lisa looked heavenward for a moment. Why did Lynnie have to be a pain in the butt in front of Sam? She sighed. "You can read at home. I'll make sure Lawrence Jr. stays out of your room, okay? I'll set him and Bridget up with a DVD or something, okay?"

Lynnie seemed to consider it. "Okay." She stood up. She looked at Sam and said, "Is that Tara?"

"What? Tara? Where did you get that idea?" Lisa had never talked about Tara to anybody, and definitely not to her sister. She must have overheard a phone conversation or something.

Lynnie shrugged.

"That's my friend Sam." She motioned for Sam to come over. "Sam, this is my sister Lynnie."

"Nice to meet you Lynnie." Sam stuck her hand out.

Lynnie politely shook Sam's hand and headed toward the playground gate.

Sam raised an eyebrow. Lisa shrugged and whispered, "I think she's got middle-child syndrome or something. I don't know."

Sam nodded, and they headed to the car. She opened the passenger door and pulled the front seat forward. "Okay, everybody, hop in."

AFTER SAFELY SECURING her siblings in the house with her mother, Lisa got back in Sam's convertible. "This is a nice car."

"Thanks. My parents bought it for me when I got my permit last year, but I have to pay the running expenses like gas, oil changes, maintenance — that kind of stuff. So where's this famous bowling alley of yours?"

"Valley Lanes? Okay, go out here." Lisa pointed the way out of her neighborhood toward the main road. "Go left on C.R. 62, and then I'll guide you once we get closer."

"Cool."

"So, how's Susie?" Lisa wasn't sure how much Sam knew about Susie and Marlee's relationship.

"Honestly, I don't know." Sam signaled left and then pulled onto the two-lane highway. "She wouldn't talk to me. She dropped me off without a word and then sped away. Something happened in Marlee's room, that's for sure."

"They were, uh, they were becoming good friends." Lisa didn't elaborate.

"Yeah, they were."

Hmm, Lisa thought, *neither of us is saying it. Maybe she doesn't know anything. Or maybe she thinks I don't know anything.* "Maybe Marlee doesn't want to have any more friends from East Valley after her trip to the hospital last night."

Sam sighed. "Maybe. Do you feel the same way?" Sam kept her eyes focused on the road.

"No," Lisa said simply. "I think I can stand to be around a few East Valley Panthers."

Sam smiled. "Good."

Sam pulled into the parking lot of the bowling alley and found a spot near the door. They rented shoes, found bowling balls, and made their way to lane twelve at the far end of the alley.

Lisa pulled on the rented shoes and was self-conscious of her size ten feet compared to Sam's size sevens. She tucked her sneakers under the bench and sat at the scorer's table. "What should I put for your name? Sam or Two?"

Sam laughed. "Marlee calls me Two because I play second base, so put Two for me and C for you."

Lisa nodded and typed it in. "I put you up first, Two."

"That suddenly sounded really silly." Sam grimaced.

Lisa laughed. "I know. Let's stick with Sam."

Sam nodded in agreement and then grabbed the electric orange ball she had selected. She took her approach toward the pins and tossed an unglamorous gutter ball.

Sam turned around and grimaced. "Maybe we should have practiced first."

"Hey, nothing says I'm gonna do any better, eh?"

Sam smiled, and Lisa wasn't sure, but she thought maybe Sam blushed. Sam hadn't changed clothes since Marlee's house, and the red, white, and blue bowling shoes looked totally out of place with her white Capri's and salmon silk shirt. Lisa felt underdressed in her blue jeans and retro red v-neck Adidas shirt with three white stripes on each sleeve.

Sam knocked down three whole pins on her next ball. "At this rate, I'll have a thirty by the time we're finished."

Lisa laughed and got ready for her first throw. The ball hit the one pin dead on and sent it and the other nine pins flying. She couldn't help her smile when she turned around.

"Nice strike." Sam held out a fist for Lisa to punch. "God, you're strong."

Lisa felt her face get warm. "Thanks." She sat down at the scorer's table, and Sam got ready for her next turn.

Lisa took a deep breath to calm her pounding heart and wondered what she was doing at the bowling alley with a girl she hardly knew. Lisa threw a thumbs-up when Sam knocked down five pins, but then she took a quick breath and pledged, *I will take this one slow. I will not fall in three minutes like I did for Tara.*

Sam pointed to the pins. "Hey, look at that."

Lisa had been too busy trying to stay sane that she hadn't noticed Sam's spare. "Geez, are you some kind of bowling shark?"

Sam waggled her eyebrows. "Actually, no. Bowling, skiing, ice skating—I suck at those. Softball, tennis, golf, and ping-pong I'm good at."

Lisa wondered what else Sam was good at.

After Sam's brief moment of greatness, her bowling skills deteriorated again to gutter balls and low pin counts. Lisa won the first game easily by a score of 130 to 65.

Sam sat next to Lisa at the scorer's table. With a shaky hand, Lisa hit the buttons to start a second game. She knew she should stand up, grab her ball, and start the next game, but she couldn't bring herself to move.

Sam asked, "You, uh, want to get out of here?"

Lisa nodded and took a slow breath.

"Okay, I'll go pay. Think of somewhere we can go to, uh, talk."

Lisa nodded again. She groaned as soon as Sam left. She was already breaking the promise she'd just made to herself.

Lisa directed Sam to the Clarksonville County Community College softball field. She'd thought about going to Lake Birch, but Marlee said she and Bobby used to go there, and she didn't want to think about Marlee.

The softball field was located in a remote back corner of the college campus. The field and parking lot were surrounded by a thick oak forest. No other buildings could be seen from the lot.

Sam pulled into a parking spot at the very end of the lot facing right field. "Nice spot," Sam said. "It's pretty secluded."

"Yeah." *That's why I chose it.* Lisa felt a rush of heat run through her.

Sam turned off the engine, undid her seatbelt, and swiveled to face Lisa. Lisa tried to swivel as well, but got caught on her fastened seatbelt.

"Oh, geez," Lisa sputtered and undid the belt. She turned to face Sam. "So..."

"Yeah..."

"Here we are." Lisa looked down at her hands.

"So, uh, you have a lot of brothers and sisters."

"Just the three." Lisa laughed. "But, it feels like an army sometimes."

Sam chuckled. "I don't have any."

"You're an only child? I didn't know that."

"Yeah. Just me."

Lisa couldn't imagine being the only kid in a family. Actually, she had been the only child until she was six and then Lynnie came along, but she barely remembered that time. "Do you get lonely?"

"Sometimes, but I don't know anything different actually. I spend a lot of time with Helene because Daddy's got his meetings, and Mother's got her committees."

"Who's Helene?"

"Helene's my nanny."

Lisa laughed. "You have a nanny?"

Sam smiled. "Well, she's not really my nanny anymore. She lives with us, and she's sort of our housekeeper, cook, and, um, well I guess she takes care of everybody. Mom, Dad, me."

"Oh, so she's everybody's nanny."

Sam laughed and tapped the console between them. "Yeah, I guess she's the nanny for the whole Payton Family."

"Payton? That's your last name?"

Sam nodded.

Lisa grinned, but then shook her head. "Samantha Payton, I hope you're not a serial killer or something, because I don't know anything about you. I don't even know what grade you're in."

"Eleventh."

"Tenth." She pointed to herself. "So, you're seventeen?" Sam nodded. "That explains why you have your license. I won't get mine until next February."

"I'll have to chauffeur you around until then." Sam reached over the console and put her hand on top of Lisa's.

Lisa's heart sped up. "It's a long way to Clarksonville from East Valley." Sam's hand still rested on hers. Oh, God, this was a Tara moment. Lisa pulled her hand away pretending she needed to push a lock of hair behind her ear.

Sam pulled her hand back as if nothing had happened. "Hey, that gate is open. Let's walk around the field."

"Okay." Lisa breathed a sigh of relief. Things were moving a little too fast. Lisa opened the car door and took a deep breath of the late afternoon air. The sun had begun to recede in the sky, and she shivered in the slight chill.

Sam opened the gate, and Lisa fell into step beside her as they headed toward home plate.

Sam took a practice swing in the batter's box. "So, why did you tell me Marlee's pitches last night?"

Lisa felt her cheeks get hot. She decided to tell the truth and see what happened. "I was flirting."

"I see."

They walked up the first base line in silence. When they stepped on first base, Lisa asked, "Why were you so friendly the first time we played you guys?" Lisa kept her eyes focused on the outfield fence, because she couldn't look Sam in the eye.

"I was flirting."

"Ah."

"Did you know?" Sam raised an eyebrow.

Lisa laughed. "No. I had, uh, other things on my mind." *Named Marlee.*

"Oh." Sam's voice held a hint of disappointment.

"I don't have those other things on my mind anymore. Well, actually, it was one other thing, but not anymore."

"Oh." There was a happy lilt to Sam's voice that time. They touched second base and headed toward third. A robin hunting for worms flew off to left field as they passed. "Can I interest you in a tour of the third base dugout?"

Lisa nodded, and when they reached the dugout, Sam held the gate open for her.

Lisa walked in and turned around. "So, how about you? Do you have other, uh, things on your mind?"

"Just one." Sam stepped closer.

Lisa's heart sped up again. "Oh, yeah?"

"Yeah." Sam touched Lisa's cheek gently. "You."

Lisa inhaled sharply. "Me?"

Sam responded by putting both hands on each side of Lisa's face and pulling her closer until their noses touched.

Lisa moved forward until their lips met. Sam's lips were warm and, oh, so soft. Their kiss was soft at first, but heated up quickly. Sam moved a hand behind Lisa's neck and pulled her closer. Lisa wrapped her arms around Sam's waist.

After several minutes, Sam pulled away, but rested her forehead on Lisa's. "Oh, my God." She was out of breath.

"I know." Lisa put a hand on Sam's chest, just beneath her neck, and spread her fingers. "I wish—I wish..."

"What?"

Lisa wanted to say she wished they could have taken things slower, but Sam had stirred her up so much, that she didn't care. "I wish you would do that again."

Sam reached down and lifted Lisa's hand to her lips. She kissed each finger in turn and then tilted her head back in invitation. Lisa put her free hand around Sam's waist and pulled her close until there wasn't room for even a single molecule between them. She kissed her. After a few minutes, Lisa finally pulled away breathless. She placed her cheek against Sam's. "You feel so good," she murmured.

"So do you." Sam nuzzled against Lisa's neck sending shivers to her toes.

Lisa pulled away and held Sam at arm's length. "Are we moving too fast?"

Sam held Lisa's gaze. "Lisa, I've liked you since last year."

"Last year? I didn't even know—"

"I know. You didn't even know I was alive. I never knew how to tell you. I mean, you're so strong and confident. And so tall." Sam laughed. "I was desperate to find a way to get to know you, and when Susie and Marlee started seeing each other—"

"I knew it." Lisa smacked her thigh.

"You didn't know about them?"

Lisa shook her head. "I didn't know for sure. I've only come out to one other person. My ex."

"You have an ex?"

Lisa looked down at her feet. "Yeah. She dumped me about a month ago."

A car drove down the road by the field. Sam tapped Lisa on the arm. "C'mon, let's go to the car."

"Okay."

They headed out of the dugout toward Sam's car.

Sam held open the gate for the field. "Is she on your team?"

"Who?"

Sam chuckled. "Your ex."

"Geez, no. I met her at softball camp. She lives on Long Island."

"That's pretty far away."

"Yeah." Lisa laughed. "I guess that's why it didn't work out. She's a senior."

"A senior? Phew, now I don't feel so bad robbing the cradle."

Lisa grinned. "Is that what you're doing?"

Sam opened the passenger door for Lisa. "Yep."

Lisa got in, reached over, and unlocked Sam's door.

"So what about all of *your* exes, eh?" Lisa raised her eyebrows. "I bet you've got them lining up out the door."

Sam started the engine and faked a frown. "What makes you think I have any?"

Liza grinned and pulled Sam to her. She put both hands on Sam's face and kissed her. "That's how."

"Oh, uh, well, yeah. I guess I do have an ex. Just the one." Sam didn't elaborate and pulled out of the parking spot. She turned on her headlights in the deepening twilight.

"Well? Who is she?"

Sam didn't answer right away. She seemed to be concentrating on pulling out onto the main road. She took a deep breath. "You don't know her."

"Try me," Lisa insisted.

"Oh, she's just a girl I played with on my summer travel team."

"Who?"

"Oh, uh, the Northwood shortstop."

"Geez, you mean when you guys played Northwood a couple of weeks ago, your ex was on the field?"

Sam nodded.

"Was that hard for you? Playing against your ex?"

"Kind of, but we went our separate ways in September when school started. We've both officially moved on I think."

Lisa wouldn't ever let on that the tiniest of flames still burned in her heart for Tara, the hoodlum from Long Island. She smiled shyly at Sam. "I think my second is turning out much better than my first."

"Me, too. Second is way better. Times a thousand." She sent Lisa a look that melted Lisa's toes.

Lisa cleared her throat and reached for Sam's hand. "I'm so glad you drove back to Clarksonville, today."

"Me, too." Sam swerved the car into an abandoned gas station and slammed the car into park. "Kiss me and show me how glad you are."

Chapter Seven

Second Base

LISA CUT BRIDGET'S hot dog into small chunks. Bridget stabbed a piece with her fork and dipped it into her mashed potatoes.

Sam grimaced. "I've never seen that, uh, particular food combination before."

Lisa's mother laughed. "You'll never know if you like it unless you try it." She held out the bowl of mashed potatoes toward Sam.

Sam shrugged. "Why not? A Memorial Day barbeque just isn't the same without mashed potatoes, right?" She plopped a small scoop on her paper plate.

"That's the spirit," Lisa's father said. "Sweetpea, pass Samantha the plate of hot dogs."

Bridget sat between Sam and Lisa at the picnic table under the maple tree in the Brown's small back yard. The tree produced enough shade to keep the bright sunlight out of their eyes. Lisa helped her little sister lift up the plate.

"Here Samtha," Bridget said.

Sam stabbed for a hot dog with her plastic fork. "Thanks." She put the hot dog on her plate, cut off a slice with her knife, and stabbed it with her fork. She held the hotdog slice poised over the mound of mashed potatoes. "Like this?"

Bridget nodded.

"Okay." Sam blew out a sigh as if steeling herself to eat octopus. She dipped the hot dog into the creamy white potatoes and took a bite. "This is surprisingly good." She took another bite.

Lisa laughed. "Hey, looks like you're one of the family now."

"Cool." Sam smiled. "Thanks for inviting me over Mr. and Mrs. Brown. My family doesn't do anything special on Memorial Day." Sam took a third bite of the hotdog-potato combination.

"That's too bad," Lisa's father said. "Sometimes we go up to Lake Birch, but I couldn't borrow my buddy's canoe this year."

"Maybe next year, honey." Lisa's mother patted his hand.

"I hope so," he said, "because pretty soon our oldest will be all grown up, off to college, and won't have time for the rest of us. Right, Lisa Bear?"

"Lisa Bear?" Sam laughed.

Lisa reached around Bridget to smack Sam playfully on the arm. "Papa, come on. In front of company?"

"What?" Her father asked innocently. "Oh, hey," the tone of his voice indicated that he was changing the subject. "How's Marlee doing? She pitched a little this week, right?"

"Yeah. She's all set to pitch against East Valley tomorrow."

Her father nodded. "Big playoff game against your biggest enemy, eh?" He looked at Sam and winked.

Sam smiled back at him.

Lisa narrowed her eyes and looked at Sam over Bridget's head. "Why yes. Yes it is. Mom, why did you invite the enemy into our home?"

It was Sam's turn to reach around Bridget to smack Lisa. "Hey, was this food poisoned? That hot dog and mashed potato thing, that wasn't an evil plot, was it?" Sam put both hands to her throat. "Arghh," she groaned as if poisoned.

Bridget and Lawrence Jr. giggled and grabbed their own throats. "Arghh," they groaned with Sam. Lynnie smiled, but didn't join in.

Lisa looked at her parents and said with a laugh, "I think you have five children now."

Lisa's mother and father laughed, and her mother said, "Yeah, I'd say Samantha fits right in. We'll have to call her Samantha Brown from now on."

Sam beamed, and Lisa's heart leaped at the sight.

"Okay, Brown children," Lisa's mother playfully including Sam in the command, "let's clean up the table and then we can play lawn darts."

"Lawn darts," Lawrence Jr. shrieked. "Hurry up, you guys." He scrambled off the bench of the picnic table and threw his paper plate in the metal trash can. He stood with his hands on his hips.

Lisa grimaced at Sam. "Are you ready for lawn darts with two kids under the age of seven?"

Sam's eyes grew wide. "Where's your catcher's gear? We might need it."

"Really." Lisa laughed.

"Hey, you guys," Sam said to Lisa's sisters and brother. "I brought you all something."

"You did?" Lynnie stood up quickly and threw her plate in the trash can.

"Yeah." Sam smiled. "Let me go get the stuff from the car." She stood up and pulled her car keys out of her pocket.

Lisa looked at Sam with one eyebrow raised. "Do you need help?"

"Nah, I'll be right back."

Sam headed around the side of the house. Lisa looked at her sisters and brother and shrugged. "Make sure you all say thank you, okay?"

They nodded, and Lisa busied herself cleaning up the table.

Sam came back around the house with a box, set it on the table, and the entire Brown clan, including Lisa's parents, gathered around.

Sam pulled out a brand new Candy Land board game and handed it to Bridget. "This is for you. Maybe we can play this later. After lawn darts."

"'Kay," Bridget said running her hand over the colorful box.

"Say thank you," Lisa's mother admonished.

"Thank you."

"You're welcome, Bridget."

Bridget took the game box to the other end of the picnic table and asked her father to help her open it.

Sam reached back in the box and pulled out a brand new Transformer action figure in a sealed box. Lawrence Jr.'s eyes lit up, but Sam held the toy out toward Lynnie. "Lynnie this is for you."

Lawrence Jr.'s face fell which caused the entire family, including Sam, to laugh. "I'm just kidding." She handed the toy to Lawrence Jr. "Of course this is for you." She winked at Lynnie who smiled back.

"Thanks, Sam." He grabbed the toy from her hands and tore open the packaging.

Sam cleared her throat and faced Lynnie. "I have something for you, too. I noticed you liked books about wizards, and I wasn't sure if you'd read these yet." She pulled out a hardcover edition of *Harry Potter and the Sorcerer's Stone*.

Lynnie reached for the book and ran her hand across the colorful cover.

"Have you read this one?"

Lynnie shook her head.

"Oh, good."

Lisa's heart swelled. Sam had found a way to bond with Lynnie right off the bat.

Lynnie clutched the book tightly to her chest and then gave Sam a hug. "Thank you."

"Oh, you're welcome." She pulled another book from the box. "I brought you the entire series, because if you're anything like me, you'll have this book finished like *that*." She snapped her fingers. "And then you'll want to read the next one right away."

"Oh, Samantha," Lisa's mother said. "That was very generous. She just recently discovered books about magic, wizards, and witches. Right Lynnie?"

Lynnie nodded, but didn't look up. She had already started reading the first page.

Sam smiled. "Well, I'm glad I could feed her need to read. Oh, and she can keep the books, by the way. I have another set at home."

"Really?" Lisa said.

Sam nodded.

"Thank you so much."

Sam blushed. "No problem."

Lisa's mother went into the house with the leftover hot dogs. Her father busied himself setting up the lawn darts with help from Lawrence Jr. and Bridget. They were all out of earshot, except for Lynnie who sat at the table, but she was so absorbed with her new book, that she didn't seem to be aware of anything else.

"You just wait until I get you alone later," Lisa whispered.

"Oh, yeah?"

Lisa waggled her eyebrows. "It's our two week, two day anniversary."

"I know. How soon until we can get out of here?" Sam whispered back.

"After the annual lawn dart competition, you can take me anywhere that's dark and secluded."

Sam blushed to her blond roots and then cleared her throat. "Hey, can you believe Susie broke up with Marlee?"

"Trying to change the subject, eh?"

Sam nodded.

Lisa grinned. "You know, I thought Marlee broke up with Susie that day we visited her after her accident. I mean, geez, Susie looked so devastated when she came flying out of the house. I feel so bad that Jeri and I didn't go back up to see if she was okay."

Lisa's mother opened the screen door and tossed a wet rag onto the table. "Honey, can you wipe the table?"

"Sure, Mom. Hey Lynnie, go inside and read, okay?"

"Okay." Lynnie got up, still reading, and went inside the house.

Sam tossed a napkin in the trash can. "You weren't out to Marlee yet, were you?"

"Not then, but we're out to each other now." Lisa grinned.

"Yeah, I know. You gotta have somebody to talk to." Sam sighed. "I hope she takes Susie back. Susie's miserable."

"If she's so miserable, why'd she break up with Marlee in the first place?" Lisa continued to wipe the table. "I mean, c'mon. You break up with someone and then two weeks later beg to come back? That makes no sense. Did you read the letter Susie wrote to Marlee?"

Sam shook her head.

"Me, neither, but Marlee said Susie wants a sign from her at our game tomorrow."

"I know what the sign is," Sam said with a grin.

"Ooh! What is it?" Lisa threw the rag on the table and sat down in a heap. "Tell me."

Sam leaned closer. "She wants Marlee to..."

"Oh, c'mon, what?"

"Nope. Marlee should be the one to tell you. I've been too much of a gossip queen already."

"Oh, you suck." Lisa smacked Sam playfully on the arm.

"Okay, everybody," Lisa's father announced. "It's time for lawn darts."

Sam stood up. "Saved by the lawn dart."

Just as Lisa stuck her tongue out at Sam, her mother came back out for the rag. "Oh, that's mature, Lisa."

"I know."

Lisa's father called, "Mama, are you in?"

"Nope. You go on ahead. I have to put the food away."

"Okay, Mama's out. Lynnie's at Hogwarts, so it's me, Bridget, and Samantha against Lisa and Lawrence Jr."

Lisa grabbed a blue lawn dart. "I think that championship game got started a day early."

"Bring it on, Lisa Bear. Bring it on." Sam ran before Lisa could smack her with the business end of the lawn dart.

Lisa and Lawrence Jr. lost the first game, so Lisa quickly challenged the other team to a best two out of three tournament. When they lost again, it quickly turned into the best three out of five. Lisa lost track of the number of games they played and was surprised when her Mom called Bridget and Lawrence Jr. in to get ready for bed.

"Mom," Lisa called once she and Sam had successfully gotten both Bridget and Lawrence Jr. into their pajamas. "Sam and I are going out for a quick ride, okay?"

Lisa's mother looked at the kitchen clock. "Okay, but be back by ten. It's a school night, and Samantha still has a forty-five minute ride home."

"Okay, Mom." Lisa took her house key off the hook by the front door. "Ready?" she said to Sam.

"Yep." Sam turned to Lisa's parents. "Thanks so much for inviting me over. I had a great time."

"Any time," Lisa's father said. "Hey, are you available on the fourth of July? We have to defend our lawn darts' championship title."

Before Sam could answer Lisa said, "Oh, you guys so cheated."

Sam laughed. "Sore loser much?"

"Go on," Lisa's mother said. "Bicker in the car." She ushered them out the door.

Sam opened the passenger door for Lisa.

Lisa got in. "You're such a gentleman."

Sam laughed. "You won't be saying that later."

"Promise?"

Sam's smoldering smile almost melted Lisa's toes.

Sam pulled into what was becoming their usual spot at the secluded Clarksonville Community College softball field. There were no other signs of life in the dark parking lot.

Lisa took off her seatbelt. She spread her fingers and matched her hand against Sam's. Her fingers were at least a quarter inch longer. She intertwined their fingers and pulled Sam closer. "Kiss me."

Lisa welcomed the warm lips against her own. Her pulse quickened. She pulled Sam closer, as if that were even possible and kissed her with a need she'd never felt before. Sam's arms went around Lisa's neck. Lisa nibbled her way to Sam's ear and nuzzled Sam's neck. She kissed her on the lips one more time and pulled back. She looked at Sam knowing her eyes gave away everything she felt for her.

"I love your hair." Lisa stroked Sam's ponytail.

Sam smiled.

"But," Lisa said, "let's get rid of this." She pulled the hair band off of Sam's ponytail. Sam shook her head to let her hair flow free. Lisa ran her fingers through the long blond tresses. "God, you are so..." Lisa bit her lip.

"What?"

Lisa felt her face get hot. "Sexy."

"So are you." Sam's grin made Lisa's heart pound. "Can I undo your braid?"

Lisa nodded.

"Turn around."

"Okay," Lisa whispered. Hot tingles settled low in her belly as she presented her braid to Sam.

Sam took the hair band off the bottom and untwisted the three separate strands. Using her fingers, she raked Lisa's long hair smooth.

Lisa moaned. "God, that feels so good."

Sam gathered Lisa's long black hair into a bundle and moved it to one side. She then kissed Lisa on the back of the neck.

Lisa shivered. "I can't believe the way you make me feel."

Sam kissed her way around Lisa's neck. She nudged Lisa's shoulder in request for Lisa to turn back around and face her.

Lisa obliged, and let Sam kiss her on the lips again. Lisa sighed when the kisses moved to the base of her throat.

Sam tugged at Lisa's shirt. "Can I take this off you?" Her voice was husky.

Lisa's stomach clenched as she registered Sam's request. Her face got warmer as she took a quick look out the windows. Not a single soul was in sight. She leaned away from Sam and lifted her T-shirt up with shaking hands. Sam helped her take the shirt off the rest of the way. Lisa was glad she had chosen to wear a lace bra instead of a sports bra.

"So pretty." Sam traced the outline of Lisa's lace bra with her fingers, reaching further still to trace the cleavage. Lisa melted when Sam's lips replaced the fingers.

Lisa lost herself in Sam's kisses, but soon demanded equal time and unbuttoned Sam's shirt. Her heart clenched when she saw the loveliness of Sam's body hidden only by her silk bra.

It wasn't long before both bras found their way to the floor of the Sebring. The girls embraced and pressed their softness against each other. Lisa couldn't believe how amazing Sam's soft skin felt against hers.

Sam stroked Lisa's face. "You are so damn gorgeous. I wish this stupid center console wasn't in the way."

"I know, but I don't care. I'm with you, so I don't care." She pulled Sam closer and kissed her again.

The town clock began chiming. "Oh, geez." Lisa scrambled for her shirt. "It's ten o'clock. I'm dead meat." She handed Sam her shirt. "You gotta take me home."

Sam frantically searched for the bras and finally found them nestled together under the brake pedal.

They tried to dress in a hurry and kept knocking elbows. Lisa burst out laughing. "I'm gonna pull a muscle."

Sam laughed and got her own shirt situated and properly buttoned. She started the car engine. She sped all the way back to Lisa's house and pulled the Sebring in front of the driveway at ten minutes past ten.

Sam stroked Lisa's cheek. "I had a great day."

"Me, too. I had no idea I'd let you get to second base today." Lisa grinned.

"Hey, I *am* a second baseman, you know, but I think if that stupid town clock hadn't rung, I'd be a third baseman about now."

Lisa smacked Sam playfully on the arm. She sighed. "I have to go in. Do I look okay?"

"You look amazing, but you'd better stop smiling."

"I can't help it." Lisa smiled even bigger and then leaned over to kiss Sam again.

The front porch lights flickered off then on again.

"Oh, geez." Lisa squeezed Sam's hand. "I hope we didn't just get caught. Oh, God. I don't care." She opened the car door and stepped out. "I'll see you tomorrow, okay?"

"Definitely."

Lisa took a few steps up the driveway and realized her braid was still undone. She gulped when she noticed her mother watching through the front window.

Chapter Eight

Win-Win

LISA SAT ON the Cougars' team bench with Jeri on one side and Marlee on the other. The championship game against the East Valley Panthers was set to get underway in under an hour. The Panthers hadn't arrived yet, but as soon as their bus pulled in, Lisa knew it would be hard not to run over to Sam. Marlee would probably have an even harder time ignoring Susie because, as far as Lisa knew, she hadn't decided whether to take Susie back or not.

Coach Spears laid her scorebook on the team bench. "You've worked hard all year, ladies, and now it's time to show East Valley," she pointed to the empty visitors' bench, "that you are the better team. This is the one game you've worked for all season." She gestured toward the team's two seniors, Jeri and Paula, and said, "I'm sure our seniors would appreciate a trophy and a shot at States. It's time to put up or shut up, ladies." She looked at her watch. "Okay, go take your warm up laps as a team."

Lisa ran her laps with Marlee, and then they warmed up in the pitching area behind the bleachers. Once she was satisfied that Marlee was properly warmed up, they walked back toward the bench. Lisa waved to her family in the bleachers as she went by.

"Play well, honey," her mother called.

"Do your papa proud," her father said.

"I'll try, Papa, I'll try." She laughed when she saw Bridget and Lawrence Jr. already covered with dirt playing Tonka trucks. Lynnie sat reading one of her new Harry Potter books.

Lisa and Marlee joined Jeri on the team bench. Jeri leaned over Lisa and said to Marlee, "She wants you to give her a sign?"

Apparently Jeri the straight girl was just as intrigued by Marlee's love life as Lisa was.

Marlee nodded. "She said that if I took off my hat today and nodded my head yes that'll mean I'll give her another chance. Otherwise, if I don't give her a sign, she'll just stay in East Valley and leave me alone."

"What are you gonna do?" Lisa and Jeri asked at the same time. Lisa smacked Jeri on the leg.

"Oh, c'mon, you guys. Honestly, I really don't know."

"Fine," Jeri grumbled. "Don't tell us. But I think...nah, it's your decision." Jeri ran off to catch pops with Paula and some of the other outfielders.

The big luxury bus from East Valley pulled in.

"Breathe, Marlee, breathe." Lisa took a deep breath of her own. She desperately wanted to look for Sam, but didn't for Marlee's sake.

A perfect day for softball had been delivered. The skies were crystal blue with puffy white clouds. It was the perfect day to take Sam to Lake Birch, or better yet, to take a ride on the back roads outside of town and find a secluded spot far, far away from people.

Even though she promised herself she wouldn't, she snuck a peek at the red and black East Valley team making its way toward the visitors' side of the field. Her breath caught in her throat when she saw Sam, hair loose, black softball bag slung over her shoulder, eyes bright. Lisa smiled. Her heart sped up when Sam smiled back at her.

"Hi," Sam mouthed from across the field and waved.

Lisa waved back. "Good luck," she mouthed.

Sam wiggled the fingers on both hands as if sending bad luck whammies. Lisa stood up, mouth open in disbelief. She put both hands on her hips and shook her head slowly. She couldn't hold the pose and laughed.

Sam laughed, too, and yelled over, "I'll talk to you after."

"After. Okay." Lisa turned away from the East Valley team and pulled out her chest protector and mask.

The Cougars took their pre-game warm-ups on the field, and then let the East Valley team have theirs. Lisa busied herself adjusting the straps on her shin guards, so she wouldn't watch Sam. She snuck a peek, though, when Sam ran off the field, blond ponytail bouncing with every step.

The umpire gestured to the Cougars' bench. "Home team, take the field."

Lisa grabbed her mitt. "We can do this Marlee, c'mon." They ran onto the field to start the game that would decide the North Country League championship.

During the first inning, Lisa settled Marlee into their usual routine of fastballs and change-ups. Later in the game, they'd introduce the rise, curve, and drop. If all went well, they'd even try the new screwball. Maybe. The fastball-change-up combination worked so well that the East Valley Panthers didn't score in the top half of the inning. They didn't even get a runner on base.

The Cougars got up to bat in the bottom half of the inning and quickly put two runners on base. With one out, Lisa headed toward the batter's box.

"C'mon, all-county batter," Marlee called from the on-deck circle. "Smack it out there."

Lisa had been named to the All-County First Team in batting, but she was about to step into the batter's box against Christy, the First Team pitcher for Clarksonville County, so she couldn't rest on her laurels.

Lisa dug her heels in and tried to find a hole in the East Valley outfield. The right-center field gap looked good. If Christy threw her an outside pitch, she'd aim for it. She waited for the first pitch. It was in the dirt. Ball one. The next was way too high. Ball two. The next two pitches were so far outside, there was no way she could have reached them, so she walked to load the bases. Marlee was up next.

Lisa took a deep breath. This was Marlee's first at bat against the pitcher that had slammed her into the hospital. No one really knew if Christy had done it on purpose, except for Christy herself, but Lisa mentally crossed her fingers that Marlee would find the nerve to stand in the batter's box.

Christy released the pitch. Lisa exploded off the base and took a larger lead than usual.

"Ball one," the umpire said.

The catcher leaped up and made a motion to throw down to first base, so Lisa scrambled back to the base. The next pitch to Marlee was in the dirt, but the catcher made an awesome stop and kept it in front of her. Ball two.

Christy's third pitch floated right down the middle of the plate, and Lisa knew instantly the East Valley team was in trouble. Marlee swung and connected. The ball sailed over Susie's head in left field. Lisa had just run past Sam when Marlee's smash bounced on the grass outside the fence.

"Yeah," Lisa shouted and pumped a fist. Marlee had just hit a grand slam homerun off the cow that had tried to kill her.

Lisa crossed the plate and waited for Marlee to cross. When she did Lisa grabbed her in a hug. "Way to go, pitcher." Lisa didn't let go, so their teammates had to hug them both.

Lisa went back to the bench and grabbed a sip of water. She took a deep breath before throwing on her catcher's gear. She knew never to count out the Panthers, but it was nice being up by a score of 4-0 with only one out in the first inning.

The Cougars didn't score any more runs in that inning or the next. In the bottom of the third, Christy walked Lisa again. Unfortunately for the Panthers, Marlee came up and smashed a double up the left field line. Lisa ran past Sam again, and scored all the way from first base. That put the Cougars up by a score of 5-0.

The score remained unchanged when the top of the sixth inning rolled around. It was the Panthers turn to bat, but they seemed like a team deflated. Batter after Panther batter fell victim to Marlee's rise ball. The third batter of the inning struck out swinging, and Lisa tossed the ball to the pitcher's circle. She hurried in and stripped off her catcher's gear since she was due to lead off the bottom of the inning. Julie helped by unhooking the shin guards.

"Thanks, White Girl." Lisa kicked off the shin guards that Julie had just unhooked.

Julie pointed toward Marlee. "Does she know yet?"

Lisa almost choked. How could Julie know about the East Valley-Clarksonville gay girl drama going on? There was no way Julie could know about the decision Marlee had to make. Oh, wait. Julie had to be talking about Marlee's perfect game. Not a single East Valley player, Sam and Susie included, had gotten on base.

"Julie, c'mon. Marlee never thinks about perfect games or no-hitters."

"You know what?" Julie laughed. "It's probably better that way."

"Yeah, you're right." Lisa picked up her helmet and bat and took a couple of swings in the on-deck circle. She watched Christy throw her warm-up pitches.

Lisa jumped when Marlee snuck up behind her and whispered, "Does the whole team know about me? Me and Susie?"

"What are you talking about?"

"Batter?" the umpire called for her.

Marlee grabbed Lisa's arm. "No one's looking at me or even talking to me."

"Geez, Marlee, you are so slow. And I shouldn't even say it, but you sound paranoid. You have a perfect game going, dorkhead." Lisa took a step toward the plate. "And you know as well as I do it's a jinx to talk to a pitcher who's on her way to a perfect game." She headed toward the plate. "Yeah, it's brain damage all right."

She dug her heels in the batter's box and waited for the first pitch. Christy hadn't given her a single strike the entire day and apparently didn't intend to because Lisa walked for the third time.

Marlee stepped into the batter's box and smacked the first pitch into the three-four hole just out of Sam's reach.

"Burned," Lisa said to Sam as she ran past her toward second base.

The right fielder tossed the ball back in to Sam who tossed it back to Christy. Sam walked over to Lisa on second base. "Burned? You just wait until I get you alone later, we'll see who burns."

"Ooh, now that sounds interesting."

Sam smiled and backpedaled to her position.

Lisa looked at Marlee who wagged her finger as if to tell her to stop cavorting with the enemy. Lisa quite maturely stuck her tongue out at her pitcher.

The Cougars couldn't move Lisa or Marlee any further along on the bases, so the score remained 5-0 going into the top of the seventh and potentially last inning.

The Panthers from East Valley had to score at least five runs or their season would be over. Lisa squatted behind the plate. She expected to be more tired at that point, but her legs still felt strong. Of course, three up and three down every single inning helped in that regard.

Lisa flashed the sign for fastball. Why mess with something that was working? She put her mitt up on the inside corner. "Just you and me, Marlee."

Marlee's pitch hung over the plate, and the leadoff batter hit a hard ground ball right back at her. Lisa ran up the line to back up first base in case of an overthrow, but Marlee fielded the ball cleanly and tossed it to Julie for the first out of the inning.

"Nice," Lisa called on her way back behind the plate. "One pitch, one out. Just you and me, one more time."

Lisa called for three fastballs. The batter swung and missed on the first two pitches, and the third pitch nicked the inside corner for strike three. There were two outs with one more to go.

Lisa tried not to smile. Marlee was one out away from a perfect game. All they had to do was get through Sam. Sam, self-admittedly, had trouble hitting against Marlee.

Lisa swallowed hard when Sam stepped into the batter's box. The feathered ends of Sam's blond ponytail stuck out from underneath her helmet. Lisa bit her lip as she remembered running her hands through Sam's soft hair the night before. She took a deep breath to clear her head.

"One more, #3. Just you and me." Lisa squatted behind the plate and flashed the sign for fastball. Marlee put her hands together to start the delivery. Lisa put her mitt up for the pitch, but then Marlee stepped back off the rubber. Sam stepped out of the box, and the umpire called for time.

Lisa, not knowing what to do, stood up. She thought for sure Marlee was about to take her hat off and nod at Susie telling her she'd take her back, but she didn't. She simply stepped back on the pitching rubber as if nothing had happened and waited for the sign. Lisa squatted back down, Sam stepped back in the box, and the umpire leaned low. Lisa flashed the sign for fastball again.

"Okay, Marlee. Just you and me." Lisa got into position. *No girlfriends or drama right now, pitcher. Just you and me.* Lisa felt bad rooting for her own girlfriend to strike out, but she kind of had to.

Marlee fired her first pitch. Strike one on the outside corner. The next pitch was inside, just missing for ball one. Lisa called for another fastball. Sam swung and fouled it off for strike two. Lisa searched for the big money pitch. The rise ball, it had to be. Sam always missed it. Lisa flashed the signal for rise ball, but the ball rose just out of the strike zone for ball two. Lisa was surprised that Sam laid off the pitch, because she usually swung at them. With the count even at two and two, Lisa called for another rise ball, and Sam laid off that one as well. The count went full at three balls and two strikes, and Lisa's heart jumped in her throat. If they walked Sam, Marlee's perfect game would be lost. There was no choice. Lisa flashed the sign for fastball and put her mitt smack dab in the middle of the strike zone. *Meatball,*

Marlee, Lisa willed. *Meatball. Let Sam hit it.*

Marlee's pitch was true, but Sam's swing was truer. Sam connected with the fat pitch and sent it flying into the eight-nine gap between Jeri and Paula. Lisa's heart sank. Why did it have to be Sam who broke up the perfect game? Marlee was going to be heart-broken.

Lisa waited for the inevitable, but then a miracle happened. Jeri, from out of nowhere, leaped for the ball, and snatched it out of the air.

"She caught it. She caught it!" Lisa yelled.

Jeri landed face down on the grass and held the ball high in her glove.

The umpire yelled, "The batter is out!"

"Holy!" Lisa ran up to Marlee. She hugged the stuffing out of her pitcher, but she didn't care. They had just won the North Country League championship game and kept Marlee's perfect game intact.

Julie, Johnna, and the rest of the infielders joined them in the pitcher's circle and celebrated, then en masse stormed Jeri in the outfield.

After celebrating with her teammates for several minutes, Lisa realized she'd lost her mitt somewhere along the way, but she didn't really care. She looked around for Marlee and found her standing with Jeri. They were looking at Susie on the visitors' bench. Susie looked haggard and drained. Lisa's heart went out to her.

Lisa walked up just in time to hear Marlee say, "You are awesome, Jeri."

"No, you are awesome, Marlee."

"No, you."

"No—"

"Shut up, both of you," Lisa said. "You're both awesome. But, Marlee, you still have that decision to make, don't you?" She gestured in Susie's direction.

"Yeah," Jeri added, "that decision, Marlee."

Marlee's smile fell away. "No, I made my decision."

Lisa's heart dropped. Susie would be so disappointed. "Oh, okay." She shrugged and turned to find her mitt.

"I decided to do this." Marlee pulled her hat off her head and nodded her head a half dozen times.

Lisa and Jeri cheered. Susie stood up, the relief on her face obvious. Sam smiled, too.

Lisa smacked Marlee on the arm for teasing them and then went in search of her mitt, so she could let Marlee approach Susie alone.

A few minutes later, Coach Spears called the team together for a post-game huddle in left field. "Girls, this game is the direct result of the hard work you've put in all season. Each and every one of you made this happen. Hitting, fielding, throwing, base running, you mastered the fundamentals and became a championship team."

Lisa and her teammates cheered and clapped.

"It's a little surreal for me, actually," Coach Spears continued. "I've been waiting a long time for just the right combination of talent, but we have to thank our biggest workhorse. To pitch a perfect game in a championship..." The words caught in Coach Spears's throat and her eyes welled with tears. Lisa felt tears brimming in her own eyes.

Marlee cleared her throat obviously trying to regain her own composure. "Listen, guys. I get credit for the perfect game, but every single one of you had a hand in this. I mean, how about Jeri's SportsCenter catch?" The team clapped for Jeri. "And Coach Spears? She kept telling me I could do anything I set my mind to." The team clapped and cheered for their coach. "But I have to give most of the credit to Lisa." Lisa's teammates clapped and hooted for her. Lisa felt her cheeks get warm.

Marlee put her arm around Lisa's shoulder. "Lisa very humbly says that I'm the train, and she just keeps me on the track, but it's so much more than that. She calls all my pitches. Even in college, the coaches call the pitches, but Coach Spears lets Lisa do it, because Lisa truly is the catching goddess of the universe." Her teammates cheered again.

Coach Spears patted both of them on the back. "I am truly blessed to have such a talented and cohesive team. Now, Jeri? Paula? I'm pleased to tell you that your high school softball careers are not over yet. At best, we'll play four more games and be the New York State Division C champions."

Lisa screeched, "Whoo hoo!" She took a deep breath. A state championship in softball was unheard of in Clarksonville High School history. Clarksonville had never even won the North Country League championship before. Ever. That honor always went to East Valley or Southbridge.

"But, ladies," Coach Spears continued, "every game is single elimination, so every game is do or die. If we lose, we're out. So all we have to do..." she looked every single player in the eye, "...is win the last game we play."

"Win the last," Lisa said.

"Yeah," Jeri agreed. Jeri put her hand in the middle of the players' circle. Lisa put her hand on top followed by her teammates. "On three everybody. Win the last. Ready? One, two, three!"

"Win the last!" the team shouted.

The meeting broke up, and everyone headed toward their waiting friends and families. Even Coach Spears headed toward a dark-haired woman whom Lisa suspected was her girlfriend.

Lisa patted Marlee on the back. "Thanks for saying those nice things."

Marlee smiled at her. "I meant every word."

"Thanks. And, uh," she gestured toward Susie and Sam waiting for them near the bleachers, "it looks like you and I are win-win today."

Marlee grinned, and they bumped both fists in double-victory.

Chapter Nine

Courage

LISA PULLED THE family minivan into Marlee's driveway. "Thanks for letting me drive, Mom." She pulled off her seatbelt and opened the driver's side door.

"Sure, honey." Her mother got out of the passenger side, and they met in front of the van. "I feel better letting you practice driving now that the roads aren't snowy and icy. Just remember this day when I ask you to chauffeur Lynnie, Lawrence Jr., and Bridget around next year."

"Geez, getting my license doesn't sound as much fun anymore."

Her mother laughed. "Samantha will bring you home by midnight, right?"

"Yeah, I think Susie's driving, though, but I'll make sure I'm home on time." She gave her mother a quick hug. "Love you, Mom. See you later."

Lisa walked up the driveway to Marlee's house. This time she wore flats and navigated the gravel drive more easily than the last time she'd been there. She heard her mother back the van out and head down C.R. 62 toward home.

Lisa smoothed down her red fitted shirt. She'd spent half that morning figuring out what to wear because she wanted Sam's eyes to pop out when she saw her. Not that long ago, she would have been smoothing out her shirt to impress Marlee and would have rejoiced in the fact that she was going out to dinner and the movies with her, but not this time. Lisa was more excited about going out with Sam, even if it was on a double date with Marlee and Susie. She knocked on the kitchen screen door.

"C'mon in." Marlee called from inside.

Lisa opened the screen door and walked in. "Hey, Marlee." The door thumped closed behind her. One day Lisa hoped to have a big bright country kitchen like Marlee's.

"I knew it was you," Marlee said from where she sat at the kitchen table. "I spied out the window."

"Anxious much? When are they getting here?"

"In about twenty minutes, I think. Susie called when they left, and that was at four o'clock." She got up from the table and put a glass in the sink. Marlee wore black jeans and a white long-sleeved Henley. Her short blond hair was still wet from a shower. "Do you want something to drink?"

"No, I'm good." Lisa sat down at the table. "So, what'd you think about Coach Spears's practices from hell this week?"

"Oh, man. She's trying to turn us into the U.S. National Team, I think."

"Stacey Nuveman I'm not."

"Yeah, right." Marlee laughed. She checked her watch and looked out the kitchen window to the driveway. "I think Coach wants us to take no prisoners when we play Overton Corners Tuesday."

"They're from the Champlain Valley region, right?"

"Yeah." Marlee opened a drawer. She pulled out a pen and a pad of paper. "I'm gonna leave my mom a note reminding her that we're going to Northwood for dinner and then to the movies over there."

"My parents thought it was weird that Susie and Sam were coming all the way here from East Valley, and then we're going ten more miles to Northwood to hang out."

Marlee looked up from her note. "Yeah, well, I hope you didn't tell them I'm the one who's paranoid about, you know, double dating in Clarksonville." Marlee blushed.

Lisa rubbed her mouth to hide her smile. "No, I didn't, but let's hope nobody knows us in Northwood, eh?"

"Oh, don't even say that." Marlee finished her note and recapped the pen. "You know, you floored me that day you came out to me. I had no idea about you, but I think after two weeks I'm finally over the shock." She sat down at the table across from Lisa.

"Sorry about that, but I had to come out to you. You looked so miserable, and I figured you might need somebody to talk you. I knew you and Susie had hooked up."

Marlee put her head down on the table, clearly embarrassed. "I can't believe it was so obvious," she mumbled into the table.

"Only to me. Like I told you that day, it takes one to know one."

Marlee sat back up. "Yeah, but I didn't know about you. Or Sam. Or even me for that matter." She chuckled and leaned closer. "Lisa, I didn't even know if Susie was, you know, gay, when I told her that I liked her."

Lisa's mouth dropped open. "You came out to Susie, but you didn't know if she was gay? That took a lot of courage."

Marlee grinned. "But it worked out, right?"

Lisa nodded. "You're lucky, but, geez, we have to fine tune your gaydar. When did you know for sure you were gay?" *Which obviously had nothing to do with me.*

"The first time I saw Susie run out to left field."

"At our first game against them this year?"

"Oh, no, no." Marlee shook her head. "Before that. Jeri and I drove out to East Valley to watch them play Southbridge."

"Oh, now I see why you were so distracted when we played them the first time. You had a little crush on a certain East Valley left fielder, didn't you?"

"Yeah." Marlee nodded and blushed again. "Sorry." She sighed. "This is all so new to me."

Lisa grinned. "So, how are things now that you and Susie are back together?"

"It's great. She's great. Man, I can't believe how much I like her."

Lisa smiled and firmly closed the lid on her short-lived crush on Marlee.

Marlee scrunched up her face in embarrassment. "She came out here last night, and we went to Lake Birch."

"Lake Birch, eh?" Lisa waggled her eyebrows.

"Oh, shut up. So how's Sam?" Marlee singsonged.

"She's amazing, absolutely amazing. And before you ask, she went after me."

"She did, did she?"

Lisa nodded and felt her face get warm.

"Sam's cool. I like her."

"Me, too." Lisa grinned.

"No kidding."

"Hey, does your Mom know about you yet?"

Marlee shook her head.

"Are you going to tell her?"

Marlee shrugged. "I guess so. I just don't know how or when or where."

"Me, neither. I'm going to tell my parents eventually. I mean, c'mon, when I was in seventh grade, I knew I liked girls."

Marlee laughed. "You knew in seventh, but it took me until eleventh to figure it out." She looked at her watch again. "I wish they lived closer."

"Especially since we can't drive out there on our own yet."

Marlee grinned. "I'm getting my license on June eleventh."

"Is that your birthday?"

Marlee nodded.

Why hadn't she known Marlee's birth date? Lisa almost laughed out loud when she realized she had been a terrible stalker, but thank goodness those days were over. She didn't know when Sam's birthday was, either. That was definitely something she had to find out fast. She wondered if Marlee knew when Susie's birthday was. Speaking of Susie...

"Hey, Marlee, why did Susie break up with you, anyway?" Lisa cringed. "Oh, geez, that was a little abrupt. Sorry. You don't have to answer that if you don't want to."

"Oh, no, it's okay. I mean I can't tell you every sordid detail, but I'll make a long story short. Christy got jealous of the time Susie spent with me. She thought Susie was telling me private stuff about her. Which she absolutely wasn't."

"Susie broke up with you over that?"

"Yeah, she couldn't stand the pressure Christy put on her. And when Christy threw that pitch at me—"

"Allegedly threw that pitch at you," Lisa said with a grin.

"Allegedly, my eye." Marlee's eyes grew wide. "Anyway, Susie thought she'd keep me safe from Christy's wrath by breaking up with me."

"Ooh, harsh. Sam didn't tell me any of this."

"I don't think Sam knows any of that stuff, either."

"Yeah, she said Susie didn't talk to her about Christy much."

Marlee nodded. "I think Christy's learning to deal with the fact that Susie wants to hang with me."

"Seems that way. She didn't throw a single pitch at your head on Tuesday."

Marlee tapped the table with her index finger. "Exactly."

Lisa heard a car and turned her head toward the kitchen window. The bright afternoon sunlight streaming through made it difficult to see whose car was pulling up the driveway.

Marlee bolted to the window and shielded her eyes. "It's them. It's them." She flung open the kitchen door.

Lisa smiled at the excitement in Marlee's voice because she felt the same excitement bubbling in her own body.

Sam was out of the car before Susie turned the engine off. Lisa ran out the door past Marlee and grabbed Sam by the waist, picked her up, and spun her around once.

"I missed you." Lisa leaned down to put her forehead on Sam's.

"I missed you, too."

Lisa snuck a peek at Marlee and Susie. Marlee had her arms wrapped around Susie's neck. They were kissing like nobody's business, so Lisa decided it was okay to kiss Sam in the light of day, right there in the McAllisters' driveway.

Lisa leaned down and gently pressed her lips against Sam's. She kissed Sam tenderly and then rested her head on Sam's shoulder. Sam slid her arms around Lisa's waist.

"I know it's only been four days since I last saw you," Sam said, "but those four days have been absolute torture."

"Same." Lisa picked her head back up and stared into Sam's playful eyes.

"I love it when you wear your hair down." Sam reached up and pushed a lock of hair off Lisa's face.

"Same." Lisa mimicked the motion and pushed a lock of blond hair off of Sam's face.

Lisa looked back at Marlee and Susie. They were obviously making up for lost time. "Geez, those two need to get a room."

"Break it up, you two," Sam called over. "You're gonna melt the gravel."

Marlee pulled ever so slightly away from Susie and grinned. "Uh,

I think you two melted your own patch of gravel over there, so don't talk."

Lisa shrugged and smiled. "Yeah, I think you're right."

"*Dios*," Susie said. "We'd better get going before Marlee compromises my good name."

"Oh, man," Marlee smacked Susie's arm. "You are in so much trouble."

"Promise, *mi vida*?"

Lisa and Sam laughed.

Marlee reluctantly let go of Susie and went back to lock the front door. She bounded back to Susie. "C'mon, let's hit the road."

Sam opened the passenger door of Susie's Toyota Celica and pulled the front seat forward. She gestured for Lisa to go into the back seat first.

Lisa cringed, not because she was claustrophobic, but because she'd have to figure out a way to fold herself in the small space. It really didn't matter since she'd be crumpled in with Sam. "Uh, oh. We've graduated to the back seat. Are you gonna compromise *my* good name back here?"

Sam grinned seductively. "Only if you want me to."

Lisa smiled back. *Oh, I want you to Samantha Payton. I want you to.*

A LITTLE OVER a week later, Monday, June eleventh, the day of the first round of playoffs finally arrived. The old yellow school bus rumbled through the oak tunnel. They were less than five minutes away from the Sandstoner Fields in East Valley.

Lisa spun around in her seat to face Marlee. "I can't believe we have to play this game in East Valley."

"Yeah, well, I guess East Valley figured they'd win the North Country title like they always do, so the state scheduled the first round game there."

"You know what?" Jeri said. "I'm glad. Their field is way better than ours."

"Yeah, no kidding," Marlee said.

"The backstop is farther behind me, though," Lisa said.

Jeri grinned. "So don't have any passed balls."

Lisa threw her hat at Jeri. "And don't you get scared by that terrifying chain link fence in the outfield."

Jeri flicked the hat back. "Where is this team from again?"

"Coach said they're the Overton Corners Hornets from the Champlain Area," Lisa said.

"Are they any good?"

"Of course they are. They wouldn't be in the first round of the state playoffs if they weren't." Lisa rolled her eyes at Jeri.

"That must mean we're good, too," Jeri said with a grin.

"Damn straight," Marlee said.

Lisa laughed and whispered low, "Straight? Not you."

Marlee leaned in close. "Hey, judging by what I heard going on in the back seat of Susie's car Saturday night, neither are you."

"Oh, shut up. There were no saints in the front seat either."

The bus pulled into the parking lot of Sandstoner Fields, and Coach Spears directed the bus driver to pull up behind the home team dugout.

"Oh, yuck." Marlee held her nose. "We have to use the East Valley dugout."

"Ewww," Lisa said.

The bus stopped, and Lisa stood up. She grabbed her gear and fell in step behind Julie. "Hey, Julie, how's Marcus?"

Julie turned around with a big grin. "Wouldn't you like to know, Brown Girl?"

"Someday you'll tell me everything, right?"

"Maybe." Julie turned around and made her way off the bus.

And maybe someday I'll spill my guts and tell you about Sam. Some day.

Lisa grabbed the green duffle bag off the front seat of the bus. The catcher's gear was always her responsibility.

Coach Spears had gotten them out of school early that day, so the stands were still empty. Even the Overton Corners team hadn't arrived from their hotel yet.

The Clarksonville players stowed their gear and then put on their cleats. Lisa was impressed with all the cubby holes for gear and helmets. At the Clarksonville field, they had to throw their stuff on the ground because they didn't even have a dugout.

"Go ahead and take your laps," Coach Spears said. "Stretch and throw after that." The rest of her teammates took off, but Lisa sat on the bench putting on her shin guards. She liked to run with them on, so they'd feel like a second skin to her.

"Oh, Lisa," Coach Spears sat down, "I'm glad you're still here." She pulled a lineup card out of her back pocket. "This is a scouting report on Overton Corners."

"A scouting report?" Lisa had never seen such a thing.

"Yes, my roommate took a road trip and watched their championship game. She took down all this information."

Lisa pressed her lips together so she wouldn't smile. *Roommate, eh? Highly doubtful.* She looked at the list. "Okay, looks like their number four batter likes to hit to the left side."

"Yes, and with power."

"She'll probably be getting some way outside pitches then, eh?"

"You got it." Coach Spears handed the card to Lisa. "Go take your laps, now, but look over that list when you get a chance."

"Gotcha." Lisa stood up and stretched her legs to shake off the bus ride. She joined the team as they finished their first lap around.

After the laps, Lisa and Marlee stretched with the team, but then made their way behind the left field fence to the cow pen. That was Marlee's name for the East Valley pitching area. They threw overhand for a few minutes and then Marlee stepped closer to start her wrist flicking routine. She backed up step by step until she was on the practice rubber.

Lisa squatted down and put her mitt up.

"Mask," Marlee said with her hand on a hip.

"Oh, c'mon. Do I have to?"

"Coach said there'll be a lot of bigwigs at these games, so we have to do everything by the rules."

"Geez." Lisa stood up and grabbed the discarded catcher's mask. She put it on. "Happy now?"

Marlee nodded.

"You're so bossy."

Marlee laughed. "Shut up and catch."

Lisa laughed and squatted down. She flashed the sign for fastball. "We're just warming up now. Don't overthrow." The first pitch popped nicely into her mitt. She threw it back.

They settled into their usual warm up routine. Lisa worked Marlee through all of her pitches, and they were just about to work the ladder one last time with the fastball, when Sam and Susie walked up.

Lisa tossed her mask aside and stood as close to Sam as she dared. "Oh, I wish I could kiss you right now."

Sam smiled. "Me, too, but actually we came on a peace-seeking mission."

Susie looked at Marlee. "*Hola, mi vida.*"

"Hi, yourself."

"*Felice cumpleaños.*"

"Thanks. Do I look mature now that I'm seventeen?"

Lisa smacked Marlee on the arm. "It's your birthday? I can't believe I forgot. Happy birthday. And no, you don't look mature at all. Never have."

"Oh, thanks a lot."

Sam and Susie laughed, and then Susie said to Marlee, "Christy wants to know if she can talk to you." She pointed to the bleachers where Christy sat watching them.

"Now?"

Susie sighed. "I know the timing is wrong, and I told Christy to wait until after the game, but she said she probably won't be staying."

Marlee looked at Lisa as if silently asking her what she should do.

Lisa shrugged. "We have time. Look, Overton Corners Hornets just got here." The big touring bus idled in the lot, and the purple and yellow uniformed players made their way toward the visitors' dugout.

Marlee shrugged and turned back toward Susie. "I guess it's okay."

Susie smiled. "You're the best." She waved for Christy to come over.

Lisa picked up her mask. "I'll see you in the dugout, Marlee."

"No," Susie said, "Christy wants all of us here."

Lisa raised an eyebrow. "Okay." She moved closer to Sam and bumped hips. Sam bumped back and smiled.

Christy made her way along the outfield fence and stood next to Susie. Lisa couldn't believe how pale Christy looked. Christy was a big girl, strong and built like an ox, but at the moment she looked small and deflated.

"Hey guys," Christy said.

Marlee nodded. "Hey."

"How are you?" Christy gestured to Marlee's head.

Marlee put a hand to her head. "I'm good. It was only a slight concussion."

Christy blinked back some tears. "I'm sorry, Marlee. Look, I'm an ass, okay? I had my priorities, like, way wrong, and I totally took it out on you."

"That's okay."

Christy smiled. "Actually, it's not okay, but thanks for saying so. I've been seeing a shrink now for about three weeks, and she says I need to take stock of the good things I have in my life and make sure I don't muck those up even further."

Susie laughed. "Your therapist told you not to 'muck' things up?"

"Well, those are my words, not hers." Christy looked at Marlee and Lisa. "Anyway, I realized all you guys from Clarksonville were some of the good things I had in my life. So, I'm sorry I took that for granted and then made you the focus of my anger. I hope you can find it in your heart to forgive me someday."

Marlee smiled. "I think I just did."

Christy took a deep breath and let out a sigh of relief. "Thanks, Marlee. I can see why Susie likes you so much."

"*Ay caramba, mi amiga por fin esta cogiendo cabeza.*"

"Damn straight I'm finally right in the head. What's your excuse?" Christy said with a laugh to Susie. "Okay, I'm gonna get going. And, hey, kick some Hornet butt today, okay?"

"We'll try," Marlee said. "See ya."

"Say hi to Jeri for me." Christy walked back toward the bleachers.

"Okay," Marlee called after her. "We will."

Lisa waited until Christy was out of earshot and said, "That took a lot of courage, you guys." Lisa caught the sad expression in Sam's eyes.

"Oh, man," Marlee said, "I feel so bad for her."

Everyone nodded and Susie said, "Thank you so much, *mi vida*. I told her you would understand."

Marlee shrugged. "I can't imagine being in her shoes. Her shrink sounds really good."

Susie nodded. "She is. I had to go to one of Christy's sessions." She pointed toward the bleachers and said to Sam, "C'mon, we'd better let these Cougars finish their warm up. They've got some Hornet butts to kick."

Lisa and Marlee waved. "I'll talk to you after the game," Lisa said to Sam.

"Same." Sam smiled, and then she and Susie turned toward the bleachers. As they walked away, Sam said to Susie, "Do hornets even have butts?"

Lisa and Marlee laughed.

"Oh, man," Marlee twirled her arm in a circle, "let's run through a few more pitches. I gotta get my head back into the game."

"You got it." Lisa put on her discarded mask and squatted. She pounded her mitt with a fist. "Fire it in here, Marlee. We'll take 'em down one Hornet at a time."

Chapter Ten

Luckiest Girl Alive

THE UMPIRE PULLED a ball out of the pouch at her waist. "Home team, take the field." She tossed the ball to Marlee.

Lisa threw on her mask and adjusted her chest protector one last time. "Okay, number three, just warming up now."

Marlee threw her five warm up pitches, and Lisa threw the ball down to second base. She purposely lobbed the ball to make the Hornets think she couldn't throw very well.

The first Hornet batter that stepped into the box was left handed, so Lisa called down to Julie at first base, "Watch for the slap." Julie nodded.

Marlee threw four pitches and quickly got behind in the count 3-1 on the first batter of the game.

"C'mon, Marlee. No lead off walks," Lisa mumbled to herself. "They always bite us in the end." She put her mitt closer to the middle of the zone. The batter swung at the pitch and popped up to Johnna at shortstop.

"One down," Lisa called. "One-two-three inning. C'mon, Cougars."

The next two batters grounded out and struck out in turn to end the top half of the first inning. Lisa tossed the ball back to the pitching circle and jogged off the field. A tall man with black hair and mustache said, "Way to go, Lisa."

She looked at him and said, "Thanks." He looked vaguely familiar, but she couldn't place him. His black leather jacket was cool, though. Maybe he was one of her teammates' dads, or maybe he went to the First Presbyterian church where her family went. Whatever. She didn't have time to think about it.

She recognized a lot of familiar Cougar fans in the packed bleachers. Her own family was there and Marlee's mom, too. Even Coach Spears's roommate sat near the dugout. Lisa had no idea who most of the other two hundred or so people were. Apparently, a state playoff game was a big honking deal in the North Country.

Lisa called, "C'mon, Jeri. Just get on base."

Jeri adjusted her helmet and stepped into the batter's box. She smacked the first pitch into left field. The left fielder overthrew her cutoff, so Jeri took off and waltzed into second safely.

"Way to go, Jeri," Lisa yelled and took off her shin guards. It looked like she'd be getting up that inning.

Lisa snuck a peek at Sam in the bleachers. Her golden hair framed her face in the late afternoon sunlight. Lisa's heart sped up. Sam turned, and her face brightened when she realized that Lisa was looking at her. Sam threw her two enthusiastic thumbs up. When Lisa took a deep breath and blew out an exaggerated sigh, Sam clenched both fists in a "you can do it" gesture. Lisa nodded and looked back toward the game.

Julie stepped into the batter's box.

"C'mon, Julie," Lisa yelled.

Julie slapped the ball to the second baseman whose only play was to first. Jeri had been running on the pitch and reached third easily, so with only one out, the Cougars had a runner on third base.

Lisa took her practice swings in the on-deck circle while Johnna, the Cougars' shortstop, took her turn at bat. Johnna swung and missed at a rise ball out of the zone. Lisa cringed. The scouting report from Coach Spears's roommate said that the Hornet pitcher's big money pitch was the rise. Unfortunately, Johnna popped up the next rise ball to the third baseman for the second out of the inning.

Lisa stepped up to bat and worked the pitcher to a two and one count. The fourth pitch looked good, so she swung and sent it whizzing past the pitcher into center field. Jeri scored, and Lisa pumped a fist from where she stood on first base. The big number one lit up on the scoreboard under the Cougars' runs column.

"C'mon, Marlee," Lisa called from first base. "Get me over. Nothing big. Just a little single."

Marlee hit a hard grounder, but the third baseman fielded the one-hopper and threw her out easily at first to end the inning.

Lisa jogged back into the dugout. She said to Marlee, "At least we scored first, eh?"

Marlee blew out a sigh. "Yeah. Hey, let's stick with the fastball-curve combo, okay?"

Lisa nodded and threw on her gear. Kerry, the backup pitcher, helped strap on Lisa's shin guards.

The Hornets' behemoth number four batter led off the inning. Lisa remembered the scouting report and set up on the outside of the plate. The batter swung and missed, so Lisa set up outside again. Another swing and a miss. Strike two. The batter then moved closer to the plate so Lisa changed the strategy and set up inside. The ball hit the inside corner for strike three and the first out of the second inning. Lisa loved scouting reports.

"Nice one, Marlee. A few more like that. C'mon number three." Lisa yelled.

"C'mon number three," Lisa's father echoed from the stands.

Lisa smiled. Like father, like daughter.

The next Hornet batter fouled off a couple of pitches before striking out on Marlee's change-up. Two outs with no runners on. Five

Hornets had gotten up to bat, and none of them had gotten on base. Lisa kicked herself mentally for even thinking about a perfect game for Marlee.

The next batter slapped a high-chopper to Corrie at second base. She fielded the ball cleanly, but the batter beat out the throw for a base hit.

"That's okay," Lisa called to her team. "We'll get the next one." *And it really is okay, because now no one, including me, is thinking about perfect games or no-hitters anymore.*

Lisa squatted behind the plate and flashed the sign for fastball. Marlee launched the pitch, and the runner on first took off for second base. Lisa bolted up, grabbed the ball, and rifled it down to Johnna waiting on second base. The runner was too fast, though, and slid in safely.

Lisa growled and readjusted her face mask. She hated when runners stole bases on her watch. *That will not happen again,* she vowed silently.

Marlee threw another fastball, and the batter walloped a line shot past Corrie into right-center field. The runner on second came all the way around to score and tied up the game 1-1.

Things didn't get better for the Cougars as the inning progressed, because the Hornets scored another run to take the lead by a score of 1-2 with two outs.

"Time," Lisa called and ran out to Marlee in the pitcher's circle. She covered her mouth with her mitt. "Hey, it's okay. They only scored two—"

"Only?"

"C'mon. We can get those back in a flash."

Marlee covered her own mouth with her glove. "Why do we cover our faces like this?" She moved her glove around.

"I don't know." Lisa shrugged. "So the other team can't read our lips?" Lisa laughed. "Anyway, they've got two outs already, and the last batter in the order is up. I think it's time to unveil the rise."

"And maybe the screw."

Lisa jogged back toward home and said over her shoulder, "Maybe, but probably not."

Just before she reached the plate, the dark-haired man with the mustache and leather jacket said, "You're doing great, Lisa."

She didn't acknowledge him, but again wondered who he was. Maybe he was one of those bigwigs Coach Spears said might come to the game. She gulped. Maybe he was a college scout. Was he scouting her? No, she was only a sophomore. He was probably scouting Marlee. She didn't have time to wonder about it as she settled back behind the plate.

She put her mitt on the inside corner. The Hornets' right fielder swung hard, but fouled the ball back into Lisa's unprotected hand.

"Mother f—" Lisa groaned and fell to her knees. Lightning bolts shot through her hand. She clutched it and rocked back and forth as the pain pulsed harder. Her hand was starting to swell already.

She finally caught her breath, and then felt a hand on her back.

Coach Spears leaned down. "Let me see."

Lisa blew out a sigh and held up her hand, but pulled it back out of reach. "It was just a foul ball. It's fine."

"Just let me see." Coach Spears grabbed Lisa's forearm and pulled the hand to her. Lisa bit her lip as Coach felt all around. "It doesn't feel broken. Let me put some freeze spray on that, and we'll see how it feels." She turned toward the dugout and motioned for someone to bring the medical kit.

The spray was arctic cold, but happily lessened the pain.

Coach Spears looked at the umpire. "Can she throw a couple?"

The umpire nodded and handed Lisa a ball. A sharp pain shot through the right side of her hand as she took the ball, but she did her best to ignore it. She tossed the ball tentatively to Marlee trying to use all her fingers except the pinky. The pain wasn't as sharp when she did that. The icy spray must have worked. Marlee tossed the ball back, and this time Lisa threw it all the way down to second base.

"It's a little stiff from the icy spray, but I think I'm okay."

"You sure?"

Lisa nodded and put her mask back on as if to end the conversation.

"All right, but you let me know the minute it doesn't feel right."

Lisa nodded again.

"Play ball." The umpire invited the batter back in the box.

Watching Lisa get hurt must have rattled Marlee because she walked that batter and then hit the next one with a pitch to load the bases.

Lisa's hand pulsed. She desperately wanted to get this last out and get some ice on her swelling hand. "Just one more you guys, c'mon."

Unfortunately for Lisa's hand, the next batter dinked a single on the left field line scoring another Hornet run. The Cougars finally stopped the hemorrhaging when Marlee struck the last batter out on three pitches. At the end of the second inning, the Hornets were ahead by a score of 1-3.

Lisa ran into the dugout. "Hey, Sarah." Sarah was the backup catcher who usually only went in if the backup pitcher Kerry was in the game.

"What's up?"

"Can you snag me a bag of ice? I don't want Coach to see me anywhere near the ice chest. Wait, not yet," Lisa whispered. "Wait 'til she goes out to the third base box."

Sarah nodded and casually leaned forward against the fence.

Coach Spears opened the dugout gate and headed toward third base. Sarah leaped into action. She grabbed an ice pack from the cooler and handed it to Lisa.

"Thanks."

"You okay?" Sarah asked.

"I think so. Don't worry. You don't have to suit up yet."

Sarah blew out a relieved sigh.

Lisa placed the ice pack on the right side of her hand, but hid behind Sarah. The ice began to numb the pain. "Geez, I never knew ice could feel so good."

She wasn't able to ice her hand for long, because the Cougar batters went three up and three down quickly. She tossed the ice pack to Sarah who snuck it back into the ice chest.

Fortunately, the Hornets' bats quieted down, and they didn't score any more runs over the next four innings. Unfortunately for the Cougars', their bats were also quiet, and they didn't score any runs, either.

At the top of the seventh inning, the Hornets came up to bat still ahead by a score of 1-3.

Lisa pumped a fist after Marlee struck out the first batter.

"One down, Cougars," Lisa yelled. "Stay tough. Let's hold 'em."

The next batter smacked a grounder right at Kym, the Cougars' third baseman, but she bobbled the ball, and the runner reached first safely.

"That's okay," Lisa called out. "We've still got one down. Infield, get two. Outfield, go three."

Lisa set up for the next batter, but a sinking feeling grew in the pit of her stomach. Her team had to score at least two runs in the bottom half of the inning, or they would lose, and their season would be over. It didn't look hopeful, either, because the bottom of the Cougar order was due up. Maybe they weren't really a state championship caliber team. Maybe East Valley was the team that should have been there.

Lisa took a deep breath and tried to shake off her doubts. She called for a fastball. The runner on first took off for second. That ticked Lisa off so much that she grabbed the pitch and threw a strike to Johnna covering second base.

"Out." The umpire threw one arm in the air.

"Yeah!" Lisa yelled. She pointed at Johnna to tell her nice job. Her hand screamed in pain, but she refused to feel it. The pain didn't matter. She simply clenched and unclenched her fist to try to keep it loose, a task that was getting more and more difficult as the game wore on. "One more out," she called to the team and set up behind the plate.

Even though there were two outs, the troubles for the Cougars weren't over because the next two Hornet batters got on base. With runners on first and second, the next batter fouled off pitch after pitch until finally lining a single to center field. The runners took off around the bases. Lisa's stomach fell to her toes. How many runs would score this time?

Jeri fielded the ball cleanly in center. The runner who had started on second base was rounding third and heading home.

"Home, home," Lisa yelled and set up slightly down the third base line. "C'mon, Jeri," she willed.

Jeri fired the ball from center field.

"Let it go. Let it go," Lisa called to Julie who had come in from first base to cut it off if needed.

Jeri's rocket bounced twice in the infield and into Lisa's waiting mitt. Lisa turned toward the runner and braced for impact. The runner slid. Lisa held on to the ball with all her might.

"Out at home!" the umpire yelled.

"Yeah," Lisa jumped up and tossed the ball to the pitcher's circle. She hugged Jeri on their way into the dugout. "Nice toss, center fielder."

"Way to hang, catcher." Jeri held the dugout door open for her. "How's the hand?"

Lisa grimaced. "We're totally not talking about that right now, okay?"

Jeri nodded and put her glove away. She grabbed her helmet and bat. "Hey, Cougars," she shouted. "We're not going down without a fight, now. Dig deep, everybody."

"Yeah," Lisa agreed. "I didn't come here to lose, you guys. C'mon, we can do this." She tore off her catcher's gear and thanked Sarah for the bag of ice. She hid behind Marlee and waited for the coolness to ease the pain in her hand.

Corrie, the Cougars' leadoff batter, must not have heard Jeri or Lisa because she struck out swinging in three pitches. Lisa's stomach churned, but there was still hope because Paula, the Cougars number nine batter was up next and had already walked twice.

"C'mon, Paula," Lisa called, "be patient." She wiggled her way in between Marlee and Julie against the dugout fence.

"This is a sucky birthday," Marlee said and stuck out her lower lip.

"Sorry, Marlee," Julie said.

"Hey, you know what?" Lisa said. "One of my famous Yankees said, 'It ain't over 'til it's over.'"

"Yogi Berra," Marlee said. "He played for the Mets, too, you know."

"Way back in the sixties, right?"

"Yeah."

Lisa nodded. "And another one of your famous Mets said, 'You gotta believe.'"

"Tug McGraw."

Lisa nodded again. "So, let's believe." Lisa bumped fists with Marlee and then with Julie. She put her hand to her mouth and called. "C'mon Cougars. Never say die. C'mon Paula."

For the third time that day, Paula walked to reach first base safely. Jeri stepped into the batter's box, and Julie grabbed her helmet and bat and ran into the on-deck circle.

Lisa called, "C'mon Jeri, You're due." She laughed. "Actually, she's gotten on base every time, but who cares? We need a hit now."

An inside screwball brushed Jeri back off the plate.

"Oh, man," Marlee said. "That was close."

"Dead." The umpire put both hands in the air and pointed toward first base.

Lisa leaped in the air. "She got hit by the pitch. We've got two runners on."

Julie stepped into the batter's box and worked the count full. Lisa clutched the fence with her good hand until the knuckles turned white. "C'mon, White Girl. It's all about you."

Lisa cheered when Julie dinked a single over the shortstop's head. All base runners advanced safely.

Lisa pulled away from the fence. "Crap, bases are loaded, and I'm on deck. Where's my bat?"

"Lisa," Marlee grabbed her arm, "chill out. Take a breath."

Lisa looked her pitcher in the eye and did as she was told. "Okay, I'm calm." She found her bat and helmet.

Johnna stepped into the box and got ready for the pitch. Lisa stood in the on-deck circle and swung lightly. If Johnna got a hit and Paula scored, they would only be down by one run. She gritted her teeth when Johnna fouled out to the catcher on the second pitch to make the second out.

Johnna slammed her bat on the ground in disgust and headed toward the dugout with a scowl on her face. "Pick me up, Lisa. You're our last hope."

Oh, no pressure there, Lisa thought and stepped into the box. The bases were loaded, but there were two outs. The odds were against them, but Lisa was determined not to make the last out to end their season.

She dug her heels in and took a quick practice swing. The first pitch was a screwball inside. Ball one. The next pitch fell under the strike zone for ball two. She took another deep breath and did her best to ignore her throbbing hand. She decided to swing only if the pitch was nice and meaty. The Hornet's pitcher took her signal from the catcher and put her hands together. She started her windup, and Lisa readied herself for the release. A change-up meatball was coming right down the center of the plate. She hesitated for a split second and exploded with her bat. The ball sailed high in the air down the left field line.

Lisa ran toward first base. "Stay fair, stay fair," she yelled as she ran. She had almost reached first base when the ball bounced off the fence and back onto the left field grass. She pumped a fist when Paula scored from third making the score 2-3. She knew Jeri would score, too, but hoped she'd hit it far enough for Julie to score all the way from first base.

Lisa headed for second base as Jeri rounded third and sprinted home. The Hornet's left fielder had just reached the ball in left field. Jeri crossed the plate safely to tie the score at 3-3. Lisa stopped at second base and watched Coach Spears wave her arms frantically for Julie to head home. The Hornet's shortstop took the relay throw from her left fielder and rifled the ball to the catcher waiting for the throw. Julie slid. Lisa held her breath.

"Safe!" The umpire threw her arms out to the side.

Lisa leaped in the air and sprinted toward her teammates mobbing Julie at the plate. The Cougars had just won their first playoff game. The people in the stands stomped their feet and cheered louder than she'd ever heard. When she reached her teammates, they left Julie and turned on her. Jeri hugged her tightly, and Marlee pounded her helmet so hard, she thought she might get a concussion.

It was hard to hear with all the pounding, but it sounded like Jeri said, "Nice hit."

"Thanks."

Lisa wriggled out of Jeri's grasp and away from Marlee's helmet pounding.

Marlee said, "You are so friggin' awesome, Lisa. What an awesome birthday present. God, I love you."

"Ha!" Lisa laughed. *Too late, Marlee. I've moved on.*

"Way to go, Amazon," Sam called from the fan side of the fence. "You're my hero." Sam batted her eyelashes.

Lisa pumped a fist in the air and pointed at her. "Don't go anywhere."

Sam shook her head and pointed to the ground as if to say she wouldn't move from that spot.

Lisa made her way to the end of the high-five line. After high-fiving the Hornets, she headed toward the dugout. Just as she reached the door, the tall dark-haired man with the leather jacket and dark mustache said, "Nice job, Lisa. I'm very proud of you."

"Oh, thanks." *But shouldn't you be talking to Marlee?* She decided to ask him if he was a scout, but then her mother walked up to the fence and said, "Great job, Lisa." She held a sleeping Bridget in her arms.

"Thanks, Mom. Geez, I thought we were goners there."

"You almost were."

Her father called from the stands. "Great job, Lisa."

"Thanks, Papa," she called up to him and laughed because her father was having a hard time getting Lynnie to close her book so they could leave.

"Are you taking the bus home?" her mother asked.

"Yeah, we've got more celebrating to do."

"Okay, we'll see you at home. I'm proud of you, honey."

Her mother turned away, and Lisa looked for the scout, but couldn't find him. She shrugged and headed to the dugout to celebrate their first round victory. The Cougars had beaten the odds and conquered the Overton Corners Hornets by a score of 4-3. The quarterfinals were in two days.

Lisa found Sam still leaning against the fence where Lisa had left her. Lisa answered Sam's grin with a grin of her own. She smiled inside, too. Although her hand hurt like hell, she was the luckiest girl on the planet.

Chapter Eleven

Tools of Ignorance

LISA SAT UP in her bed on Tuesday night too wired to sleep. The school day had dragged on and on and then practice after school was long and intense. Coach Spears must have been feeling the pressure, because if they lost the quarterfinal game against Whickett High School the next day then their season would be over. Lisa wished she could sleep in the next morning until it was time to get on the bus for the three hour ride to the game, but Coach Spears was making them go to homeroom and then first period. After that they'd head to the locker room to change into their uniforms, get their gear, and get on the bus that would take them through the Adirondack Mountains all the way to Warrensburg.

She opened her journal to the last entry and laughed. The last time she had written in it was on April 27, over a month and a half before. She rooted around in her drawer for her favorite blue gel pen, but couldn't find it. She settled on a cheap green ball point instead and uncapped it.

June 12

I can't believe I haven't written in this journal for so long. My last entry said I thought Sam was flirting with me. Well, yeah, she was. We've been together exactly one month today. We got together on May 12. I wish I could have seen her today, but we both had school. East Valley's way too far away. If I had my license, we could hang out more. Especially because the time we do hang out goes by way too fast. I miss her all the time.

I thought I was in love with Marlee at the beginning of softball, but I think I was just lonely or depressed or something. Tara hadn't been calling me, and in the back of my mind I knew she was going to break up with me. But who cares? Tara's a thing of the past, I'm way over Marlee, and Sam is awesome.

Sam, Sam, Sam. Her full name is Samantha Rose Payton. She's as pretty as her name. She doesn't seem to mind that I'm, like, five inches taller than she is. She plays second base for East Valley. And speaking of second base, we went there again this weekend. I can't believe the way I feel when she touches me like that. I can tell she likes it when I touch her, too. I'm so freakin' nervous about third base. I think Sam is, too. I almost went there with Tara, but I got too scared. I think I could go with Sam. She makes me feel so...

Lisa's heart pounded as she thought about the last time they went to the Clarksonville CCC softball field. She chewed on the end of her pen. It was hard to articulate how Sam made her feel. Wanted? Loved? Needed? Yeah, all of those.

Sam makes me feel so many things. I think I love her. Ahhh! I can't believe I just wrote that. This is so scary. I think about her all the time. Sometimes I pretend we live together in a cute little house, and we have babies and dogs and cats and a fenced in yard with flower gardens everywhere. Our friends come over for barbeques in the summer, and we have game nights in winter. Sam met Mom and Papa already. They like her, and I think she likes them, too. Bridget adores her and so does Lawrence Jr. Lynnie's coming out of her shell around her, too, which is awesome. Lynnie's halfway through all those Harry Potter books Sam brought her. I haven't met Sam's parents yet. That'll be scary.

Okay, I gotta change the subject because I miss her too much. Sooooo, anyway, we play Whickett High School tomorrow. They're the winners from the Capital District near Albany. According to Coach, the scouting report says they have a pitcher who is really fast. Faster than Marlee and faster than Christy. Of course, Coach didn't say it that way. She said something like, "She's faster than anything you've ever seen before." Ha-ha. We know what that means, eh?

Okay, a few more things and then I have to get some sleep.
1. Coach Spears is totally gay. Her "roommate's" name is Anne, and she's really nice.
2. Bridget is sleeping so cute right now.
3. I think there's a college scout looking at Marlee. He was at the game yesterday when we creamed Overton Corners. He's really tall, too.
4. Oh, yea, (duh) I hit a game-winning double yesterday!!! My hand still hurts, but it wasn't so bad at practice today. I'm fine!! (Yeah, right.) The whole right side of my hand is black and blue. I didn't tell Coach.
5. Marlee and Susie make an awesome couple. I really like Susie. I think Marlee's in love with her. I think they're in love with each other. Her full name is Susana Torres.
6. I think Mom saw me and Sam kissing a coule of weeks ago.

She didn't say anything, so maybe not.
7. I love Sam Payton!

Lisa put her journal and the cheap green pen back in the drawer. She yawned, snuggled down, and pulled the covers up around her neck. The second she closed her eyes, though, they flew open again. Crap, she hadn't done her first period geometry homework. Maybe Mrs. Pacheco wouldn't check it. Whatever. It was too late now. She closed her eyes again and willed sleep to come quickly.

THE CLARKSONVILLE SCHOOL bus entered the Adirondack Park on its way to Warrensburg. Tall pines and birches stood majestic in their mountain setting, and Lisa scanned for deer and black bear as the the bus whizzed by the wilderness. All she saw were a couple of wild turkeys running near the side of the road. Looking for wildlife was a lot more interesting than the unopened geometry review book in her lap.

Coach Spears stood up in the front of the bus. "Girls, can I get your attention please?"

Lisa sat in the next to last seat on the bus. Julie sat in the seat next to hers. They would have been in the way back, but Marlee and Jeri always claimed the very last seats. Lisa couldn't see Coach Spears over the high-backed green seats, so she slid toward the center aisle.

"Girls," Coach Spears continued, "we'll stop at the McDonald's in Tupper Lake to use the rest rooms, but that'll be it until we get to the Warrensburg Sports Complex. So, go easy on the liquids, okay?"

Lisa laughed along with her teammates. She had a couple of bottles of water in the lunch cooler at her feet.

Coach Spears smiled. "I suggest you eat somewhere between here and Blue Mountain Lake. I don't want you full and lethargic when we get there."

They had about two hours to Blue Mountain Lake and then another hour or so after that to Warrensburg. Lisa wasn't hungry yet, so maybe she'd wait until Long Lake to eat the peanut butter and jelly sandwiches she and Bridget made together that morning.

Coach Spears continued, "When we get closer we'll talk about our strategy for the game, but here's what's coming up for us. If we win this afternoon—"

"Coach?" Jeri interrupted and raised her hand in the back seat.

"Yes?"

"*When* we win this afternoon."

Coach Spears laughed. "Okay, you're right. *When* we win, we'll move on to the semi-finals on Saturday. We'll take a bus to Binghamton on Friday, and yes, you'll miss the entire last day of classes."

A cheer went up in the bus.

"Sorry seniors, I bet you're heartbroken about missing your last day."

Jeri called up to the front, "Not a chance, Coach."

"I didn't think so. Anyway," Coach Spears continued, "we'll check into a local hotel, practice that evening, and then play in the semi-final game on Saturday morning. If, oops sorry, *when* we win the semis, we'll play in the finals that very afternoon."

Lisa grinned at Julie. They bumped fists across the aisle. It would be so cool to go all the way to the finals.

"Okay, that's it for now. Remember to eat by the time we get to Blue Mountain Lake."

"Hey, White Girl," Lisa called over to Julie, "come help me with this." She waved the geometry review book at her and slid toward the window to make room.

Julie sat next to her and reached for the geometry book. She opened the book to a page with practice proofs.

Lisa groaned when she saw the proofs and pulled her new cell phone out of her jacket pocket. "Hey, check out my new phone first."

"You are so stalling, Brown Girl."

"I know." Lisa grinned.

Julie turned the phone over in her hand. "Cool phone."

"My mom gave it to me this morning just as I was leaving to catch the bus for school. She said it was about time I had one."

"Far out." Julie slid the phone open. "I wish my mom would up and give me a phone like this. Oh, cool. You've got a Qwerty keyboard. That's a lot easier for texting."

"I know. I texted my friend Sam this morning. She's in school, though, so she can only text me in between classes."

Julie handed the phone back, and Lisa put it in her jacket pocket. Julie pointed to the first problem. "Let's go over this one."

"I hate proofs."

"Everybody hates proofs, except Mrs. Pacheco, I think. I can't believe she gave you a zero for not having your homework this morning."

"I know, geez. She can't cut me some slack? We're playing in the state quarterfinals today. What's more important than that?"

"Uh, let's see." Julie put her index finger on her chin and looked up. "Maybe the Regents' exam on Tuesday?"

"Ugh," Lisa groaned. "Don't remind me."

Julie shrugged. "So," she said casually, "did I tell you?" She shut the book and clamped her lips together in a grin.

Lisa leaned in close. "Oh, my God. He finally asked you out, didn't he?"

Julie nodded and her eyes grew wide in excitement.

"Did you guys go out yet?"

Julie nodded.

"Where?"

Julie cheeks flushed "He wanted to take me to D'Amico's, but I wasn't sure if Jeri would be working that night, and I..." She shrugged.

"What?"

"I don't know. I didn't want Jeri teasing me in front of people. They'd, like, stare at the white guy and black girl on their first date, you know?"

"I get that." *More than you know.* "So what'd you do?"

"Okay, but don't laugh." Julie smiled.

"I won't." Lisa crossed her fingers just in case.

"We went to the Northwood Firemen's Brass Band concert."

"In the Northwood town square?"

Julie nodded. "Yeah, we were surrounded by all these white-haired senior citizens. Oh, and he brought a blanket and French bread and cheeses and little pepperonis. Oh, my God, Lisa, it was so nice. I like him so much."

"Me, too. Oh, not in that way, but Marcus is cool." Lisa smiled. She wanted to tell Julie that she felt the same way about Sam and how they had to hide from the world, too. Instead she said, "You know, it sucks that people judge you guys just because you're black and he's white."

"Tell me about it. I wish you were dating somebody, 'cuz then we could, like, double date or something."

A little ache spread across Lisa's chest. Maybe she'd tell Julie about Sam once school let out for summer in a couple of weeks. She cleared her throat. "People can be so freakin' ignorant, eh?"

Julie rolled her eyes and nodded. "I know. I can't change the color of my skin. It's not like I have a choice here. I wish..."

"What?"

"I wish people would judge me by me and not what they think black people are supposed to be like. I'm just Julie, you know?"

Lisa nodded. "You're more than 'just Julie,' but you're right. Stereotypes suck." *And, geez, I wish I had the nerve to come out to you right now, but I just can't.*

"Yeah," Julie said, "people grow up prejudiced I guess. They think it's okay to put down anybody that doesn't look like them. They don't think for themselves."

Lisa nodded. "Yeah, really. It's like they live in a vacuum. They cling to their tools of ignorance."

"Tools of ignorance?" Julie cocked an eyebrow.

"That's what my catcher's equipment is called, actually."

Julie shook her head. She looked totally confused. "Your catcher's equipment?"

"I didn't make it up. I swear. My father told me that some catcher a long time ago had to play in a heat wave, and when he put on his catcher's stuff, he called them his tools of ignorance." She shrugged.

"That's funny. I could never be a catcher."

Lisa laughed. "But 'tools of ignorance' fits those stupid people, eh?"

"Yeah. They need tools of enlightenment, I think. If Marcus likes me as much as I like him, then maybe we'll just have to make people deal with it. Let them see us together, you know? Maybe that would enlighten more people."

Lisa cringed inside. "Easier said than done, I imagine." *I don't 'imagine' how hard it would be because I* know *how hard it will be.* Lisa looked out the window at the lonely forest the bus was passing by. She needed to take her own advice. She and Sam needed to be more visible, too, but how?

"C'mon," Julie said breaking the silence. "Let's practice some of those proofs. I predict a proof about quadrilaterals on Tuesday."

Lisa let out an exaggerated sigh. "Do we have to?"

"We have to."

Just as Julie opened the review book, the bus slowed down to a crawl. Lisa looked out her window. Construction cones lined the two-lane highway. The bus came to a full stop and didn't move for several long minutes. Lisa groaned. "This better not make us late."

Coach Spears stood up. "Can anybody get a cell phone signal? Mine won't connect." She held up her phone.

Lisa slid open her phone to see if she had a signal. "Here Coach." She held it in the air. "It's weak, but it's got one."

"Oh, excellent." Coach Spears walked to the back of the bus. "I want to call the tournament director and let her know that this construction is slowing us down." She looked at her watch. "Thank goodness we left so early."

Coach Spears sat down in Julie's vacated seat and punched in the number. "You know there are only two seasons in the Adirondacks, right?"

"Winter and more winter?" Lisa guessed.

"No, but good guess." Coach Spears smiled. "Winter and construction."

Julie and Lisa laughed. Coach Spears put up a finger when the call connected. She began explaining their delay to the tournament director.

Lisa and Julie exchanged a worried glance. "Hey," Lisa said, "don't worry. They can't start the game without us."

"Yeah," Julie said with a grin, "especially not without the world's greatest catcher and her tools of ignorance."

"Oh, shut up and teach me geometry."

Chapter Twelve

Quarterfinals

LISA PICKED UP her catcher's gear from the front seat and hopped off the bus. Julie fell in step with her, and they headed to the field at the Warrensburg Sports Centre. The construction in the Adirondack Mountains slowed them down, but Coach Spears reassured them they would have plenty of time to get warmed up.

Lisa and Julie stepped into the visitors' dugout and settled in to put on their cleats. The Whickett High School pitcher was warming up from the pitching rubber on the field.

"Geez!" Lisa pointed. "Coach was right." She rubbed the side of her bruised hand.

Julie's eyes widened. "We're never gonna hit that."

Lisa blew out a sigh and shook her head. "We gotta figure out a way." She clenched and unclenched her fist. Her pinky still wouldn't close all the way.

Lisa ran Marlee through their usual warm up routine, and then the infield and outfield took their warm ups. In a quick thirty minutes, the Clarksonville Cougars were ready to start the quarterfinal round. As the visiting team, the Cougars were up first. Jeri got up to bat and sat down quickly having struck out in three pitches. Apparently the rockets launched from the Whickett pitcher were too much for her. Julie managed to foul off one pitch, but she too struck out. Lisa stood in the on-deck circle watching Johnna swing and miss at the first pitch.

"No wonder this team made it so far," Lisa muttered under her breath. She had no idea how she could swing fast enough to hit the supersonic pitches. Lisa wondered if maybe Coach Spears would make them all start bunting or something, so they wouldn't strike out.

As if to prove Lisa's point, Johnna struck out swinging to end the inning, so Lisa hustled back to the dugout to put on her gear.

Marlee kneeled down to help Lisa strap on her right shin guard. "Let's try the screwball today."

Lisa tightened her chest protector. "Okay."

"Yea." Marlee pumped both fists in the air like a kid who had just gotten permission to stay up late. She ran out toward the pitcher's circle.

"But not in the first inning," Lisa called after her.

The bottom half of the first inning didn't go well for the Cougars. The first batter for Whickett High School smashed one of Marlee's fastballs into the left-center field gap for a double. The next batter reached first base safely when Kym couldn't handle a hot grounder at third.

With runners on first and second and no outs, Marlee got two quick strikes on the third batter. Lisa flashed the sign for fastball. Marlee shook it off. Lisa flashed the sign for change-up. Marlee shook that off, too. *No screwballs in the first inning.* Lisa flashed the sign for rise ball, and Marlee must have liked that selection because she put her hands together to get ready for the pitch.

The rise ball flew over Lisa's head, but despite her best efforts she couldn't reach it. She ran for the ball near the backstop. Marlee covered the plate, but there was no play because the runners only moved up one base. Thank goodness because it seemed to take forever to get to the ball. The backstop seemed so much farther away than the one at their home field.

"Time," the umpire yelled and put her hands up in the air.

Lisa tossed the ball back to Marlee. "That's all right, Marlee. We'll get the next one."

But they didn't get the next batter because she smacked a two-run single into right field scoring two runs. The fourth Whickett batter singled to center to put runners on first and third with no outs.

Lisa stood up and called for a timeout. Coach Spears had given her the scouting report before the game, but it didn't seem to be helping. Lisa had to come up with something else, so she walked out to Marlee in the pitcher's circle, and waved for the infielders to join them.

"Okay, you guys," Lisa said. "Let's shake off that long bus ride and get in this game." She gestured toward the runner on first. "I think she's going to steal second. So Johnna, get ready to cut off my throw and fire it back home if the runner on third tries for home. Okay?"

Johnna nodded.

They put their hands together, and Marlee said, "Cougars on three. One, two, three."

"Cougars!" They hustled back to their positions.

Lisa ran back toward the plate and noticed the college scout sitting on the visitors' side of the bleachers. He had on the same cool black leather jacket he'd worn at the Overton Corners game. *He's not going to recruit Marlee now if we don't get our act in gear. I wonder if Coach Spears knows he's here.*

Lisa squatted behind the plate. Marlee fired her pitch, and the runner on first took off for second. Lisa leaped up to grab the pitch, but the batter bunted the ball onto the infield. Marlee fielded the bunt cleanly, checked the runner on third, and threw the batter out at first base. Julie then ran toward the pitcher's circle with the ball held high as if daring the runner on third to try for home.

Marlee finally found her groove and struck out the sixth and seventh batters to end the disastrous first inning. The Cougars ran back to their dugout down by two runs.

Lisa led off the top of the second inning. She adjusted her helmet and stepped into the batter's box. She decided to let the first pitch go by just to see how fast it actually was. The pitch whizzed by her and smacked into the catcher's mitt for strike one.

Holy Jesus! Lisa thought. *This ain't gonna be easy.*

She readied herself for the next pitch and swung late for strike two. She stepped out of the box and took a deep breath to hide her embarrassment. Coach Spears had been right. This chick was fast. Lisa took a deep breath and stepped back in. The next pitch came right down the center of the plate. She swung and missed the ball by a mile. The Whickett pitcher had fooled her with a very sneaky change-up.

"Son of a..." Lisa grunted and did the slow walk of shame back to the dugout after striking out.

Julie patted her on the helmet. "You'll get 'em next time."

Lisa blew out a sigh. "I don't know." She put her helmet in the rack. "She's freakin' fast." She looked up just as Marlee swung and missed the first pitch. "C'mon number three. Smack it out there."

Marlee missed the next pitch for strike two. Lisa studied the pitcher carefully, but couldn't detect a difference in her delivery when she threw the change-up to Marlee on the third pitch. Unfortunately, Marlee missed it and struck out for the second out of the inning. Kym got up to bat, but went down just as quickly with the same fastball, fastball, change-up combination to end the top half of the second inning. The Cougars were still losing by a score of 0-2.

Luckily, the first two Whickett batters in the bottom of the second inning struck out, but the top of their order was due up next. Marlee quickly worked the batter to a one ball, two strike count. Marlee shook off Lisa's signs for change-up, fastball, and rise ball. Marlee grinned. *Okay, fine.* She flashed the sign for screwball.

Marlee threw a perfectly delivered screwball right into the batter's hip.

"Dead," the umpire yelled and pointed toward first.

Lisa shook her head and pointed at Marlee. "No more screwballs," she mouthed.

"Okay, okay." Marlee put her hands up in defense and walked back to the circle.

With one runner on first base and two outs, Marlee threw a beautiful rise ball that the batter popped up into foul territory. Lisa threw off her mask and looked up. She ran toward the backstop and lunged for the ball. She caught it in her mitt for the last out, but her bruised hand smashed against the chain link fence. She whimpered, but refused to let the pain show.

"Out," the umpire called.

Lisa flipped the ball from her mitt to the umpire's outstretched hand. She kept her back turned away from the dugout, took a deep breath, and squeezed her throbbing hand tight.

The college scout in the stands looked concerned. "Are you okay, Lisa?"

"What?" She hadn't realized she was standing right in front of him. She waved her bad hand. "Oh, it's nothing." She smiled back and headed for the dugout.

Sarah handed her a bag of ice.

"How did you know?"

Sarah shrugged. "You usually sprint right back in the dugout on the third out."

"Oh." She put the ice on her hand. "Does Coach know?"

Sarah shook her head. "Nope."

"Let's keep it that way, okay?"

"Should I get my catcher's gear ready?"

Lisa shook her head. "Nope, I'm fine."

"Okay." Sarah nodded in obvious relief and moved in front of Lisa so the ice pack would remain hidden from their coach.

Marlee nudged Lisa on the shoulder. "You okay?"

Lisa shrugged. "I guess."

Marlee sighed. "Just tell Coach if it gets too bad, okay?"

"Okay." Lisa knew there was no way she'd ever let herself get taken out of the game over a stupid little bruise. No way.

Alicia, the Cougars left fielder, stepped up to bat and promptly swung and missed the first fastball.

Lisa looked down at her hand and wondered how she hadn't judged the distance to the backstop properly. She frowned. She thought the backstop was farther away than it was. She looked at the fence where she'd smacked her hand and gauged the distance to the Whickett catcher. It was farther than the field at home, but not as far as the East Valley field they'd played on two days before. The Whickett catcher flashed a sign to her pitcher, and the change-up was on the way.

"Hey Marlee, did you see that?" She pointed toward the catcher.

"What?"

"The catcher. She relaxed when she called for the change-up. She sat up taller and kept her right hand on her thigh instead of behind her back. Geez, the catcher totally gives away the change-up." Lisa grabbed Marlee's sleeve. "Oh, my God, Marlee. She only has two pitches. The supersonic fastball and the change-up."

"Oh, man, I think you're right. Hey Jeri, c'mere." Marlee waved her over.

"What's up?" Jeri plunked her batting helmet on her head since she was up soon.

"Lisa figured something out. It's too late for Corrie because she's already up to bat, but we can tell Paula. Hey, Paula," Marlee called to her in the on-deck circle.

Paula ran over. "You want to administer last rights or something before I get up?"

Lisa laughed. "No. That pitcher only has two pitches. Fastball and change-up. We think we can tell when the change is coming. We'll yell, uh—" she turned to Marlee. "What should we yell?"

"Delta?"

Lisa looked at Marlee with one eyebrow raised.

Marlee laughed. "Delta means change in math, like in slope."

"Oh, yeah," Lisa said sheepishly. "How could I forget?"

"Guys," Paula said, "hurry up and decide. I gotta get back."

"Okay," Lisa said, "we'll yell, 'delta' when the change is coming." Paula scurried back to the on-deck circle. Lisa turned to Marlee. "I am so gonna fail my Geometry Regents."

"You are not. I'll help you." Marlee nudged her in the shoulder.

"Seriously?"

"Yeah, I'm up to a B in Calculus now."

"Brainiac."

Marlee laughed. "Your Regents' exam's on Tuesday, right?"

"Yeah." Lisa nodded. "Thanks for helping me. I may be a lost cause, though."

"Stop. You'll be fine." Marlee pointed to the Whickett catcher. "Look, you were right. She relaxed." A change-up floated over the plate for strike three.

"Girl, you are good," Jeri said to Lisa. "I think we might be able to do something with this team, now." She headed toward the on-deck circle.

Paula stepped up to bat with two outs in the top of the third inning. She swung and missed on the first two pitches. The catcher relaxed, and Lisa and Marlee cried at the same time, "Delta!" Paula adjusted and smacked a single to right field.

Lisa and Marlee taught the rest of the team how to read the catcher's body language for the change-up. "And, you know what?" Lisa said. "Every single one of us can hit her fastball."

Julie looked back from the on-deck circle and rolled her eyes. "What are you smokin', Brown Girl?"

Lisa laughed. "No, really. We can hit her. She doesn't throw a rise, a curve, a drop, or anything else that I've seen. All you have to do is swing when you see the ball come off her hip. And, don't swing hard, either. She's providing all the power."

Jeri smacked a single down the right field line as if to prove Lisa's point. Julie hit a single which scored Paula from second base. The Cougars were down by one run when Johnna stepped into the batter's box. She swung at the first pitch and sent a hard grounder toward the second baseman. The second baseman looked surprised that anything was coming toward her and didn't field the ball cleanly. All runners were safe.

Lisa stepped into the box and got ready for the pitch.

"The bases are full of Cougars, Lisa!" Marlee shouted from the on-deck circle. "Just a little single gets in two."

Lisa got ready for the first pitch.

"Delta!" Marlee and her teammates yelled.

Lisa waited the right amount of time and swung. The ball sailed into the right-center field gap. Lisa headed toward first base, and Kerry waved her toward second. Lisa cheered when she saw Julie score right after Jeri.

"Slide," Coach Spears yelled out to Lisa as she was approaching second base.

Lisa slid. She was safe at second base, and the Cougars were up by a score of 3-2.

Once the Cougars unlocked the secrets of the rocket-launching pitcher, they were able to score runs on a regular basis and beat the Whickett High School Wolves by a final score of 10-2.

After the high-five line, Jeri called the team together, and they put their hands on top of hers. "Delta on three, Cougars. One, two, three!"

"Delta!" the team yelled and then laughed.

Lisa nudged Marlee in the ribs. "There he is." She pointed to the dark-haired man with the leather jacket.

"Who?"

"That college scout I told you about. The tall guy talking into his cell phone."

"Man, he's tall. What college is he from?"

Lisa shrugged. "I don't know. I asked Coach, but she didn't know who he was either."

"Should we ask him?" Marlee whispered.

"Nah, I'm sure he'll contact you or something. I mean, geez, he came all the way to Warrensburg, so he must be interested in recruiting you."

Marlee shrugged. "I guess. C'mon, let's get going. I want to get on the bus so I can call Susie and then my mom."

"Oh, me too. I can finally call Sam from my own cell phone instead of borrowing yours all the time."

On the bus, Lisa talked with Sam for over a half hour, and when they hung up, she hugged the phone as if hugging Sam. Sam and Susie were going to drive down to Binghamton on Saturday to watch them play in the semi-final game. She stood up and leaned over her seat to look at Marlee. Marlee was still on the phone with Susie.

Lisa pointed to Marlee's phone. "They're coming down Saturday."

Marlee grinned. "I know."

Lisa smiled and slid back into her seat. She re-opened her cell phone to call home.

Her mother answered the phone. "Lisa Bear. How'd it go? Hey, everybody, it's Lisa."

She heard a chorus of "Hi, Lisa" from her family.

She laughed and said, "We won."

"Oh, that's wonderful, honey. How did you play?"

"Okay, I guess. Their pitcher was fast, but we figured out how to hit her. I hit a triple and two doubles. I think I had, like, six RBI's."

"That's wonderful. Okay, okay. Hang on a second. Bridget's tugging at my sleeve."

Lisa smiled when she heard her mother try to convince her little sister to be patient because Lisa would be home in a few hours. Apparently Bridget would have none of it, because she grabbed the phone. "Weesa?"

"Hi, Sweetpea."

"Are you coming home?"

"As fast as I can. You'll be asleep when I get there, though, but I'll see you in the morning."

"No, I'm staying up."

Oh, no. Sorry, Mom.

Her mother got back on the phone, and they talked about the game for a few more minutes. Lisa remembered the dark-haired man. "Oh, that college recruiter was at the game scouting Marlee again."

"Recruiter?"

"Yeah, he was at the Overton Corners game, too."

"Has he talked to Marlee yet?"

"No, that's the weird thing. He just watches the game and then leaves. Oh, you know what though? He talks to me sometimes."

"He talks to you?"

"Yeah, and he knows my name. Oh, geez, maybe he's recruiting me." Lisa stomach knotted.

"What does he look like?" her mother asked.

"Oh, he's really tall and has dark hair with a dark mustache. He wears this cool black leather jacket, too."

"Uh, huh," her mother said as if she remembered him.

"Did you see him at the Overton Corners game or something, Mom?"

"Yes, something like that."

Lisa heard an odd tone in her mother's voice. "Mom, what's wrong?" The cell phone crackled.

Her mother sighed.

"Mom, are you still there?"

"I'm here." She sighed again. "Your, uh, your father wants to meet you."

"Papa?" Lisa shook her head confused. "Papa wants to meet me where?" She waited, but her mother didn't answer. "Mom?"

She pulled the phone away and looked at the tiny screen. Signal lost.

Chapter Thirteen

Honesty

AFTER THE QUARTERFINAL win against Whickett High School that Wednesday, the Clarksonville school bus made its way through the mountains, and Lisa's cell phone finally re-established a semi-decent signal in Tupper Lake. She called her mother back immediately.

When the Clarksonville school bus pulled into the high school parking lot at 11:30 that night, Lisa was still dazed by the bombshell her mother had dropped on her. After saying goodbye to her teammates, Lisa hopped into the passenger seat of the minivan.

"Hi, Mom." Lisa shut the car door and hugged her mother.

"I'm so glad you won, honey." Her mother pulled back from the hug and smiled a sad sort of smile.

"Mom?"

"Yes, honey?"

"Why now?"

Her mother sighed. "I wasn't counting on this day coming for a few years yet." She started the engine and backed out of the parking spot. "Apparently he's getting married and wants to be open and honest with his fiancée. That includes meeting you, I guess."

"Oh." Lisa sat with her hands folded in her lap.

"Lisa, you don't have to meet your father if you don't—"

"Mom?" Lisa interrupted.

"Hmm?"

"Can we not call my bio dad my father?"

Her mother looked at her with sympathetic eyes. "Okay. You're right. Let's call him William then, okay?"

Lisa nodded. "What's his last name?"

"Dowell."

Lisa watched the houses go by in the darkness for a moment. She turned to face her mother. "Why'd he leave you, Mom? I mean you were so young and alone. You must have been so scared."

"You know, I was scared at first, but I had Grandma and Grandpa. They were so supportive that I knew it would be okay. I didn't start showing until after graduation, so that helped, too."

"Did you ever think about," Lisa looked down at her hands, "you know."

"Having an abortion?"

"Yeah," Lisa said quietly and looked up at her mother.

"Not for a second." Her mother caught her gaze and smiled. She looked back to the road and both were quiet for a few minutes. Both she and her mother were pro-choice when it came to women making decisions about their own bodies, but she was relieved to hear that her mother hadn't considered an abortion.

"Mom?"

"Yes, honey?"

"Why did William leave you?"

Her mother sighed. "Well, when I told him I was pregnant he said he wasn't ready to be a dad. We sat down with his parents and with Grandma and Grandpa and decided that I'd have the baby on my own. With my parents help, of course."

"Didn't that make you mad? That he had nothing to do with any of it?" Lisa couldn't believe somebody would just leave like that.

"I was relieved, actually."

"How come?"

"I didn't want to marry him. I wasn't in love with him anymore. We were heading for a break up when I realized I was pregnant with you."

Lisa looked out the window. "Mom, I don't know if I want to meet him."

"You don't have to decide right now, okay?"

Lisa nodded. "Okay."

Her mother added, "But I think he's coming from a sincere place now."

"I have to think about it, Mom."

A thousand different thoughts swirled around in her mind. What would she say to him? What would her real father think? How would Lynnie and Lawrence Jr., and Bridget react? Did he look so familiar because she saw herself in him?

"Mom, does Papa know William wants to meet me?"

Her mother shook her head. "I'm going to break it to him on Friday when you leave on the bus for Binghamton."

Lisa felt an ache in her chest. The last thing she wanted to do was to hurt her father.

Her mother pulled the minivan up the driveway and turned off the engine. They went inside the house, and Lisa went straight to her room. She laughed when she saw Bridget sleeping soundly in the wrong bed. Apparently her little sister had been trying to wait up, but couldn't stay awake. Lisa took a quick shower and then got in bed next to her sister. The pain she felt about possibly hurting her family subsided somewhat.

THE NEXT DAY, Lisa tried to stay upbeat and positive during her last day of classes and then later at practice. No one seemed to notice that she was preoccupied, thank goodness. After dinner, her mother let her skip her usual dish washing chore to get caught up on homework. After an hour and a half of homework, she'd had her fill and went outside to call Sam. Her mother didn't make a fuss, because she must have known Lisa was bursting to talk to someone. Lisa strolled to the deserted playground trying to figure out what to say to Sam.

She jumped up on a swing. The distant street light was the only source of light in the darkness. A few bats flitted overhead diving for insects.

She slid open her phone and said, "Sam."

Sam picked up on the other end almost instantly.

"Well, hi stranger," Sam said, her voice happy.

"Hi." Lisa pushed off the ground and let her feet dangle as she swung back and forth.

"I love this new cell phone of yours. I get to talk to you more. Are you ready for tomorrow's big bus ride?"

"Um hmm." Lisa's chest tightened, and she started to cry into the phone.

"What's wrong, baby? Are you okay?"

Lisa swallowed hard and choked out, "No."

"Okay, I'm putting my shoes on and getting my car keys. I can be there in forty minutes."

"Oh, no, Sam. I'll be okay, really. I just didn't know who else to talk to."

"Are you sure you don't want me to drive out there?"

"I'll be okay, I guess."

"Well, if I were there I'd pull you into my arms right now."

Lisa took a breath. "And I'd snuggle into you and lay my head on your shoulder."

"And, then I'd start stroking your back. So, now that I'm holding you tight, tell me what's wrong."

Lisa's face scrunched up again as she tried not to cry. It didn't work. She knew Sam heard it.

Sam said softly, "And right now, I'm kissing your tears away."

"Um hmm." Lisa's throat was still tight.

"Oh, Lisa, c'mon, what's wrong? I know you're not upset about the playoffs in Binghamton tomorrow."

"No."

"You're not breaking up with me, are you?"

"Oh, no, Sam. I—" She had been about to say, "I love you," but stopped herself. Instead she said, "Never." She attempted a smile hoping Sam would hear it on the other end. "It's nothing like that. I just..." God, where to start?

"What, baby?"

"I haven't been completely honest with you." Lisa pushed herself higher on the swing. "My father isn't..." She took a big breath. "My father isn't my father."

"What do you mean?"

"I mean, my mom is my biological mom, but my father isn't."

"Oh," Sam said with understanding. "Did you just find out?"

"No. My father married my mom when I was six. Lynnie, Lawrence Jr., and Bridget are all his. They don't know that I'm not their full sister, though, and I don't want them to ever find out."

"Is that what's got you so upset?" Lisa heard the sympathy in Sam's voice.

"Partly." Lisa felt her chest tighten again.

"Okay, and now I'm stroking your cheek. Ooh, maybe I should be kissing you."

Lisa laughed. "Geez, what took you so long?"

Sam laughed. "There you go. That's my Lisa. So what else has you upset?"

"Well, nobody knows that my father isn't my father, except you now."

"It'll be our secret."

"Thanks. He adopted me, you know." As soon as she said that, everything came bubbling up to the surface, and she told Sam some of the things her mother had told her the night before. "I feel so stupid thinking my bio dad was some college scout." She took a deep breath. "He wants to meet me."

"Whoa. Why now?"

"He's getting married and wants to be honest with his new wife or something. I'm not sure if I'm ready to meet him, though."

"I don't blame you."

"I mean, I used to bug my mom about him all the time, but she kept telling me to stop thinking about him. When I wouldn't let up, she'd say we shouldn't make my father, my real father, I mean my..." Lisa groaned. She didn't know what to call him.

"Lawrence Brown, Sr. *is* your real father, Lisa. He always will be."

"I know. I guess maybe that's why I'm so upset. I love my dad, and I don't want to hurt him. I don't want Lynnie and Lawrence Jr. and Bridget to get confused, either. It's such bad timing."

"I just kissed the palm of your hand."

Lisa smiled, "Thanks."

"You know what?"

"What."

"I think any time would be bad timing for something like this."

"I guess."

"Hey," Sam said, her voice upbeat, "I've got an idea."

"What?" Lisa put her feet out to stop the swing.

"You referred to William Dowell as your bio dad earlier, so why don't we just call him your 'bd,' just to keep things straight."

"My bd?" Lisa laughed. "Okay, but that's the only straight thing I ever want to do."

"Same." Sam laughed.

Lisa's heart swelled at the sound of Sam's laugh. "Sam?"

"Yeah?"

"Promise me we'll always be honest with each other."

"Absolutely."

Lisa stood up, opened the gate to the playground, and headed toward home. The moonless night would have made her feel lonely, but Sam was her lifeline. "I want to know everything about you, Sam. I want to meet your parents and see your house. I want to meet your nanny, too."

"Absolutely. When school's out, I'll pick you up and bring you to my house. We can spend the whole day out here. That way you can see and know everything about me." There was something in Sam's voice that Lisa couldn't quite put her finger on. It almost sounded like resignation, like Sam didn't really want Lisa to come over.

"Are you sure?" Lisa asked tentatively.

"Yeah, why wouldn't I be?"

"I don't know," Lisa said. She must have misread Sam's tone. "Maybe Marlee could drop me off, so you wouldn't have to come all the way out here to be my chauffeur."

"I didn't know Marlee had her license already."

Lisa laughed. "Actually she doesn't have it yet. She was supposed to get it on Monday, but we played Overton Corners that day, and since we keep winning, she can't get out to the DMV in East Valley to take her test."

"Bummer."

Lisa paused for a second. "Sam?"

"Yeah?"

"I'm sorry I'm such a downer tonight. It doesn't exactly set the mood, does it?"

"Lisa, everything doesn't have to lead to me taking your clothes off. Even over the phone." She laughed. "I mean, that part is amazing actually, but it's only a small part of why I like being with you."

"Really?"

"Of course, but right now I'm putting my arms around your neck and kissing you."

"Mmm, that's nice. I'm kissing you back." Lisa felt a shiver as she imagined kissing Sam.

"Mmm."

"I wish you were here, Sam."

"Me, too."

"I guess I'll see you in Binghamton on Saturday."

Sam laughed. "Oh, great. Now I'm a softball wife."

"Could you imagine if we combined our teams? An East Valley

and Clarksonville merge? We would be so awesome. Susie in left, you at second, me catching, and Marlee pitching."

"Let's do it this summer."

"What d'ya mean?"

"Well," Sam said, "Susie, Christy, and I play for a traveling team. Coach Gellar is always looking for good players. You guys should play with us."

Lisa's spirits lifted. "That'd be so cool. I'll ask my Mom and Dad. Hey, maybe I can see you after church on Sunday. We can, uh, you know go for a drive and stuff."

"Mmm, the 'and stuff' part sounds yummy."

She paused on the front stoop. "Okay. I'll text you tomorrow when we're on the bus."

"Goodnight, baby."

"Goodnight." Lisa wanted to add, "I love you," but didn't. She hung up her phone and smiled. It felt great to finally tell somebody about her bio dad, her bd. A great weight she hadn't known she'd been carrying lessened slightly.

LISA PLOPPED DOWN on the bed in the Binghamton Oaks Motel and closed her eyes. She hadn't slept well the night before worrying about meeting her bio dad. She tried to sleep for at least part of the four hour trip on the bus, but couldn't pass up Julie's and Marlee's help with geometry.

She had just dozed off when Marlee threw a towel on her. "Lisa, c'mon. Coach wants us changed for practice and on the bus in five minutes."

"Okay, Mom, I'm up." Lisa sat up and rubbed her eyes.

"Oh, man. You look terrible."

Lisa threw the towel back at Marlee. "Thanks a lot."

Marlee laughed. "Did I wear you out exposing the secrets of geometry proofs to you?"

"No." Lisa stood up and stretched. "I didn't sleep well." She didn't elaborate, and Marlee didn't ask. What would she have told Marlee, anyway? That her bio dad showed up out of the blue and wanted to get back in her life? She wasn't ready to reveal that big secret to her friends yet, other than Sam.

"Hopefully, you'll sleep better tonight." Marlee grabbed her softball bag and headed toward the door. "I'm gonna head to the bus, okay?"

Lisa nodded. Once Marlee left, Lisa threw some cold water on her face and then changed into her practice clothes. She ran to the parking lot with her softball bag slung over her arm. Coach Spears gave her a stern look when she walked up late.

The Binghamton Softball Complex was a short five minute ride from the motel. Lisa was still in slow motion, so she and Marlee were the last ones to step off the bus.

Lisa whistled when she saw the meticulously groomed fields. "Maybe someday our field can look like that."

"Pfft," Marlee spat. "Not in our lifetime."

"Yeah, what was I thinking?"

They walked up the pathway between fields one and four toward the concession stand at the geometric center of the complex.

Lisa's stomach fluttered when she saw that a couple teams were already practicing. "I can't believe we're in the state playoffs."

"I know. It's surreal. Somebody needs to pinch me." Marlee blew out a sigh.

Lisa laughed. "Nah, I don't usually pinch people I like."

"Yeah, actually, I kind of want to take that part back." Marlee pointed to their teammates who had gathered around a wooden A-frame sign in the middle of the walkway. "What's everybody looking at?"

"The brackets, I think."

"Oh, cool."

Their teammates moved on toward field three, their assigned practice field, so Lisa and Marlee had the sign to themselves.

Lisa pointed. "Look, here's where we beat Overton Corners in the first round, and then Whickett in the quarterfinals."

"Final four, man."

Lisa bumped fists with Marlee and then followed the bracket to their next game. "We play Central Leatherstocking High School at nine tomorrow."

"Who do we play after we win that game?"

Lisa raised an eyebrow at Marlee. "Geez, optimist much?"

"Why not?"

"Okay then. Let me see." Lisa moved her finger to the other side of the bracket. "Looks like we play the winner of tomorrow's eleven o'clock game. That'll be either Arsdale High School or—oh, crap." She leaped away from the sign as if bitten.

"What's wrong? You look like you got shocked or something."

Lisa pointed to the sign.

"Brookhaven High School?" Marlee clearly didn't understand.

"Tara's school."

Marlee's eyes grew wide. "Tara as in ex-girlfriend Tara?"

Lisa nodded. She grabbed the bracket board and took a deep breath. Seeing Tara was the last thing she needed on top of everything else.

Chapter Fourteen

Central Leatherstocking

LISA SOMEHOW MANAGED to get a decent night's sleep in the motel, and felt infinitely better when she woke on Saturday morning.

"C'mon, slowpoke," Lisa said to Marlee. "I need to be the first one on the bus so Coach doesn't give me the hairy eyeball again." She held the door to their motel room open.

"Okay, okay." Marlee grabbed her softball bag and her small suitcase and slid past Lisa in the doorway. She looked up. "Oh, man. What a great day to play."

"I know. Blue skies, puffy white clouds that better not have a single drop of rain in them."

"Yeah, really."

The bus driver opened the door to the bus and let Lisa and Marlee in. Besides the driver, the bus was empty, and they made their way to their usual seats. Coach Spears stepped on the bus barely a minute later and looked surprised to see them. She winked at Lisa and then turned away to go over their schedule with the bus driver.

The rest of her teammates trickled on the bus and within fifteen minutes they pulled up to the Binghamton Softball Complex. Lisa looked around for Tara. There was no sign of her, thank God. She didn't see Sam or her parents, either, but that was probably for the best for now, because she had to find a way to focus her attention on the game against Central Leatherstocking High School.

She and Marlee warmed up in the pitcher's area, and then Lisa helped Coach Spears with the infield and outfield warm ups. Once they were through, Lisa grabbed the bag of balls and headed back to the dugout. Her family was just walking up.

"Hi Mom. Hi Papa," she called.

"Hi, honey." Her mother waved. "Play well."

Her father ushered Lynnie, Lawrence Jr., and Bridget ahead of him to a front row spot on the bleachers. "Do Clarksonville proud, honey."

"Will do, Papa."

Bridget saw her and broke free of her father's grip to rush the fence. "Hi, Weesa."

Lisa squatted down in front of her littlest sister. "Hi, Sweetpea. That was a long car ride, wasn't it?"

"Yeah, Warence spilled his juice all over. Mama got so mad."

"I bet she did."

Marlee walked up behind Lisa and pointed toward the stands. "Hey, there's that college scout."

Lisa looked up and saw William, her bio dad, sitting on the far end of the bleachers. "Oh, yeah."

Marlee smacked her on the arm. "I'll be in the dugout."

"Okay."

Lisa stood up. "Hey, Bridget, go on back to Papa. I have to go play now."

"Okay, bye." Bridget ran back to their father.

Lisa knelt down by the fence and retied her cleats one at a time. In actuality, she was really watching her bio dad out of the corner of her eye. He was focused on his cell phone, so he didn't see her watching him. Lisa wondered if she had inherited his dark black hair. And his chin. Yeah, she definitely had his chin. She couldn't get a good look at his eyes under his glasses, but she wondered if she had his brown eyes, too. He flipped his phone shut, so she looked away quickly and hoped he hadn't seen her watching him.

Lisa headed toward the dugout, but stopped dead in her tracks when a voice from her past said, "Holy crap. If it isn't my favorite apple picker from the North Country."

Lisa turned toward the sound and her heart jumped. She hadn't seen Tara in almost a year. She swallowed hard when she locked eyes with the baby browns on the other side of the fence. The tiny flame that still burned for Tara flared inside her heart.

"Hey, Tara," Lisa said simply. Memories of Tara at summer softball camp came rushing back. Their kiss, second base, almost third. She felt her body flush all over.

"Who knew a bunch of apple pickers could make the final four."

Lisa cleared her throat. "I see you and your hoodlums made it, too."

Tara smiled and then looked her up and down. She leaned against the fence. "You're lookin' good. Real good. Maybe I was a little hasty breaking up with you."

"Shhh." Lisa looked around to see if anybody was within earshot. "Somebody'll hear you."

"Oh, you always were a worry wart." She whispered, "Remember how scared you got that someone would walk in on us in my dorm room?"

Lisa flushed at the memory. "Uh, listen, I gotta get ready for the game. I'll talk to you later, okay?"

"Count on it, apple picker. Count on it."

Lisa headed back to the dugout, but felt Tara watching her every step. She plopped down on the bench and took a deep breath.

Marlee sat next to her and whispered, "That's Tara?"

Lisa nodded and put her face in her hands.

"Oh, man, Lisa. She's friggin' hot."

"Shhh," she sat up and looked around. "At least Sam's not here yet, thank God."

"Man, oh, man," Marlee said. "What's with you and all the hot girlfriends? You're a chick magnet."

Lisa grinned and shrugged. She didn't want to think about it at the moment. She had a game to get psyched for.

The beefy umpire looked toward the Cougars' dugout. "Home team, take the field." He pointed toward the field.

Lisa grabbed her catcher's mask and helmet and ran back behind the plate. Marlee took her five warm up pitches, and the first batter of the New York State Class C semi-final game stepped into the batter's box.

Lisa still felt Tara's gaze on her, so she took a deep breath to try and clear her head. She couldn't let Tara or William or anything else interfere with the game ahead. She squatted behind the plate and pounded her fist in her mitt and called for Marlee to throw an outside fastball at the knees.

"Strike!" The umpire yelled.

"Nice one, Marlee." Lisa threw the ball back.

Lisa called for another outside fastball, but the ball hung over the plate too much, and the batter smacked a single through the three-four hole into right field.

Lisa pointed to Johnna at second base. "Get ready for the steal."

Johnna nodded and pounded her glove. On the first pitch, the runner took off for second base, and Lisa fired the ball toward second. Her adrenaline must have been on overload because her throw sailed clear into center field.

"Dammit," Lisa muttered under her breath when the runner ran safely to third.

She wondered what William thought about her error. He was probably shaking his head. Tara was probably laughing her head off.

Lisa took a deep breath and refocused on the next batter. Marlee got two quick strikes, and Lisa called for the change-up. The batter swung and missed for strike three, but the ball hit the heel of Lisa's glove and bounced away. Since Lisa didn't catch the third strike, the batter raced toward first base trying to make it there before Lisa could pick up the ball and throw her out. Lisa leaped up, snagged the ball, made sure the runner on third didn't take off for home, and threw the ball to Julie covering first.

Lisa knew instantly that her throw was wild. Julie lunged for the ball, but couldn't get it. "Crap," Lisa muttered under her breath as the ball skipped into right field. She watched helplessly as the runner from third base scored, and the batter, who should have been out on strikes, ran all the way to second base.

Lisa kicked the dirt. "Get a freakin' grip, Lisa," she muttered to herself. She hoped Sam wasn't there yet to see her second glorious error.

Thankfully the Cougars managed to get out of the inning with only the one Central Leatherstocking run. Back in the dugout, Sarah brought ice to put on her already aching hand. So far, she had successfully hidden her black and blue hand from Coach Spears. Whenever Coach asked, she always said it was fine. Thanks goodness Sarah was good at slipping her ice without Coach knowing.

The Cougars got up to bat in the bottom half of the inning, but Jeri and Julie made two quick outs. Johnna got hit by a pitch and was awarded first base. Lisa took a deep breath and stepped into the box. If she could hit a long one, maybe Johnna could score from first and make up for her two colossal errors.

The first pitch was high, but Lisa swung anyway. She missed for strike one, and stepped out of the box.

"C'mon, Lisa," Coach Spears called from third base. "Swing at strikes, kiddo. Just strikes."

Lisa nodded and stepped back in the box. The next pitch came inside, and she swung hoping to pull it down the left field line. She couldn't believe she missed that one, too. She took a deep breath and willed herself to hit the next one. The next pitch came in nice and fat. She pulled her bat back, swung with all her might, but stumbled off-balance when she missed the change-up for strike three.

Lisa slammed her bat on the ground. She hated striking out. She looked into the stands as she slunk back to the dugout. Sam was sitting next to Lynnie. Her long blond hair fell deliciously in front of both shoulders and framed her tanned face and brilliant smile. Lisa couldn't help the grin that took over her face, her strikeout instantly forgotten. Anybody who looked at her would know immediately that she was completely and totally gone in love.

Tara laughed, and Lisa watched in horror as Tara turned to look straight at Sam. An evil smile crept up Tara's face. Lisa slammed the dugout door open. Not only did she freakin' strike out in front of everybody, but now Tara knew about Sam. She slammed herself down on the bench and strapped on a shin guard. Sarah helped with the other.

Coach Spears squatted in front of her. "Kiddo, I don't know what you've got on your mind right now, but you need to snap out of it, okay? Let it go. You are the rock of this team, so take a deep breath, and let it go."

"Yes, Coach." Lisa stood up and put on her chest protector. "Sorry." She hustled onto the field.

Lisa took a deep breath, pounded her mitt, and squatted behind the plate. With new determination, she helped her team keep Central Leatherstocking High School from scoring in the top half of the second inning. She even ended the inning by snagging a runner trying to steal second base.

Julie ran off the field behind her and clapped her on the back.

"That runner got caught with her hand in the cookie jar. That'll teach her to try to steal a base against Lisa Brown and her tools of ignorance."

Lisa bumped fists with her first baseman and purposely avoided looking into the stands. Her focus had to remain on the field. They didn't make it this far only to lose in the semi-final game.

Lisa finally remembered how to use her bat and smacked a double in the third inning and a single in the fifth. But even though the Cougars got several base runners over the next five innings, they didn't score a single run and were still losing 0-1 when it was their turn to bat in the bottom of the seventh inning. If they didn't score, they would lose and be out of the tournament. Their season would be over.

Lisa tried not to let her misery show. She was the one who had committed the string of errors that allowed Central Leatherstocking's lone run. Sarah tried to hand her another ice pack for her hand, but she waved it off. The pain in her hand didn't matter at this point.

Julie stepped into the box to lead off the inning. She swung and the ball bounced deep into the hole between short and third. The shortstop fielded the ball cleanly and made a good throw, but Julie beat it out by a toenail.

Lisa rattled the chain link fence. "Way to go, White Girl." She grabbed her bat and helmet and walked to the on-deck circle.

Johnna got up to bat next and successfully sacrificed Julie to second. Lisa was up. She took a deep breath and wouldn't let herself think about making amends for her errors. Instead she pictured a smooth stroke that connected solidly with the pitch. With a 1-1 count, a hittable pitch came down the pike, and she swung, putting all of her five foot nine inches into it. Her efforts paid off as the ball towered over the center fielder's head. She rounded first and saw the ball careen off the fence. She headed toward second. Coach Spears waved her on to third.

"Down, down, down," Coach Spears yelled.

Lisa slid, and the third baseman put the tag on her hip. The umpire in the field threw both arms out to the side. "Safe."

"Yes." Lisa leaped up and threw a fist in the air. Julie had scored from second base and the game was tied. She didn't dare look into the stands, because she was the winning run and had to stay focused.

"C'mon, Marlee," Lisa called from third. "Just a little single. Nothing big, number three."

Marlee worked the count full. The Central Leatherstocking pitcher went into her motion and sent the pitch rocketing toward home plate. Marlee swung and made contact. Lisa leaped into the air when the ball landed in shallow right field for a hit. She sprinted all the way home to score the winning run.

Lisa's teammates burst out of the dugout and mobbed her at the plate. They left her standing dizzy to mob Marlee coming back from first base.

Lisa tried not to smile too much when they walked the high five line with the Central Leatherstocking team. The Cougars headed back toward their dugout, and Lisa smiled. Sam was at the fence.

"Great game, Lisa." Sam's blue-gray eyes glistened.

"Thanks." Lisa's heart swelled. She wished she could take Sam somewhere and kiss her. "I'm so glad you made it."

Sam leaned closer and whispered, "Baby, I wouldn't have missed it for anything."

Lisa was just about to whisper back when Tara walked by. "Lucky game, apple picker. Give us a minute to beat Arsdale, and we'll see you in the finals."

Sam looked at Lisa with a puzzled expression. "That girl is kind of cocky. I hope you don't have to play them."

Lisa nodded. "Me, too."

Chapter Fifteen

Never in a Million Trillion Years

AFTER THE WIN against Central Leatherstocking in the New York State Class C semi-finals, the Clarksonville Cougars from the North Country Region advanced to the finals for the first time in school history. They would play whichever team won the next game. Lisa kept her mental fingers crossed that Arsdale would beat Tara's Brookhaven team.

Lisa grabbed her catcher's gear and followed Julie out of the dugout.

"There she is." Julie pointed to Coach Spears's roommate who was handing out Subway sandwiches.

"I'm not really hungry," Lisa said, "but I guess we need to eat before the finals."

"Eeee," Julie gushed. "Can you believe we're in the finals?"

"Not really. This whole season has been crazy."

"No kidding."

They reached Coach Spears's roommate. "Great job today, girls. Keep it up." She handed each of them the subs they had ordered.

Julie grinned. "Win the last, right?"

Coach Spears's roommate nodded with a smile.

"Win the last." Lisa knocked sandwiches with Julie.

They headed toward the bleachers to find their families. Lisa looked around for William, but he was in line at the concession stand, and Tara, of course, was on the field getting ready for her game against Arsdale, so the coast was clear. She relaxed a little.

A couple of black girls walked past them. They looked at Julie and said, "Hey."

Julie nodded back. "Hey."

Lisa waited until the girls were out of earshot and asked, "Do you know them?"

Julie shook her head.

"Why'd they say hello to you?"

"It's a black thing."

"Oh," Lisa said, "like black solidarity or something?"

"I guess. I'm not sure why we do it." She laughed. "It's not like it's in the handbook or anything."

Lisa laughed.

Julie looked back at the girls they had passed. "Actually, now that I think about it, they were kind of rude saying, 'hey' just to me and not to you."

"Guess I'm a little too white, eh, White Girl?"

Julie laughed. "Probably, Brown Girl, but you know what? Just 'cuz those girls were black doesn't mean we'd even like each other. Color isn't automatic when it comes to friends." Julie bugged her eyes out at Lisa and grinned.

Lisa grinned back. "Friend, I feel the same way, too." She readjusted her softball bag on her shoulder, and they stepped off the path so they wouldn't get run over by a Little League softball team scampering toward the concession stand.

"Hey," Julie said, "nobody's the same, anyway, right? People are different in all kinds of ways, not just color."

"Yeah." *I hope you'll accept the fact that I'm different when I finally get up the nerve to come out to you.* "Being different makes us unique."

"Exactly, and you, Lisa, are definitely unique."

"Hey, what do you mean by that?"

Julie looked at her wrist as if she were wearing a watch. "Gosh, would you look at the time?" She pointed to the top row of the bleachers. "There's my mom and dad. I gotta go."

"Oh, way to get out of that one, White Girl."

Julie laughed. "I'll see you later, Brown Girl." She bounded up the bleachers.

Lisa smiled when she saw Susie sitting with Marlee and Marlee's mother near the top of the bleacher seats. She spotted her own family sitting with Sam on the bottom bleacher. Apparently, Sam and Susie were both sucking up to the future in-laws.

She walked over to her family and wondered if gay people acknowledged each other the way Julie did with those two girls. Did gay people nod and say, "Hey," when they passed each other in the mall? Not everybody had good gaydar, though. She'd have to ask Tara about it later.

Whoa, Tara? Where the hell did that come from? Lisa shook her head and hoped she didn't slip up in front of Sam. She desperately didn't want Sam to know that Tara was there. Never in a million trillion years did she think that Sam and Tara would ever be in the same place at the same time.

"Hi guys," she said to her family when she reached them.

"We're very proud of you, Lisa Bear," her father said.

"Thanks, Papa." She gave him a hug and then patted Lawrence Jr. on the head. She hugged Bridget who sat sandwiched between her father and mother for safe keeping.

Her mother gave her a quick hug. "You played so well, honey."

"Well, I don't know about that. I had a rocky start."

"But you worked it out," Sam said with a smile. "Marlee pitched really well, too."

"Oh, geez, I know. She's even got her screwball working today."

Lisa squished in between her mother and Sam. She looked past Sam and said, "Hi, Lynnie."

Lynnie waved. "I was cheering for you."

Lisa smiled. "I heard you. Thanks." She smiled inside, because Lynnie used to complain about getting dragged to her softball games.

Lisa opened her sandwich. She took a bite and realized she was starving. She took another bite before she had even finished the first.

"Slow down, honey," her mother scolded.

"Sorry," Lisa said with her mouth full. "I'm famished."

Lisa followed her mother's gaze toward William where he stood in the concession line. She said, "Larry, why don't you go play soccer with Lawrence Jr."

Her father followed her gaze. "Ah, okay. We'll see you later, girls." He herded Lawrence Jr. away from the bleachers toward an open patch of grass near the parking lot.

"Honey," her mother turned toward Lisa, "can you watch the girls? I've got something to take care of."

"Okay, Mom. C'mere, Bridget, slide over next to me."

"'Kay." Bridget crawled in her lap.

"Oh, okay." Lisa handed her sandwich to Sam until Bridget got situated.

"Weesa?"

"Yes, Sweetpea?" Lisa took the sandwich back with one hand. She held Sam's gaze for an extra long second before concentrating on her little sister.

"Papa took me to the 'session stand." She pointed toward the concession stand.

"Me, and Wynnie, and Wawrence got orange pop."

"Did Lawrence Jr. spill his pop all over the place?"

"No." Bridget giggled. "You're siwee, Weesa."

"Oh, yeah? Let me ask Sam. Am I silly, Sam?"

Lisa and Sam locked eyes over Bridget's head. God, how she wished she could be alone with Sam and kiss her.

Sam broke their gaze and winked at Bridget. "Lisa, you're the silliest person I know."

Bridget giggled.

Lynnie, who was sitting on the other side of Sam, laughed and said, "Lisa, you are kind of silly sometimes."

"Everybody's picking on me today. I'm going to go sit on the other set of bleachers."

"No, you have to stay here so we can torture you some more. Right, girls?"

"Yeah," Lynnie and Bridget said with gusto.

"I'm so insulted." Lisa handed her sandwich to Sam and stood up holding Bridget tightly with her left arm, legs dangling.

Sam reached up and grabbed Lisa's right hand and started to pull her back down.

"Yeeow," Lisa cried and sat down with a thump. She clung tightly to her sister with her good hand and pulled the bad one close to her chest.

"What? What happened?" Sam's eyes were wide with fear.

Lisa didn't have a chance to answer because Sam's face lit with understanding. She leaned close and whispered, "You told me that hand was okay."

Lisa took a couple of deep breaths as the pain subsided. She shrugged.

"Let me see," Sam demanded.

Lisa knew she had no choice. She laid her hand in Sam's.

"Oh, my God, Lisa." She lowered her voice. "This bruise is gross. Look how swollen this is. You shouldn't be playing with your hand like this." She rubbed the bruise with a feather-light tough as if trying to see how bad the injury was.

The pain was so intense that Lisa pulled her hand back. "It's fine."

"It's not fine," Sam sighed, "but I know I won't be able to convince you not to play."

Lisa shook her head. "Nope."

The Brookhaven team ran onto the field, and Lisa was glad they had something else to focus on. She watched Tara warm up at shortstop. So pretty. So athletic. So— She sighed in mid-thought. Watching Tara was dangerous territory. She looked for her mother instead.

Her mother stood with William on the side of the concession stand away from other people. She was shaking her head emphatically, and Lisa could tell she was pissed. Lisa almost laughed when she noticed William drop his gaze as he got scolded. He was trying to get a word in, but her mother wouldn't let him. She wagged a finger in his face, spun on her heels, and marched back toward the bleachers.

Lisa could only imagine what her mother had said to him. She probably reamed him out for showing up at the game. Lisa still hadn't decided if she wanted to meet him or not.

"Hey, Sam?" Lisa turned to look at Sam.

"Hmm?"

"My bd." She lifted her head and pointed her chin toward William.

Sam looked where she pointed and took a quick breath. Her eyes grew wide, and she nodded her head slowly as if to say she could tell that he was her biological father.

"Really?" Lisa asked.

Sam nodded again.

Lisa sighed and decided not to think about her bio dad at the moment. She took another bite of her sandwich.

Tara's team got the Arsdale team out one-two-three in the top of the first, and it was Brookhaven's turn to bat.

Sam pointed to the dugout closest to them. "I don't like that team."

"Brookhaven?"

"Yeah." Sam made a sour face. "I hope Arsdale wins."

"I just want to play whoever we can beat." Secretly Lisa prayed that would be the Arsdale team because facing Tara was the last thing she wanted to do, especially in front of Sam.

Sam chuckled. "Yeah, that's probably a better plan."

Tara stepped into the on-deck circle right in front of them. Lisa cursed the fact that her family decided to sit so close to the field. She looked at her feet trying not to be seen. She felt Tara's gaze on her.

"Hey, Lisa," Tara called.

Lisa groaned. She had to look up. She had no choice.

"Is that my replacement?" Tara pointed at Sam with her bat.

Lisa closed her eyes mortified. *Geez, Tara, tell the whole friggin' world, why don't you?* She pursed her lips together in anger and glared at Tara without saying a word.

Tara laughed. "Thought so." She took another practice swing and walked toward the plate.

Lisa felt her cheeks turn blazing hot. She turned toward Sam.

"You know her?"

Lisa nodded slowly, but couldn't find any words.

Someone on the Brookhaven team yelled, "C'mon, Tara. Get a hit."

Lynnie leaned over Sam and said, "That's Tara? She's pretty, but I like Sam way better." She looked up at Sam with admiration.

Me, too, Lisa thought, *but how the hell do you know who Tara is?*

Sam smiled at Lynnie, but then glared back at Lisa. "Um, I think we need to talk."

Lisa nodded and smiled at her mother who had just come back from her talk with William. "Mom, is it okay if Sam and I go for a walk?"

Her mother sat down. "Go ahead. I've got the girls."

Lisa and Sam made their way off the bleachers in silence. They headed toward the concession stand, but then Lisa spotted William.

"Uh, let's go the other way." She nodded her head toward William.

"Oh, yeah. Your bd."

They turned around and headed toward a maintenance shed on the far side of the right field fence. They walked behind the shed out of sight.

Sam confronted Lisa. "Were you ever going to tell me?"

"Yes."

"I mean, who is she? Is that your ex-girlfriend Tara? The one you told me about? The one you said you had no more contact with?"

Lisa took a deep breath and started to explain, but Sam interrupted. "You were the one who said we needed to be honest with each other, and here's your ex-girlfriend parading around right in front of us, and I don't even know it."

"I was going to tell you."

"When?" Sam put her hands up in the air. "Or were you, like, hoping I'd never find out?"

"I wanted to wait until after the finals. That way it wouldn't be so complicated."

Sam's eyes held a certain sadness that tore at Lisa's heart.

Lisa stepped closer. "I'm sorry you had to find out this way. Honestly, I didn't know her team had made the tournament." She wanted to brush a stray lock of Sam's hair off her face, but checked herself just in case anyone could see them.

"Hell, Lisa. Even Lynnie knew who Tara was." Sam's cheeks turned a dark red from anger or maybe it was embarrassment, Lisa wasn't sure which.

"Look, I have no idea how Lynnie knows about her. Maybe she answered the phone when Tara called me or something."

Sam seemed lost in thought, but then said, "Tara's kind of hot, you know, and that's got me more than a little annoyed."

"Annoyed?" Lisa was confused.

"Yeah, I always pictured your first girlfriend as some ugly duckling."

"Why?"

"To make myself feel better."

Lisa laughed.

"Baby," Sam said, "I know she broke up with you, but are you..."

"What?"

Sam looked Lisa in the eye. "Are you still in love with her?"

Lisa looked at the ground trying to extinguish the small flame flickering for Tara inside her chest. "No, I'm not in love with her."

"You hesitated."

"I'm in shock that we're having this conversation. Sam, I..."

"What?"

Lisa couldn't believe what she was about to say, but she mustered up the courage. "Sam," she grabbed both of Sam's hands with hers not caring who saw them, "I love you. I've loved you since that first time we went to the bowling alley. Even before you kissed me, I knew I was in love with you." Her chest tightened. "I...I don't love Tara anymore," she stammered. "You have to believe me."

Sam's expression softened. She leaned in closer and whispered, "I love you, too." She squeezed Lisa's hands, but Lisa ignored the shooting pain. "I have since forever. I'm sorry I got jealous."

Lisa's heart swelled. "I want to kiss you so bad right now."
Sam bit her lip. "I've been thinking the same thing all day."
Lisa sighed. "We can't risk it." She let go of Sam's hands.
"I know." I wish I could hold your hand, though. I wish people weren't so..."
"What?"
"I don't know. Judgmental? Ignorant? Stupid?"
Lisa laughed. "All of the above I think. We could..." she trailed off and waggled her eyebrows.
"We could what?"
"Walk back holding hands."
"Uh, that would be no. Your entire family would have a collective heart attack, and your teammates don't need that distraction right now."
"You're right." Lisa stuck out her lower lip. "But the more people see two girls holding hands, the more they'll get used to it, eh?"
"Yeah, I guess," Sam shrugged, "but I'm not up for it today. Come on. Let's get you back to your family."
They went back to the bleachers and watched Tara's Brookhaven team run up the score against Arsdale High School. At the start of the fifth inning, Coach Spears motioned for the Clarksonville players to come down off the bleachers to get ready for their game.
Lisa stood up. "Looks like we'll be playing Brookhaven." She looked at Sam. "Wish me luck."
Sam gently touched Lisa's bruised hand. "Be careful."
Lisa smiled. "I will." She mouthed, "I love you."
"Same," Sam said.
Her family wished her good luck, and she headed toward her teammates gathering behind the Arsdale dugout.
Lisa wondered how in the world her little apple picking team from the North Country would ever survive against Tara's cocky hoodlums from Long Island.

Chapter Sixteen

Brookhaven Hoodlums

LISA PICKED UP the ball bag after the short pre-game warm up.

"Bring it in, girls," Coach Spears called to the team. The Cougars ran off the field and gathered around her. "There isn't anything more to be said. Just do the things that got us here. Stay alert. No mental mistakes." She stepped back from the group and put her hand on Marlee's shoulder. "Oh, and girls? Let's win the last." She headed back to the Cougars' dugout.

Jeri put her hand in the middle of the circle of players. "Win the last on three. One, two, three."

"Win the last!" the team yelled and ran back to the dugout.

"Captains?" The umpire gestured at the Cougars' dugout with her facemask.

"You're on, you guys," Lisa said to Marlee and Jeri. "Pick tails," she called after them.

Marlee and Jeri headed toward home plate, and Lisa wasn't surprised when Tara walked toward the plate as the captain for her team. Lisa plopped on the bench with her mask, mitt, and chest protector draped over her lap waiting for the coin toss to determine home team. If they won the toss, then she'd have to scurry and put on her gear since they'd be on the field first. She leaned forward to listen.

The umpire went over the ground rules and then reminded them about good sportsmanship. She asked Tara to call the flip since her team had traveled farther to get to Binghamton.

"Heads," Tara said after the umpire flipped the coin in the air.

The three captains and the umpire bent their heads toward the ground. "Tails," the umpire announced.

Lisa put on her chest protector.

"Cougars," the umpire looked at Jeri, "I assume you wish to be home team?"

Jeri nodded.

"Okay, then. Home team, take the field when you're ready."

Jeri and Marlee ran back to the dugout. "Home team, guys."

"Whoo hoo," Julie and a few of the other girls hooted.

Lisa grabbed her mitt and mask. She was headed toward home plate when Tara yelled toward her, "Good thing you won the toss, Cougars, because that's all you mofo's are winning this afternoon." Her Brookhaven teammates laughed.

The first Brookhaven batter stepped into the batter's box. Lisa squatted behind the plate and signaled for a fastball. Just as Marlee got ready to throw her first pitch, Tara yelled from the on-deck circle, "She ain't got nothin', Brenda. Nothin'."

Marlee's first pitch smacked into her glove for strike one. *Nothing, eh?* Lisa tossed the ball back to Marlee. Two pitches later, the batter was out on strikes.

Tara stepped into the box. "How ya been, apple picker?"

Lisa ignored her and signaled Marlee for a fastball on the inside corner. Her plan was to brush Tara off the plate for the first few pitches and then have Marlee sneak a change-up on the outside corner.

"Ball," the umpire said.

"Inside, Lisa?" Tara said. "C'mon, that's my favorite spot."

Lisa called for another inside pitch. Tara ripped it foul down the left field line.

"Told ya."

Tara fouled off the next inside pitch to bring the count up to 1-2. "Nice little blondie you got there, Lisa. You didn't take long to replace me, did you?"

Lisa remained mute and set up on the outside corner of the plate. She signaled Marlee for a change-up. Tara must have been expecting it, though, because she smacked the ball to the right-center field gap in between Jeri and Paula. Lisa pounded her mitt on her thigh as she watched them run after the ball. Jeri fielded the ball just before it hit the fence, turned, and fired it to Johnna on second base. Tara slid.

"Safe." The umpire in the field threw his arms out to the side.

"Dammit," Lisa mumbled. She knew from camp that Tara was aggressive on the bases and would try to steal third the first chance she got. Lisa flexed her throwing hand. It still felt tight from the first game. Maybe she should have put some ice on it in between games, but she didn't want Coach Spears or anybody else to know her hand still hurt.

"Kym, be ready," Lisa called down to alert the Cougar third baseman of a possible steal.

Kym nodded and took a microstep closer to third base.

Lisa took a deep breath and got ready for the third Brookhaven batter. As expected, Tara took off on the pitch. The batter swung late, but Lisa caught the pitch, moved the batter out of the way with her gloved hand, and rifled the ball to Kym waiting on third. Tara slid under Kym's tag.

"Safe!" the umpire in the field yelled.

"Yes!" Tara smacked the hard dirt.

Lisa cursed under her breath.

Coach Spears stormed the home plate umpire. "Interference, Blue." She pointed to the Brookhaven batter.

The umpire shook her head.

"Oh, c'mon, Blue. Get help." Coach Spears pointed to the other umpire.

The home plate umpire pointed to the umpire in the field. He threw his arms out in a safe gesture.

The fans in the stands groaned their disapproval at the call.

"Oh, c'mon," Coach Spears growled. She headed back toward the dugout. "You owe us one, Blue," she muttered and slammed the dugout gate shut.

Lisa took a deep breath and called to her teammates, "C'mon, Cougars. One down. Hold the runner. Get the out."

The Brookhaven batter stepped back into the box and hit a soft grounder to Johnna at shortstop. Lisa threw her mask off in case there was a play at the plate. Johnna looked Tara back and rifled the ball to Julie at first base. Tara took off for home on the throw.

"Out at first," the umpire yelled.

"Home, home, home," Lisa yelled. Julie threw the ball home. Lisa caught it and threw her body in front of the plate. Tara lowered her shoulder and barreled into Lisa. Lisa, ready for the impact, took the shoulder in the chest protector and toppled backward. Tara landed on top of her with a grunt. Lisa held on to the ball with both hands.

"Safe!" The home plate umpire yelled and threw her hands out to her sides.

"What?" Lisa pushed Tara off her and scrambled up to her knees. Tara leaped to her feet, and, somehow, whether accidentally or on purpose, kicked Lisa with infield dirt. Lisa brushed it away with her free hand and said, "I was laying on the plate, Blue! How is she safe?"

The umpire didn't respond, so Lisa scrambled to her feet and faced the umpire. "You gotta be kidding me." She pointed to plate again. "I had her, Blue. I had her."

By that time, Coach Spears took up the argument and nudged Lisa away with her arm. Coach Spears complained that Tara didn't slide, but the umpire explained that Lisa was blocking the plate, and the runner had no choice.

Marlee pulled Lisa away from the argument and dragged her toward the pitcher's circle. "Give me the ball, Lisa." Marlee held out her glove.

Lisa slammed the ball into Marlee's glove and let herself be led away from home plate. "She was so out." Lisa kicked the dirt.

"I know, but there's nothing we can do about it now. Let's just get this next batter out."

"Okay." Lisa sighed.

"Is your hand okay?"

Lisa realized she had taken her mitt off and was massaging the side of her throwing hand. She threw her mitt back on. "Yeah. Never better." She stormed back behind the plate.

Thankfully the next batter grounded out to Corrie at second base to end the inning.

Lisa plopped on the bench and took off her chest protector. Sarah snuck over and handed her an ice pack. "Thanks, Sarah."

"Is it okay?"

"Yeah, yeah." Lisa lied. "T—" She'd started to say Tara's name, but thought better of it. "That girl smashed right into it at home plate, but I'm okay."

Sarah frowned as if she didn't believe her.

"It's okay, really. Don't worry. You won't have to suit up. I promise."

Lisa bit down a smile at the look of relief on Sarah's face.

Marlee turned to Lisa. "Jeri walked."

"Cool." Lisa took off her shin guards and stood up. With luck she'd get up to bat that inning. She leaned against the dugout fence next to Marlee.

Julie was up. She swung hard and ripped the pitch foul inches outside the left field line. The third baseman backed up to normal depth.

"Oh, man," Marlee said, "they're falling for it."

"C'mon, Julie," Lisa called out. "Smack another one, just like that." Lisa knew better, though. They wanted the Brookhaven team to think Julie was hitting away, but Coach had put the bunt sign on for the second pitch.

Julie squared around at the last second and pushed the bunt up the third base line. The third baseman looked startled, but sprinted in to grab the ball. She threw it to first base a split-second ahead of Julie.

"Out," the umpire said.

Julie was out, but Jeri stood safely on second base.

Lisa grabbed her helmet and headed to the on-deck circle. She bumped fists with Julie as she ran back to the dugout. "Nice sacrifice, White Girl."

Julie smiled. "Just hit her in, Brown Girl."

"No pressure there, eh?"

"Hey, it's what you do best."

Lisa took her practice swings and called out to Johnna up at bat. "C'mon, Johnna. Just a little one. Move her over." She blew out a sigh when Johnna popped up to Tara at short. She tried hard not to watch Tara's athletic movements. That was done, over, finished.

"Pick me up, Lisa," Johnna said on her way back to the dugout.

Lisa dug her feet into the batter's box. The first pitch hit the inside corner for strike one. The next pitch missed inside for ball one. *I know this ploy,* Lisa thought. *Keep brushing me back and then pop a curve or change on the outside.* Just as she finished the thought the curveball came and tailed out. Lisa swung and made solid contact. The ball landed in the same gap that Tara had hit to. Lisa ran toward first, and Kerry waved her on to second base. She pumped a fist when Jeri scored. Coach Spears put up a standing stop sign, so she eased up into second base.

"Lucky hit, apple picker." Tara caught the ball from her right-fielder.

"Oh, and yours was skill?"

Tara shrugged as if to say, "Of course." She tossed the ball back to her pitcher.

"You've changed, you know," Lisa said.

"Nah, I think you're the one that changed." Tara trotted back to her position. She called back to Lisa on second base. "And besides, I can be anybody I want to be."

Lisa frowned. It was right at that moment, standing on second base in the championship finals, that she realized she had been totally played by Tara the summer before. She was probably just another one of Tara's conquests, another notch on her bedpost. Something black boiled inside Lisa's gut permanently extinguishing the flame that had been burning there for Tara. A surge of adrenaline ran through her, and she decided that there was no way her team was going to lose to a bunch of cocky hoodlum posers.

"C'mon, Marlee," Lisa called out to Marlee who had stepped into the batter's box.

Marlee let three pitches go by and swung at the fourth. Tara made a nice back handed grab and threw her out at first base to end the inning with the score tied 1-1.

Lisa ran back to the dugout to get her gear on. "C'mon, you guys. We are not losing to this team today."

Neither team scored a single run during the next five innings. At the top of the seventh inning, Brookhaven almost scored the go-ahead run in a heart-stopping play in which their runner tried to score from second base on a ball hit to the outfield. Jeri rifled the ball to Johnna who relayed it home to Lisa. The runner slid, and even though it was close, Lisa held on and the umpire thankfully called the runner out.

Unfortunately, in the bottom of the seventh inning, the Cougars went down one-two-three forcing the game into extra innings.

In the top of the eighth inning, Tara swung hard, but hit a dinky grounder to Marlee to end the Brookhaven half of the inning. Lisa burst out laughing. She couldn't help it. In the bottom of the eighth, Johnna hit a long fly ball to right field, but the right fielder made an awesome over the shoulder catch for the first out. Lisa stepped into the box hopeful that the Brookhaven pitcher would give her something to hit. Instead the pitcher walked her on four pitches. Lisa had mixed feeling. Even though she'd gotten on base, she wanted to get an extra base hit to put herself in scoring position.

Marlee stepped in the batter's box and hit a hard grounder to Tara. Lisa ran like the wind, but Tara threw her out at second base. The Brookhaven second baseman threw to first trying to turn the double play, but Marlee was too fast and reached first safely. It didn't matter, though, because Kym, the Cougars third baseman, got up to bat next and popped out to the center fielder to end the inning.

In the top of the ninth, Brookhaven managed to get runners on first and second, but Marlee single handedly got all the outs by striking out two batters and then fielding a soft grounder hit right back at her.

Lisa ran back in the dugout, and sat on the bench, but didn't bother taking off any of her gear because the bottom of their order was up. Alicia, Corrie, and Paula hadn't done much so far up at bat, so Lisa wasn't hopeful. Sarah handed her a bag of ice, which Lisa gratefully accepted although it didn't seem to be helping anymore. Her bruised and swollen hand ached constantly.

True to Lisa's prediction, Alicia flew out to left field, Corrie struck out, and Paula grounded out to Tara ending the bottom of the ninth inning quickly. Lisa curled her lip and growled. She stood up to head out to the field for the tenth inning.

"C'mon, girls," Coach Spears encouraged. "Stay strong. Stay alert. No mental mistakes, now. It's gonna come down to whoever makes the first error."

Lisa tried to close her right hand and couldn't. It was so swollen that she was having trouble throwing the ball back to Marlee.

"C'mon, Cougars," Sam yelled from the stands.

Lisa wished she could turn and wave, but she had business to attend to. The bottom of the Brookhaven order was due up.

A left-handed pinch hitter stepped into the box.

"New batter," Lisa called out to the team. Lisa was so weary she couldn't remember what the scouting report said about the batter. She looked at Coach Spears and shrugged. Coach Spears looked surprised, reached into her pocket for the scouting report, and then flashed Lisa the fastball sign three times.

Lisa nodded, and three fastballs later, the batter was out. The next batter grounded out to Marlee for the second out, but the third batter of the inning swatted one of Marlee's fastballs into left field for a single. Marlee had hung the pitch out over the plate. Lisa figured Marlee was getting tired.

"C'mon, Marlee," Coach Spears called. "Stay strong."

Marlee nodded.

Lisa blew out a sigh. Dammit, Tara was up.

"You apple pickers have a lot of stamina." Tara dug her heels into the batter's box. "I'm surprised."

"Yeah, whatever." Lisa squatted.

"Brenda's gonna steal second base on you, you know." Tara pointed toward the runner on first base.

"Doubt it." Lisa flashed the change-up sign to Marlee. Marlee shook it off, but Lisa insisted. She knew Tara wouldn't be able to resist the slower pitch, and she'd hopefully chop at it and make the third out. Normally she'd have Marlee pitch to Tara, but she was trying to arrange things so she didn't have to throw down to second base with her swollen and practically useless right hand.

Marlee threw the change-up, and the runner from first base took off for second. *Swing, swing, swing,* Lisa urged Tara in her mind.

Tara did Lisa's silent bidding and swung at the pitch. She was so far ahead of the ball that it glanced off her bat and popped up in foul territory. Lisa threw off her mask and looked up for the ball. She took three steps to her left and lunged for it. It thwacked into her mitt for the last out.

"Out," the umpire said softly.

"Damn it!" Tara slammed down her bat.

Lisa grinned at Tara and then rolled the ball to the pitcher's circle.

Marlee opened the dugout gate. "Lisa, you've lost your mind. A change-up on the first pitch with a runner stealing second?" She shook her head.

"I knew Tara wouldn't lay off it." Lisa plopped down on the bench. She took off her gear.

"You must be psychic, man." Marlee sat on the bench next to her.

Sarah came over with the bag of ice, but Lisa shook her head. She might get up to bat that inning, and she didn't want her hand to be completely frozen. As it was, her hand was almost dead.

"C'mon," Marlee smacked Lisa on the thigh. "Jeri's up."

"I'm coming." Lisa grunted and stood up. She leaned against the fence and watched Jeri get ready in the batter's box.

Jeri swung at the first pitch and sent the ball rocketing over the head of her center field counterpart.

Lisa jumped and cheered with the rest of her teammates. "Go, Jeri, go."

Jeri rounded first and headed toward second, but didn't slow down as Coach waved her on to third base. She slid into third, but there was no play, and she was safe.

Lisa bumped fists with Marlee. "A lead-off triple."

"Oh, man. We've got this. Just a long fly ball and we win the game."

Julie dug into the batter's box and swung hard, but the ball bounced right to Tara. Lisa groaned. Tara scooped the ball up cleanly and looked over to check Jeri at third base. She reached for the ball in her glove and did the unthinkable. She dropped it. Julie was safe at first, and Jeri was still safe at third.

"Yeah," Lisa yelled and pounded the chain-link fence with her teammates.

She grabbed her helmet and bat and ran to the on-deck circle. She wanted to sneak a peek at Sam, but didn't dare.

"C'mon, Johnna," Lisa called. "You're due."

Coach flashed the steal sign to Julie. If Julie could steal second base, then at least the double play wouldn't be a possibility. Julie took off for second on the pitch, but the catcher didn't even throw down. Jeri might've taken off for home if she had.

"It's all you now, Johnna," Lisa called to her teammate.

Johnna swung and hit a slow roller to the second baseman. The second baseman fielded the ball cleanly, checked Jeri at third, and threw to her first baseman. Jeri faked a few running steps toward home in order to distract the first baseman. It worked. The first baseman pulled her foot off the bag too soon and threw the ball home. Everybody was safe and the bases were loaded.

Lisa walked to the batter's box with no outs. She kept one foot out of the box to get the signs from Coach Spears. She knew there would be no other sign than to hit away, but she needed a second to calm her nerves.

She got back in the box and took a quick practice swing. Her swollen right hand made it hard to grip the bat handle, but all she needed to do was hit a long lazy fly ball so Jeri could tag up and score. The pitch came in nice and fat down the middle of the plate, but as Lisa swung, her right hand slipped off the bat. A soft grounder trickled toward Tara at shortstop. Lisa cursed and ran toward first base. Out of the corner of her eye, she watched Jeri sprint toward home plate. Tara rifled the ball to her catcher, but to Lisa's amazement, the ball sailed way over the catcher's head, and Jeri slid safely into home plate.

Lisa leaped into the air and screamed, "Ahhh," as she hit first base. Jeri had just scored the winning run. Lisa turned and ran back toward home plate to jump on the dogpile with Jeri at the bottom.

"New York State champs!" Marlee yelled and leaped on to the pile.

Somebody, Lisa wasn't sure who, threw a glove in the air. That started a chain reaction of Cougar gloves and mitts getting tossed high in the sky.

"Yee haw," Julie yelled into Lisa's face. "Can you believe it?"

"Ahhh," Lisa yelled back in answer.

The team celebration continued for several more minutes until Coach Spears gestured for them to be good sports and high five the Brookhaven team. Tara didn't even look Lisa in the eye when they met in the high-five line. Lisa simply shrugged. At least that chapter was finally finished.

Coach Spears called them together in the dugout to wait for the awards ceremony which would begin as soon as they placed the table and trophies on the infield.

Lisa was exhausted, but her adrenaline kept her going through the ceremony. Tara and the rest of her Brookhaven hoodlums became uncharacteristically quiet on their side of the field. Whatever. Who cared? The better team had won that day.

Lisa gathered up her gear and clapped Marlee on the back. "Way to go, Miss Tournament MVP."

Marlee smiled. "Thanks."

"You so deserve it. Geez, I think you could have pitched another ten innings."

"I don't know about that." Marlee shrugged with a sheepish grin, and they headed off the field toward their families. Marlee made a bee-line for her mother and Susie.

Lisa started to make her way toward Sam and her own family when she noticed William standing off to the side. She made a split second decision and walked up to him. She stuck out her bad hand and said, "Hi, I'm Lisa. I don't think we've met."

Chapter Seventeen

Surprises

LISA WALKED UP to her bio dad with her right hand outstretched.

He looked surprised, but extended his own hand. "Hello. I'm William."

Lisa grimaced when he grasped her swollen aching hand, but at least it took her mind off her pounding heart for a second. He was, after all, her biological father. "My mom told me a little about you."

"Oh, she did, did she?" He smiled. "Nice game, by the way." He gestured toward the field.

"Thanks." Lisa blew out a sigh. "That was a tough one."

"Brookhaven's a good team, but your team was better."

"Oh, yeah?" She smiled at him.

He smiled back. "Yeah, you have the better pitcher and catcher, of course, but you worked as a team more, too." He leaned closer and said in a low voice, "I don't want to alarm you, but your mother is glaring at us."

Lisa looked behind her. The entire Brown family and Sam stood behind her waiting. Her mother looked a little lost, like she didn't know how to handle the situation.

Lisa turned and said, "It's okay, Mom. I'll meet you guys in the parking lot, okay?"

Her mother nodded and then glared at William with fire in her eyes. Lisa tried not to laugh when she noticed his cheeks turning red.

Bridget ran up to her and squeezed her legs. "Hi, Weesa."

"Hi, Sweetpea. I hope you were a good girl."

Bridget didn't answer, but stared up at William.

"Oh, sorry. William, this is my littlest sister Bridget. Bridget, this is William."

He squatted down and put his hand out for a shake, but Bridget had other ideas. She released the stranglehold she had on her sister's legs and threw herself at him for a hug.

"Oh, wow." William laughed and hugged her back.

"C'mon, Bridget," her mother said sternly. "Let Lisa talk to her friend."

"'Kay. Bye Wiwim. Hurry, Weesa. Mama said we can get McDonalds."

"Okay, I'll hurry."

Lisa's father held a sleepy Lawrence Jr. in his arms, but he gave her a quick one-armed hug anyway. "Nice job, today, honey."

"Thanks, Papa."

He walked on followed by Lynnie and then Sam. Sam shot her a sympathetic glance that said she understood how hard it must be meeting her bio dad for the first time.

"Sam, wait for me in the parking lot, okay?"

Sam nodded and sent a look of soulful encouragement.

Once Sam and her family were out of earshot, Lisa sat on the lowest bleacher.

William joined her. "I bet you're wondering why I've resurfaced after all these years."

"I was kind of surprised, but Mom said you were getting married or something."

He nodded. "I know you have a lot of questions, and I want to answer them all, but..." He took a breath and sighed. "This is hard."

"It's hard for me, too."

Tears welled up in his eyes. "You turned out great, Lisa. I'm so proud of you. You were always on my mind, but every February twelfth was always an extra special day for me."

"My birthday." She looked down. "I thought about you, too."

His face brightened. "You did?" He stabbed at the tears in his eyes and cleared his throat. "Your mom thought it would be best if we waited until you were eighteen years old for us to meet, but Evelyn..." His voice caught in his throat.

"Evelyn is your girlfriend?" Lisa tried to reassure him with a gentle smile.

"Yes, she's my fiancée. I wanted to tell her all about you, but then I realized that I didn't know you at all."

Marlee came running up on them. "Lisa, Coach wants to know if you're coming back with us on the bus or going home with your folks."

"Is everybody going on the bus?"

Marlee nodded.

"Okay, it's the bus then. I'll be there in a minute."

"Cool." Marlee ran back toward the yellow Clarksonville school bus.

Lisa stood up. "I guess I have to go."

William picked up Lisa's softball bag for her, and they headed toward the parking lot together. "I have so much I want to say to you, Lisa. Can I take you to lunch one day? Once school's out for you? I'll call your mother to make sure it's okay. She can even chaperone, if she wants."

Lisa laughed. "Yes, I would like that."

She walked him to his car, an old rusty Ford Taurus. He unlocked the door and pointed to her right hand. "I'd get that x-rayed right away."

"How did you..." Lisa clutched the hand protectively.

"You winced when I shook your hand, and that lovely shade of black and blue kind of gives it away, too."

"Okay, I'll get it looked at." She turned to go. "I'll talk to you later."

"Thank you, Lisa."

She smiled at him and headed toward her family and Sam. Her father and the kids were already in the minivan, but her mother and Sam waited for her outside.

Her mother put a hand on Lisa's shoulder. "Are you okay?" She looked as nervous as an expectant father.

"Yes, Mom. I'm fine. Stop worrying. He's going to call you about taking me out for lunch to talk some more."

"Okay." She pulled Lisa in for a hug. "Oh, I thought I had another two years before this moment." She released her daughter and then hugged Sam. She headed toward the passenger side door of the van. "We'll pick you up at the high school."

"Okay, Mom." After saying goodbye to her sisters and brother, she leaned in the van's driver's side window and hugged her father. "I love you, Papa."

"Love you, too, Lisa Bear."

"Papa?"

"Yes, honey?"

"It'll be okay."

He took a deep breath. "I know. Hey, we'll see you back at the school, okay?"

"Okay."

As her family pulled away, she linked arms with Sam, and they skipped toward the bus. Coach Spears was still talking to the tournament director, so Sam didn't have to leave right away.

Lisa kicked at the pavement with her cleat. "I wish Marlee and I could go home with you guys." She nodded to Marlee and Susie leaning against Susie's car.

"Me, too." Sam reached for Lisa's right wrist and held up the swollen and bruised hand. "Show your Coach this as soon as you get on the bus."

"Okay," Lisa lied. She didn't plan on showing Coach Spears for fear of getting yelled at. She didn't want to ruin the celebration on the bus. "Hey, will I see you tomorrow?"

Sam sighed. "I wish, but I made a deal with my parents. They said I could come here today, but I had to stay home and study for final exams all day tomorrow."

Lisa sighed. "Yeah, I should, too, I guess. School sucks."

Sam laughed. "Hey, we only have two more weeks and then the summer's ours."

Lisa gazed at Sam wishing she could run her fingers through her long blond hair and then kiss her right there in front of her teammates, but she knew she couldn't. She wasn't quite ready to challenge the world, yet.

"Sam, I meant what I said behind the shed." She gestured toward the maintenance shed.

"I know." Sam looked up at her with soft eyes. "I did, too."

"Lisa. Marlee," Coach Spears called, "we're ready to go."

"Okay, Coach." Lisa turned back to Sam. "Somewhere in here," she lifted her softball bag off her shoulder, "I have an almost fully charged cell phone. We can text each other all the way home."

Sam pulled out her own cell phone. "I'm ready when you are."

Lisa gave Sam a quick hug, wishing it could be more, and then ran up the steps to the bus. She started a chorus of "We are the Champions" at the top of her lungs. Her teammates joined her at matched volume.

LISA WOKE UNABLE to move. Her shoulders and legs were sore and stiff. She blinked open her eyes and stared at the white ceiling of her bedroom. She closed them again and smiled. Everything was going so right. The championship. Sam. School almost over. Even William seemed like an okay guy. She rolled over and blinked a few more times to focus on the clock. Ten thirty.

Ten thirty? She leaped out of bed and yelled, "Mom? We're late for church." She hurried around her room and grabbed some things she needed to get ready. She threw her green and white print dress on her bed.

Her mother hurried in the room. "Honey, honey, honey. Slow down."

"Aren't we late?" Lisa stood with a pair of pantyhose in one hand and lace bra in the other.

"No. Your father decreed that the Brown family is sleeping in this Sunday."

"Oh, we are?" Lisa put her pantyhose and bra back in the drawer. "Cool."

Bridget came dashing in the room and grabbed Lisa's legs. "Mama tode me to hush up so you could sweep. Did you sweep?"

"Yes, I slept, Sweetpea. Thank you."

"Yea." Bridget jumped up and down, smashing her head into Lisa's bad hand.

"Yeow," Lisa cried out and cradled her hand.

"What happened?" Her mother came over.

"Nothing," Lisa said. "Just my hand from the Overton Corners' game."

"Last Monday?"

Lisa nodded.

"Let me see."

Lisa held up her hand, pinky side out. The swollen black and blue skin was now tinged with green.

"Lisa Ann Brown, why didn't you tell me this was such a mess?" She ran her fingers gently down Lisa's pinky and the side of her hand. "I'm taking you to the emergency room to get this looked at right after we show Coach Spears."

"Coach Spears?"

"Yes. She called for a team meeting today at noon."

"Today?" Lisa was confused.

"Yes, today. You were too busy talking with William yesterday to hear the announcement. Okay, swelling like this needs ice." Her mother turned toward the bedroom door. "I'll get you the ice, but you'd better start getting ready for your team meeting. I think Lynnie's out of the bathroom."

"Okay." Lisa scurried to the empty bathroom to get ready.

After a shower, breakfast, and twenty minutes of fairly successful practice with geometry proofs, Lisa climbed in the minivan behind Lawrence Jr. and Bridget. "Why is everybody going, Mom?"

Her mother opened the passenger door. "We're going out for lunch after your meeting."

"That okay with you, Lisa Bear?" Her father started the engine.

"Yeah. No church. Sunday lunch out. This is a special day."

Lynnie climbed in the minivan with another one of the Harry Potter books that Sam had given her three weeks before. Lisa had no idea how many of the books she had devoured already.

Lisa slid the minivan door shut. Her father pulled onto the main road, and Lisa pulled out her phone. She and Sam had texted all the way home from Binghamton, and there was another text from Sam waiting for her that morning. "How does it feel 2 b NYS champs?"

Lisa smiled and texted back, "Amazing! Can I c u 2day?" She hit the send button and waited. The cornfields whizzed by, but Lisa barely noticed. She hoped Coach's team meeting would be short, and Sam could pick her up after the family lunch, and they could —.

Her phone blipped with an incoming text.

"Can't. Got 2 study 2day. Remember?"

Lisa's shoulders drooped. "Oh, yeah. Darn. SIGH!" she texted back and then laughed.

"What's so funny?" Her mother asked.

"Oh, nothing." She held up her phone. "Just Sam."

"That was nice of her and her friend Susie to drive all that way to the tournament yesterday."

"Yeah, it was."

"Tell Sam hello from us." Her mother turned back to face front.

"Okay," Lisa said. She texted, "Parental units say hi."

There was no return text, but Lisa wasn't worried. Sam always got back to her eventually. She held the phone in her lap just in case.

Her father pulled the minivan into the parking lot of the high school, and Lisa's jaw almost hit the floor. Over a hundred people were lined up in the parking lot. The Clarksonville High School marching band stood in formation in their royal blue and white uniforms.

"Mom," Lisa demanded, "what's going on?"

"It's not every day Clarksonville has something to celebrate, honey."

"They're having a parade for us?"

Her father nodded.

"Really?" Lisa knew her mouth still hung open, but she couldn't wrap her brain around all the people.

Her father pulled the minivan into a parking spot designated for the softball players and their families. Lisa slid open the van door. Bridget grabbed her bad hand as they got out, but Lisa barely noticed. It seemed like every single one of Clarksonville's community groups had shown up for the parade. The Elks Club, the Rotary Club, the Lions Club, the American Legion, a Girl Scout troop, a Cub Scout troop, and even the Kiwanis club were there. They were all decked out and ready to march. Bridget and Lawrence Jr. were very excited, especially when they spotted the fire truck and police motorcycles.

"Oh, look Bridget, even the Dairy Princess is here." Lisa pointed to a young woman wearing a white sash, white gloves, and jewel-encrusted tiara.

Bridget waved with all her might at the Diary Princess. She squealed with delight when the princess waved back.

"I want a crown wike hers," Bridget said without taking her eyes off the pretty young woman.

"Sure, Sweetpea. We'll get you one soon."

"'Kay."

"Some girls like tiaras and others like softball hats. I bet there are even a few who like both." Lisa smirked and figured Sam was one of those.

Her father pointed to the end of the organized throng. "The softball team is lining up in the back. I think you're the last ones because you're the guests of honor today."

"Oh, geez." Lined up at the end were five convertible sports cars. Marlee waved to her from the back seat of Jeri's Mustang. Lisa waved back.

They entire Brown family walked toward the Mustang. Lisa turned to her father. "Papa, did you know about this?"

He nodded. "Coach Spears's roommate, Anne, organized the whole thing. I don't think Coach Spears knew about it."

"Oh, wow." Lisa swallowed around the sudden lump in her throat.

They reached the car, and Marlee jumped out of the backseat. "Did you know?"

"No. It's awesome, though."

"I know."

Jeri called from the driver's seat. "You're riding with us. You, me, Marlee, Julie, and Paula."

"Cool," Lisa said.

"Okay, honey," Lisa's mother said. "You're in good hands, so we're going to meet you after the parade at D'Amico's for the luncheon."

"Oh, a *luncheon*," Lisa repeated with mock aristocracy. "We're living like the Rockefellers, eh?"

Her mother nodded and then successfully herded the two older Brown children back to the minivan. Her father, holding Bridget's hand, wasn't as successful. Bridget broke free and ran back to Jeri's Mustang. Her father scurried after his youngest.

"Sweetpea, you can't come with us," Lisa said. "I'll see you at D'Amico's in a little while, okay?"

Bridget stuck out her lower lip.

"You and me'll share a cheese pizza."

Bridget continued to pout, so her father squatted down and said, "C'mon, Bridget. I'll carry you backscratcher style."

She didn't answer, but climbed on his back and threw her arms around his neck. The barest of smiles started at the corners of her mouth.

Her father hooked his arms around her legs and stood up. "C'mon, kid, start scratching." He wiggled around as if he had an itchy back.

Bridget giggled and scratched her father's back with one hand while holding on with the other. The girls in the car laughed.

Julie and Paula ran up to the Mustang. Paula carried five royal blue T-shirts. "Look what Coach's roommate got us, you guys." She held one of the shirts up and read the front. "Clarksonville Softball New York State Champions." She handed each of them a shirt.

Jeri said to Paula, "Seniors in the front. Let the children have the back."

"Cool," Paula slid into the front passenger seat.

Julie put the T-shirt on over her own shirt and hopped into the backseat with Lisa and Marlee. "This is so awesome. Did you guys know?"

Lisa, Marlee, and Jeri shook their heads. Lisa held out her good hand and bumped fists with Julie.

"Oh, man." Marlee pointed to the lead car. "Is that Coach Spears with Mayor Bradley?"

Coach Spears turned to wave at them and grinned as if wondering what she was doing in a convertible with the mayor of Clarksonville.

Lisa texted Sam, "They r having a parade 4 us. Wish u were here." She waited for a return text, but when she didn't get one, she didn't sweat it and slipped the phone in her pocket to check later. For now, it was time to celebrate. Jeri put the Mustang in drive as the parade for the Clarksonville softball team began.

Chapter Eighteen

Secrets

HUNDREDS OF PEOPLE lined Main Street as the Clarksonville celebratory parade went by. Lisa saw Reverend Owens from her church in the crowd along with a few other people she recognized from Sunday services, but an hour into the parade, she was getting tired of waving, especially with her right hand. Thank goodness they only had a couple more blocks to go before D'Amico's Restaurant. Jeri said the mayor was going to speak, and then they would have their team luncheon.

Coach Spears's roommate—nah, Coach Spears's girlfriend, Lisa decided—did a lot of work putting the whole parade together. Lisa felt happy that Coach Spears had such a loving life partner. Sam would have done the exact same thing if Lisa had been the coach. Lisa was sure of it. Lisa wondered if Coach and her girlfriend were married. Maybe they'd gone to Canada or Massachusetts or even Iowa to get married. If they did, it kind of sucked that Coach never talked about it and nobody knew.

Lisa shook the disheartening thought away and sat up taller on her high perch in Jeri's backseat. Marlee sat on one side, Julie on the other. Lisa leaned toward Marlee. "Geez, this is madness."

"You ain't kiddin'. Clarksonville loves their parades I guess." Marlee waved to a group of little girls in softball uniforms. "Looks like we're big role models or something."

"Cool." Lisa waved to the young team as well. She turned toward Julie. "Hey, there's Marcus." She pointed to their blond shorts-clad classmate in the crowd.

"I know," Julie gushed. "Isn't he cute?"

"I guess." *If you like that sort of thing.*

"He's coming over later. We're going to study for the geometry exam together."

"Oh, yeah? Wish I could crash your party." At Julie's bugged out eyes, Lisa said, "Don't worry. I won't." The look on Julie's face told her everything. "Geez," Lisa slowly pointed back and forth between Marcus and Julie, "you guys have hooked up already, haven't you?"

Julie grinned. "Well, not *hooked up* hooked up, but, yeah, we're officially going out." She hid her face behind her hands. She peeked out and said, "Let's leave it at that, though, okay?"

Lisa smiled knowingly. She twisted an imaginary key over her lips and tossed it behind her.

"Promise, okay?" Julie pleaded.

Lisa nodded.

"We're going out again next Friday."

"Oh, yeah? Another Firemen's Brass Band concert?"

Julie laughed. "No, he's taking me to the last drive-in movie theater on the planet."

"In Southbridge?"

Julie nodded.

"Why are you guys going so far away?"

They waved to a group of senior citizens. Even though it was hard to hear over the Clarksonville High School marching band, Julie leaned close and whispered in Lisa's ear, "Same reason we went to Northwood the first time. I don't want to hear any Clarksonville redneck jerks harassing us." She pulled back. "I just..."

"What?"

"I just wish the whole world was either blind or would mind their own business."

Lisa laughed. "No kidding."

They chatted for a while about prejudice and the general stupidity of the entire human race until they were almost at the restaurant. Lisa's heart skipped a beat when she saw Sam leaning against a streetlamp, her blond ponytail pulled back delectably to show the curve of her neck above her blue peasant blouse. Lisa almost jumped out of the moving car, but thought better of it and waved frantically. Sam's smile lit up the whole block. Susie was there, too, and Lisa vaguely registered Marlee waving at her. Sam hadn't told her they were coming to the parade. She obviously kept good secrets.

"That's your friend from East Valley, right?" Julie pointed to Sam.

"Yeah," Lisa said without taking her eyes off Sam. She knew her voice betrayed her, so she cleared her throat. She tried to look normal, as if the love of her life wasn't on the sidewalk waving at her, but she knew she wasn't pulling it off.

Julie stared at Lisa with narrowed eyes as if trying to figure something out. Lisa felt herself turn crimson to the roots of her jet black hair under Julie's gaze.

Julie pointed back and forth between Sam and Lisa and raised both eyebrows in question. Lisa knew it was time to fess up. She held her breath and slowly nodded. She couldn't help the smile sneaking out between her locked lips.

Julie wagged her finger in Lisa's face and said with a grin, "I guess I'm not the only one with secrets, hmmm, Brown Girl?"

Lisa closed both eyes and opened one slowly. "Yeah." She opened both. "I hope you're okay with that. I wanted to tell you..." She didn't know what else to say.

"Lisa, it's cool. It's cool. She's really pretty."

Lisa laughed and nodded in agreement.

Julie laughed with her and leaned in to whisper, "We both like blondes, don't we?"

Lisa burst out laughing and pushed Julie away good naturedly with her good hand. In front of the hardware store, she saw William holding hands with a pretty brunette woman who looked to be about his age. Lisa figured the brunette must be his fiancée Evelyn. She waved at them and said, "Hey, there's my—" She stopped herself short of saying "bio dad." Instead she mumbled, "William."

Marlee and Julie waved at them, too. Marlee asked, "Who's William? You said that was a college scout you were talking to yesterday at the fields."

"No," Lisa said, "he's an old friend of my mom's. I just didn't realize it."

"Oh, okay. That's cool." Marlee looked confused, but Lisa just looked away and waved to the people on the other side of the street.

A near miss on that one, Lisa thought and was glad she didn't have to come out twice in one parade.

Jeri parked the car behind the brick and mortar building of her family's restaurant. Lisa and Julie hopped out of the backseat on one side, Marlee on the other. Lisa clapped Marlee on the back. "Geez, who knew Clarksonville softball was such a big honkin' deal."

"This really is crazy."

Jeri and Paula caught up to them. Jeri said, "My mom and dad didn't tell me about having the team lunch here. I hope they don't expect me to work."

"Really." Paula laughed. "I can't believe none of us knew about the parade. I don't know how they pulled this off without any of us finding out."

Marlee said, "I think we were all exhausted."

Everybody nodded.

Lisa grimaced. "Geez, you guys. What if they had planned all of this and we'd lost to Brookhaven yesterday?"

"Girl," Jeri said, "how could we lose? We had the tournament MVP on our team." She punched Marlee playfully in the arm.

Marlee laughed. "And the catching goddess of the universe." Marlee punched Lisa playfully.

"With her tools of ignorance," Julie threw in.

"Her what?" Jeri asked, one hand on her hip.

Lisa laughed and rolled her eyes. "It's a long story. I'll tell you guys, later."

"Oh," Julie said, "I see my parents. I'll see you guys inside."

"Okay, White Girl."

Julie skipped off to join her parents just as Bridget came bounding up to them.

"Give me a ride, Weesa."

"Okay, Sweetpea, but it has to be tree trunk today."

"'Kay." Bridget clamped on to Lisa's right leg and sat down on Lisa's foot. Lisa stiff-legged her sister toward the front of the restaurant.

Marlee laughed. "Oh, so that's how you stay in shape."

Lisa smiled. "Yeah, pretty much."

As they emerged from behind the brick restaurant onto Main Street, cheers went up from the crowd. Coach Spears's roommate, Anne, instructed the team to gather in front of the make-shift podium set up on the sidewalk in front of D'Amico's.

Lisa stood with her teammates, Marlee to her left and Julie to her right. The lone seniors, Jeri and Paula, stood by themselves in front of them. Lisa's parents, Lynnie, and Lawrence Jr. stood in the crowd to her left, but Bridget still clung tightly to her leg. Lisa lifted her leg off the ground every now and then causing her sister to giggle. Lisa craned her neck looking for Sam, but couldn't find her in the mass of people crowding the barricaded Main Street.

Mr. D'Amico stepped behind the podium. His large frame belied the fact that he liked his own cooking. He put both arms out to his sides and said, "Welcome home, champions." This incited thunderous applause and cheers from the crowd. He gestured toward Jeri's mother. "Francesca and I would like to thank all of you for this wonderful parade and for supporting our daughter, Jerida. Oh, and the rest of the softball team, too."

Marlee laughed and playfully pushed Jeri from behind. "Hey, Jerida."

"Shut up," Jeri said, but didn't turn around.

Mr. D'Amico invited Mayor Bradley to speak, and the mayor practically leaped behind the podium. He'd probably just come from church, because he was dressed in a blue suit with a white shirt and a plain blue tie. His hair was almost completely white. Lisa pegged him to be somewhere in his sixties.

The mayor cleared his throat. "It's a proud moment for our little village of Clarksonville. We are gathered here today to honor some of Clarksonville's finest citizens. They fought hard and conquered all that challenged them."

The crowd cheered, and Lisa wanted to clap, but her hand had started to throb again. She held it up against her chest to get some relief.

The mayor went on to thank the school board, the high school principal, and the athletic director. Lisa looked around and finally caught sight of Sam in the crowd. Her breath caught in her throat. Sam was so freakin' gorgeous. *How did I get so lucky?*

Sam grinned when she noticed Lisa watching her. Lisa smiled and waved back. Sam put up one finger and then looked down for a moment. Lisa's cell phone chimed. A text message had just come in. It was from Sam. "I luv u."

Lisa hid the phone quickly, but Julie saw it. "Brown Girl, you are so caught."

"Shut up," Lisa said and texted Sam back. She typed in, "SAME!" Sam's grin got even bigger.

The applause from the crowd refocused her attention to the podium as the mayor introduced Coach Spears.

Coach Spears coughed once and grabbed on to the podium as if she were afraid she'd fall over if she didn't. "I am so overwhelmed with all of this." The crowd cheered, and Lisa smiled when Coach Spears blushed.

Coach Spears smiled. "First of all, I must thank my Anne for putting all of this together. I understand she was the mastermind behind it all." Coach Spears smiled sweetly at her girlfriend.

Lisa and the rest of her teammates hooted their approval.

Coach Spears's girlfriend smiled back and then turned to acknowledge the applause and cheers with a couple of nods.

"She's been my support for many many years, so thank-you, Anne."

"Way to go, Coach," Lisa whispered under her breath. Coach Spears had kind of just come out, but not so overtly that people would get weird about it.

It was just like she and Sam had been saying. If more people saw and heard gay people, then maybe it wouldn't be so strange and terrifying.

"And," Coach Spears continued, "I want to thank the team." She gestured to the team in front of her.

"Whoo hoo," Sam yelled loud enough for Lisa to hear. Lisa whipped her head around and scrunched up her face in a smile.

"From our two seniors down through our lone freshman, these girls worked together through thick and thin. They hung in there during two tough ones against East Valley—" Coach Spears had to wait because a chorus of boos had begun somewhere in the back.

Lisa laughed, but shot Sam an embarrassed look. Sam waved her down as if to say it was okay, and she wasn't offended.

"No, no," Coach Spears said, "East Valley has an exceptional team. We, however, were just a little more exceptional this year." The boos turned to cheers.

Coach Spears said a few more words and then handed the microphone back to the mayor. She was about to walk away, but Mayor Bradley grabbed her by the shoulders.

"Not so fast, young lady," he said. He turned toward his assistant who handed him a plaque of some sort. "By the power of the office of the mayor of Clarksonville, I am pleased and honored to give the key to the village of Clarksonville to you, Coach Dorothy Spears."

"Whoo hoo!" Lisa yelled and slapped her thigh, careful not to hit Bridget who still clung to her leg.

Coach Spears said, "Thank you, everyone." She held up the

plaque with an old-fashioned key attached to the front. "Thank you." Lisa saw the tears in her coach's eyes and squeezed her own shut. She didn't want to start crying, too.

Mr. D'Amico moved behind the podium and said, "Thank you all for coming. I would like to invite the team members and their families to come eat. *Mangia*!"

The rest of her teammates headed toward the restaurant, but Lisa, Bridget, and Marlee waited for Sam and Susie.

Lisa greeted Sam with a quick hug. She smiled at Susie. "Hey, Susie."

"Hey, Lisa. Congratulations."

"Thanks. Sorry about those boos for East Valley, you guys."

"Oh, *Dios*," Susie said. "You guys just wait until next year."

"And you," Lisa turned toward Sam. "You didn't tell me you were coming, you sneak."

Sam grinned. "It would have given away the surprise."

"So you guys knew all along?"

Sam and Susie nodded and grinned. Everyone laughed and headed toward the front door to the restaurant. Lisa's leg was getting tired, so she pulled Bridget up into a standing position. Sam reached for one of Bridget's hands while Lisa held on to the other. Lisa's family stood out front talking to Coach Spears.

"Lisa Anne Brown," Lisa's mother said sternly as she approached.

"Yes, Mom?" Why did it sound like she was in trouble? Sam, Marlee, and Susie stopped dead in their tracks wide eyed.

Her mother reached for Lisa's right hand and held it up for Coach Spears to look at. "This is what she's been hiding from all of us."

Lisa felt her face flush.

"Oh, Lisa." Coach Spears looked at the bruising. She felt around the side of Lisa's hand, and Lisa winced. "As soon as this is over, your Mom said she's taking you to the emergency room for an x-ray. You will call me as soon as you know anything. Understood?" She looked Lisa in the eye.

Lisa almost wilted under her coach's glare. "Yes. Sorry, Coach."

Coach Spears sighed and turned to Lisa's mother. "Do you have a pen and paper? Let me give you my cell phone number."

"Yes." Lisa's mother dug around in her purse and handed the requested items to the coach.

Coach Spears wrote her phone number on the paper and handed it and the pen back to Lisa's mother. "She really should go right now, but I think you're right. She's waited this long, another forty-five minutes won't matter, but please call me the minute you hear anything, okay?"

Lisa's mother sighed. "Yes, of course."

Coach Spears turned to Lisa. "In the meanwhile we need to RICE you."

"Rice?" Lisa followed her Coach into the restaurant thoroughly confused.

"It's an acronym for rest, ice, compression, and elevation. I'll send Annie to the car for an ace bandage, but I think Jeri's dad will happily give us some ice."

"Okay. Sorry, Coach."

Coach Spears headed over to her girlfriend, Anne.

Marlee smacked Lisa on the arm. "Man, that looks bad Lisa."

Susie said, "*Dios Mio, amiga.* Does that hurt?"

"Uh," Lisa hedged. "Yeah, I guess it kind of does."

Sam hooked her arm in Lisa's. "C'mon, go sit with your team. Me and Susie'll sit over there." She pointed to a remote part of the restaurant.

Before Lisa could object, Mr. D'Amico came barreling up to them. "Could this be Samantha Rose? All grown up?"

Sam blushed. "Yes. It's nice to see you again, Mr. D'Amico."

He pulled her into a smothering hug and then held her out at arms' length. "I hope your mother and father are well?"

"Yes, sir."

"Good. You tell them to come to D'Amico's, and we take care of them. Okay?"

"I will, sir. Thank you."

Mr. D'Amico headed back toward the kitchen, and Lisa turned to stare at Sam. "How do you know him?"

Sam looked at Susie as if to get help, but Susie grinned and said, "Samantha Rose Payton, I guess it's time for you to finally come out and tell these guys who you really are."

Sam grimaced, obviously uncomfortable, and hid her face in her hands.

Chapter Nineteen

Closets

AT FIVE O'CLOCK in the afternoon, Lisa, her mother, and Sam were still sitting in the emergency room at the Clarksonville-Northwood Hospital. They had been there going on three hours and were still waiting for the results of Lisa's hand x-ray.

Lisa's mother stood up. "I'm going to step outside to call your father. I'm sure he hasn't even thought about making dinner."

"Okay, Mom."

Lisa's mother headed toward the automatic sliding doors, but then stopped and looked back as if remembering something. "Samantha, will you please get me if the doctor comes out with Lisa's results?"

Sam nodded. "Yes, of course."

Once her mother was out of sight, Lisa slowly turned to glare at Sam. "Were you ever going to tell me?" This was the first moment they'd had alone since Sam's news.

Sam sighed. "Yes."

"When?"

"Soon."

The silence between them lasted for the longest twenty seconds of Lisa's life, until Sam blurted, "I was going to tell you when you came over. You'd see it all, anyway."

"But Sam—"

"I know," Sam interrupted. "I should have told you that my family owns the D'Amico's Restaurant building. I should have told you that we own half of East Valley, parts of Clarksonville, Southbridge, and Northwood, and that I live in a mansion. I should have told you that I'm really Samantha Rose Payton, heiress to the East Valley Payton's fortune."

Lisa shook her head still not quite able to wrap her brain around why Sam had kept it secret. "I can't believe you own the Payton Arena. I never put that together."

Sam simply shrugged.

"So, you're telling me that when I saw Jewel last summer, I was sitting in a building you own."

"Well, not me. My family."

"Oh, and do you own anything yourself?"

Sam grinned, and Lisa's heart fluttered, but she wouldn't give in. Sam had kept something important from her, and she didn't want to be distracted by Sam's smile, or her silky blond hair, or the pendant dangling dangerously above her cleavage. Lisa cleared her throat and looked away from Sam's blue-gray eyes, so she wouldn't get sucked in.

Sam took a deep breath. "You really want to know?"

"Yeah." Lisa snuck a peek for her mother, but the coast was still clear.

"You know that McDonald's billboard on County Road 62 just outside of Clarksonville?"

"Yeah?"

"I own that."

"A billboard?"

"Yeah. That one and a few dozen others."

Lisa knew a look of disbelief crossed her face. "Oh, geez. I remember the little sign on the bottom that says, 'Payton.' Oh, my God, and all this time it stood for Samantha Rose Payton."

"Could you not call me that?" Sam pulled her knees up and hugged them tight.

"Call you what?"

"Samantha Rose."

"Oh, sorry."

"I don't..." Sam rested her chin on her knees.

"You don't what?"

"I don't want to be *Samantha Rose*." She looked up at Lisa with pleading eyes. "I just want to be 'Sam' with you, like before. For once, I didn't want to have to be Samantha Rose Payton, dutiful daughter of Gerald and Mimi Payton. My life is so much of a dog and pony show that I'm sick of it, actually."

"Oh, yeah," Lisa spat. "It must be tough having more money than God. Geez." Lisa looked away.

Sam groaned, and Lisa felt bad instantly, but the black hole in her heart wouldn't let her give in. Lisa had been embarrassed at the restaurant in front of her friends, when Susie blindsided her with the news about Sam's wealth. According to Susie, Sam's family was East Valley royalty and Sam was its princess. When Jeri and Marlee turned to look at Lisa with accusing eyes obviously wondering why Lisa hadn't told them, she had no answer. She hadn't known herself, which made her feel incredibly stupid because Sam's family owned the building they were standing in. Even Jeri hadn't known.

Lisa's mother walked back through the automatic doors. The physician's assistant scurried up to her from behind the nurses' station.

"Dr. Sternberg sent me out here to fetch you," the physician's assistant said. "The x-rays are done."

Lisa turned to say something to Sam, but Sam sat stonily with her face hidden in her hands, so Lisa left without saying a word.

Dr. Sternberg wasn't in the examination room yet, so Lisa hopped up on the green exam table. Her mother sat in a gray metal folding chair at the foot. Lisa noticed the x-ray in the viewing box. "Is that my hand?"

Her mother didn't have a chance to answer because Dr. Sternberg breezed into the room, salt and pepper hair pulled back in a bun, white coat billowing behind her.

"Yes, it is, and," she switched on the viewing box, "you have a break right here just at the neck of the fifth metacarpal bone." She used a pencil to point to a small fracture on the x-ray below Lisa's pinky finger. "You must have clenched your fist just before the ball hit you. The force of the impact compressed the knuckle in the pinky finger which snapped the bone."

Lisa's stomach churned at the doctor's description of her injury, and she had to turn away from the x-ray.

The doctor reached for a box that the physician's assistant left on the counter near the sink. "Your injury is called a Boxer's Fracture, and it's fairly common. As long as you stay away from catching and other contact sports for a while you'll be okay. Wear this soft cast religiously, and you should heal up in six to eight weeks. Twelve weeks maximum." The doctor undid the Velcro straps on the soft cast to get it ready for Lisa's hand.

"Mom, I have softball camp in two weeks."

Lisa's mother sighed. "I know, honey. We'll figure something out."

Dr. Sternberg showed Lisa how to place her injured hand gently into the soft cast and tighten the Velcro straps. "You may want your mom to help you out at first. It's kind of tricky trying to do it with your non-dominant hand."

"Okay," Lisa said. *This sucks.*

"You can take the cast off for showers and to air it out, but I want you to wear it faithfully."

"Okay, I will. Thank you, Dr. Sternberg."

"No problem. If you don't have any questions, I've got a snake bite on its way in." She looked at them expectantly.

Her mother shook her head. "Thank you, doctor."

"Okay, then. Good luck to you, Lisa."

"Thanks." Lisa took a deep breath. Her life had seemed so perfect a mere three hours before, but now not only did she have a broken hand, but she had a broken relationship, too.

It wasn't her fault that stupid foul ball broke her hand. Lisa steeled her jaw and told herself it wasn't her fault that Sam broke her trust, either.

AFTER SAM DROPPED them off, Lisa held her new cast high in

the air in the living room. Lawrence Jr. seemed the most impressed and wanted to try it on, but their mother herded them all to the kitchen table to eat. Lisa's father had made the Brown Family specialty of hot dogs and instant mashed potatoes. Seeing the combination made Lisa even more tired because it reminded her of Sam.

Lisa sat down at the table, and just after her family said grace, her cell phone vibrated.

Sam's text read, "I wanted u 2 myself 4 a while. I didn't want 2 share u with my complicated life. Sorry." After reading the text, Lisa decided that her phone had been off, and she hadn't received it yet. She powered down her phone and let her father plop a scoop of mashed potatoes on her plate.

After dinner she excused herself to study for her English exam the very next morning. Once in her room she changed into sweats and a T-shirt. She knew she should have pulled out her backpack and opened up her English book to study, but instead dug into her top drawer for her journal. She pulled the cheap green ballpoint pen out and sighed. Where the hell was her favorite blue gel pen? She rooted around the drawer for a few more seconds, but came up empty.

She opened the journal to a new page.

> Today started out so great. Clarksonville was so proud of our softball team and Coach Spears that they threw us a parade. Hoo-daddy! Oh, speaking of "daddies," William was there with his really cute fiancée Evelyn. Mom made a tentative lunch date for me and him next Saturday. That's cool. I have so much I want to ask him, like, do I have another set of grandparents? Do they want to know me? Do I have cousins? Aunts? Uncles?

Lisa sighed and decided not to go down that road just yet. Maybe he'd volunteer information about his family when they met. They might not even want to know she existed. Kind of like he didn't seem to know she existed for sixteen years. She started a new paragraph.

> Oh, I fractured my hand in the quarterfinal game against Overton Corners on Monday (seven days ago). Geez, that sounded kind of melodramatic. To be precise, I broke the fifth metacarpal bone on the pinky finger of my right hand. I have to wear a soft cast that you Velcro on. I'm glad I don't have to wear a hard cast. Writing isn't so bad, either. I was worried about final exams this week and next, but I'll be okay, I think. Anyway, Mom made me call Coach Spears when we were on our way home. Sam drove us, but more about Sam in a minute. Coach Spears was surprised that there was an actual break. She yelled at me again for hiding it, but

c'mon! I wasn't gonna take myself out of the playoff games. We needed to win a championship, right? Shoot, Mayor Bradley even gave Coach Spears the key to the village after the parade.

Oh, speaking of the parade, I freakin' came out to Julie (White Girl) today. I didn't even mean to. Sam was on the sidewalk as we drove by during the parade, and Julie figured it out from the dumb-ass look on my face. She told me her uncle is gay, but he moved because he didn't fit into the North Country any more. She said he moved to "San Francisgay." When I burst out laughing, she laughed, too and then told me that her uncle called it that. I wonder if I'll have to move out to San Francisgay or somewhere else, so I won't get harassed. I don't know what my future holds. I don't even know what college I'm going to. I want to be a firefighter or a police officer. Do I have to go to college for that? What college is Sam going to? No, I'm not thinking about Sam yet.

But, see? Julie didn't freak out about me, because she already knew somebody that was gay. So there. My theory is correct. If straight people know at least one gay person, then it makes it so much easier for the rest of us to come out. We perpetuate our own "Tools of Ignorance" by staying in the closet. Ha! I am so philosophical tonight.

Hey, queers everywhere! Come out, come out, wherever you are. Make it easier for me, please. Geez, I'm such a hypocrite, 'cuz I don't know if I can be open and public about it, either.

Oh, Julie told me some more bummer news. She said that a long time ago it was a law (a stinking law! GEEZ!) that blacks and whites couldn't even get married. Kind of sound familiar now? Gays can't get married, either. Well, not really. I think you can go to Toronto or Boston or something to do it — even Iowa now — but the good old Federal government in the good old USA won't recognize it. Everybody gets so excited about civil unions and such. Sounds like second class status to me. Why are gay people okay with being second class citizens? Maybe 'cuz then we're not, like, the scum of the earth anymore? I think I want to hold out until marriage is real for everybody. Life is so unfair sometimes.

Okay, yeah, remember how I said the day started out great? Well, it's not ending so well. Sam and I are in a fight. Yeah, Sam is as rich as Paris Hilton. Well, maybe not, but Sam or Samantha Rose or whoever she is didn't tell me any of this. Susie laughed at me 'cuz I didn't know. I felt like such an idiot today. My heart hurts so much. How can you love someone, but feel your heart sink when you think about them?

Seems like everybody's in one kind of closet or another. Me, Sam, Marlee, Susie, and Coach Spears are all in our gay closets. Julie is in the closet about her inter-racial relationship with Marcus, and William was in the closet about my very existence. Hell, even Sam was in the closet about being rich, and she still would be if Mr. D'Amico hadn't outted her. I don't know if I can trust her now. Grrr! I don't want to think about this right now.

Lisa signed off and closed her journal. Instead of tossing it in the back of her top drawer, she stood up and pulled out the Rubbermaid step stool she kept in her closet. She stashed the journal on the top shelf under some sweaters.

She felt satisfied that she had gotten a lot of thoughts on paper, but also felt like a lot of things still weren't cleared up. She still had to have her heart to heart talk with William, she wanted to talk to Julie some more about being gay, and she needed to digest all that she learned about Sam, but before any of that, she an English final exam to study for.

She fished her English notebook out of her backpack and pulled out the handout entitled, "English – Eleventh Hour Notes." She shimmied down the bed and rested her head on the soft downy pillow. She blinked her eyes wide to try and stay focused, but the day's events got the better of her, and she couldn't keep them open anymore. The last thing she heard was Bridget flying into the room asking if she was awake. Lisa kept her eyes closed.

Chapter Twenty

There Are Ways

LISA SAT IN the front passenger seat of the family minivan watching the purple and yellow wildflowers as the car whizzed by on highway 81.

She jumped when her mother spoke. "Are you excited about softball camp?"

"Yeah." Lisa looked at her mother in the driver's seat. "Why are you letting me go, Mom? I can't do anything." She held up her broken hand in the soft cast.

Her mother laughed softly. "I know you won't get to play any softball, but the camp director said you could still be useful as a CIT."

"Counselor in Training?"

"Um hmm. And when she cut your camp fee in half, that convinced me you would still benefit from a week away from home."

"Trying to get me out of the house, eh?" Lisa grinned.

"Honey," her mother's tone was serious, "I'm proud of you for getting all A's and B's on your report card. I know how hard you worked on your studies, and I, for one, am especially proud of your B-plus in Geometry."

"I guess." Lisa knew she didn't sound very enthusiastic so she added, "I guess I knew more geometry than I thought. Julie and Marcus both got A-plusses, though."

Her mother laughed. "Well, you can't be the best at everything, but you're the best sixteen year-old daughter in the world, you know. You're a godsend when it comes to your sisters and brother. And, this week away at camp is our way of letting you have some alone time. I don't ever want you to think that Papa and I take you for granted. It's important to us that you get time for yourself."

"Thanks, Mom."

Lisa tried to sound upbeat, but couldn't find enthusiam for much of anything these days. She and Sam were still in a fight, and it had been two weeks already. Sam texted her every day, and Lisa texted back, but her responses had been minimal and non-committal. Neither one had suggested seeing the other, but now Lisa was heading off for camp, and Sam was at her summer house on Lake Bonaparte for two weeks. Geez, who owned two houses? It seemed kind of wasteful to Lisa, but what did she know? Maybe Sam had twelve houses, and maybe Sam had twelve girlfriends, too. Maybe that's why Sam never invited her over. Or, more likely, Lisa thought with a frown, maybe

Sam was too ashamed of her poor girlfriend from the poor side of Clarksonville.

Sam wasn't all that was on her mind either. Lisa still wasn't quite sure where she fit into William's life even after their lunch the Saturday before. Lisa stared out the van window. The exit for Syracuse Airport was coming up. She wished she could get on a plane and go somewhere, anywhere, so she wouldn't have to deal with any of it. She sighed and pushed her sunglasses up the bridge of her nose against the early afternoon sun.

"What's up, Lisa Bear? You're kind of quiet today. And yesterday. And the day before."

"I know, Mom. I'm sorry." She didn't know how to talk to her mother about Sam without actually coming out to her, so she said, "William wants me to go to his wedding. He wants me to be one of Evelyn's bridesmaids."

"Oh?" A hurt look crossed her mother's face, and Lisa cringed. "You didn't tell me about the bridesmaid part."

"I'm sorry, Mom. I just...I don't know if I want to go at all."

"When is the wedding?"

"Two weeks. A week after camp."

"Lisa, that's pretty close. You need to tell William and Evelyn right away, because they need to fit you for a bridesmaid dress, and there are rehearsals and such."

"Oh." She hadn't thought of that. "Hey, Mom?"

"Yes?"

"William's kind of okay. He's nice."

Her mother looked at her with a gleam in her eye. "I know. I've always thought so, but I didn't want to confuse you until you were old enough."

Lisa burst out laughing. "Mom? You wanted to confuse me when I turned eighteen?"

Her mother laughed so hard that the van swerved a little. "Oh, sorry." She caught her breath. "No. I hoped you wouldn't get confused at all when you were eighteen and mature."

"You mean I'm not mature?" Lisa crossed her eyes and let her tongue loll out of her mouth.

Her mother laughed again. "Apparently not." She blew out a sigh. "But you need to decide soon and call William from camp. I'd say sooner rather than later. Okay?"

"I will." Lisa kind of wanted to be in William and Evelyn's wedding, but wasn't sure how William's family would react to his bastard kid suddenly showing up after sixteen years. She sighed and decided not to think about it just yet.

They rode along in silence for a while until her mother said, "I wonder how Papa's doing at home with the kids."

"He's probably in shock. I can see Bridget now, pulling on his shirt begging to go to the playground."

Her mother laughed. "And Lawrence Jr. kicking his soccer ball around the house until Papa plays with him."

"What about Lynnie?"

They both laughed and her mother said, "Lynnie will be whining to stay in her room and read the Harry Potter series over again. You know she finished all those books that Sam gave her."

The mere mention of Sam's name put an immediate end to Lisa's temporary good mood. In silence, she watched a semi-tractor trailer pass them.

"Honey?" her mother asked. "Talk to me."

Lisa took a deep breath. "What?"

"C'mon. Whenever I bring up Sam's name you clam up and get moody. What happened between you two?"

Not now, Mom. The last thing she wanted to add to her troubles was a heart to heart with her mother about Sam. She wasn't in the mood to pretend that she and Sam were just friends who'd had a misunderstanding. *Is that all it was? A misunderstanding?*

"Honey?"

"Sorry." Lisa sighed. "We just..."

"You like Sam, don't you?"

It wasn't really a question. "Yeah." She didn't elaborate.

They sat in silence for a few long minutes. Lisa knew her mother was digging for something more, but she hadn't planned on coming out to her mother that day. Someday, of course, but not then. Not with so many complicated things going on in her life.

"I mean, you *really* like Sam," her mother pressed.

Lisa exchanged a silent glance with her mother, but then stared at the truck in front of them. *I don't know if I'm ready to tell you, Mom.*

"I don't want to make assumptions, so you're going to have to help me out here."

"Mom, c'mon," Lisa said in frustration. "Not today, okay?"

"If not today, when?" Her mother sighed and tapped the steering wheel with her index finger as if trying to figure out what to say next. "I want you to talk to Reverend Owens."

Lisa groaned. "Why? There's nothing wrong with me." She looked down at her hands.

"I know." Her mother put a defensive hand up. "I just want you to be sure you know what you're getting yourself into. I mean, this could be a phase. Or Sam could be taking—"

"Taking what, Mom?" Lisa whipped her head around to glare at her mother. "Sam could be taking advantage of me? Me? What the hell do I have to offer her?"

"Language, young lady."

"Sorry. Sam's got everything in the world she could ever want." Lisa sighed and sat quietly for a moment before adding, "She's not the kind to take advantage of people." Something clicked in her head, and she decided to get it over with. She braced herself and said, "Sam and I have been...Sam's my..." She sighed and scratched at the soft cast on her right hand.

"You're in love with Sam?" her mother suggested.

"Yeah." Lisa let out the breath she didn't know she'd been holding. "I'm sorry."

"Sorry for what? That you love somebody?"

Lisa nodded.

"Oh, honey. I hope your father and I haven't ever given you reason to think we'd love you less because you love a...because you love somebody. I just want you to make sure this is what you really want. This kind of lifestyle won't be easy. Talking with Reverend Owens might help you."

"What does Reverend Owens know about any of this?"

"He's a counselor for the church."

Lisa groaned. "Yeah, a marriage counselor for *straight* people." She almost choked at saying the word straight with such derision in front of her mother. She quickly added, "What if Reverend Owens tells me I'm going to hell?"

Something primal crossed her mother's face. "Then we will find someone else for you to talk to."

"So you don't think I'm going to hell because I'm gay?"

"Oh, Lisa. Don't use that word. We don't know if you're *gay*."

"How about lesbian? Or queer? Pick a label, any label. They all fit." Lisa shrugged. *But whatever label you pick, Mom, I like girls and that's the way it is.*

Her mother hesitated and then said, "Please talk with Reverend Owens before you label yourself."

"But Mom—"

"Please, honey. At least grant me that." The pleading look in her mother's eye silenced any more of Lisa's objections.

"What about babies?" her mother asked. "You always talked about having a houseful."

"I still want babies."

Her mother tapped the steering wheel, alone in her thoughts. "There are ways, I guess."

"Ways of what?"

"Having babies."

"Mom!" Lisa groaned again, but inside she smiled a little. Maybe her mother was coming to terms with her eldest daughter being gay.

"What? I want grandchildren." She smirked.

"Mom, we had this talk in fifth grade, remember?"

"We didn't have the two mommies talk, did we?" Her mother laughed. "I would have remembered that."

Lisa pulled her sunglasses down and rubbed the bridge of her nose. "So, you're okay with, you know, me and Sam?"

"Well, I still haven't quite wrapped my brain around the whole thing yet, but I will love you regardless. I do need to ask one more thing of you, though."

"What's that?"

"Be respectful around the little ones. I don't think they'll understand."

"Are you ashamed of me?" Lisa stared down at her hands.

"Oh, honey, of course not. I just need time to get used to the whole idea. I think I'll be making my own appointment with Reverend Owens."

"You will?"

"Maybe."

"Well, you may not have to."

"Why not?"

"There may not be a 'me and Sam' anymore."

"Oh?" Her mother glanced over. Lisa couldn't read the expression.

"I don't know, Mom. She's Samantha Rose Payton, East Valley royalty."

"To be honest, Papa and I felt a little self-conscious when she came over for our Memorial Day barbeque."

"You knew who she was?"

Her mother nodded. "We thought maybe you'd be embarrassed that we're just working class folks. A hair dresser and a handyman."

"I'm proud of you guys, Mom. I would never be embarrassed by you." Lisa had always admired the hard work her parents put in at their jobs. She loved the way her mother was equal parts psychologist and hair dresser with her customers. And she loved the way her father could fix anything—even mean old Mr. Muller's furnace which her father fixed for free all the time. She'd learned a lot of skills from both of her parents. From her dad she learned stuff like the difference between a ball-peen and a claw hammer. From her mom, she learned how to have patience and listen carefully to other people. *Which I think maybe I forgot.*

Lisa looked at her Mom. "Her family owns half of Clarksonville County or something, and she didn't tell me."

"And so now you feel a little betrayed?"

"Geez, wouldn't you?"

"Yes, I guess I would, too." Her mother nodded. "Maybe Sam was embarrassed."

"Yeah, maybe, because I'm not sophisticated or something. Like I wouldn't know which fork to use or whatever."

"Oh, no, honey. I meant maybe she was embarrassed to show you how she lived."

"Why?"

"Maybe she's self-conscious about how much wealth her family has that others don't."

"Like me."

"Yes, like us. You know, that was an awfully quiet car ride back from the emergency room."

"I know. Sam and I are in a fight, I guess. Susie, that's Marlee's friend, told us that Sam was stinkin' rich, and I was embarrassed, because I didn't know. Marlee was looking at me like I should have known all along. That I should have told her." The words tumbled out in one continuous stream. "I felt like the stupidest person in the world. I mean, was I so selfish that I never asked Sam about herself? Geez, was it all about me, me, me the whole time?"

"Honey—"

"I don't know, Mom," Lisa interrupted. "I'm confused. I mean, I still love her." Lisa tensed. She'd just said the word *love* and *her* in the same sentence.

Her mother cleared her throat obviously uncomfortable by Lisa's confession. "Hey, our exit is coming up. Do you want to drive the rest of the way to camp?"

"Sure." Lisa nodded. Normally she would have been excited to get more driving practice, but she couldn't find the energy. The talk with her mother had worn her out. And on top of that, her broken hand had started to ache. Her mother flicked the turn signal on and eased into the exit lane.

Lisa's phone chimed announcing an incoming text. She looked at the display. It wasn't Sam, because the number had a 516 area code. The number looked familiar, though, but she couldn't quite put her finger on it.

She clicked open the text. "r u on ur way, apl pckr? I miss u."

Lisa stared at the screen as her mind frantically tried to make sense of the message. The only person in the whole universe that called her apple picker was Tara. Lisa froze when her brain finally understood. Tara was at camp and waiting for her.

Chapter Twenty One

Trust

LISA CHECKED BEHIND her to make sure she wasn't being followed. She didn't see any sign of Tara, so she left the path and headed into the woods toward the old shooting range. She still hadn't made up her mind about going to William's wedding, so she skipped lunch to find a quiet place, away from camp and away from Tara, where she could call him.

She picked her way along the trail, and even though the summer day was warm, she shivered as the forest closed in around her. She kicked up the dry leaves and inhaled the woodsy smell, which took her right back to the summer before when Tara had first brought her out there.

Lisa managed to steer clear of Tara during her first night at camp and most of that morning. The second night, though, Tara apparently didn't like being avoided and pounded on Lisa's dorm room door. Lisa kept her door locked tight and told her to take a hike. She thanked all the gods in the universe when Coach Greer flung open her door to find out what all the ruckus was about. Lisa couldn't hear what lie Tara came up with, but as long as Tara went away, she didn't care.

Lisa breathed in the summer forest and wondered for a second if she had taken the wrong trail because she didn't remember the old shooting range being this far away from the camp. The concrete structure finally came into view, so she relaxed. Memories flooded her mind before she could stop them. Tara standing close to her in the clearing. Tara touching her. Lisa closed her eyes and remembered feeling Tara's lips on hers for the first time. She moaned out loud at the remembered softness and the urgency. No, she would not give in to the memory, and with effort opened her eyes. The Tara in her memory was a very different Tara than the one who had slammed into her during the championship game. No, that year-old memory could never be recreated.

She took a deep breath and sat on a boulder near the edge of the clearing. Before pulling out her phone, she said, "William Dowell," out loud to the forest. She smiled. If her mother had married her bio dad, Lisa's name would have been Lisa Dowell.

"And now, batting for the Clarksonville Cougars, number fifteen, Lisa Dowell, Dowell, Dowell," Lisa echoed into the quiet forest.

Wait, she thought, *William lives in East Valley now.*

"Oh, geez." She put a hand over her mouth. "I would have been an East Valley Panther. Ewww." She laughed. "I would have been Christy's catcher."

She tried not to, but couldn't help picturing herself catching for the East Valley team. She'd be wearing red and black and squatting behind the plate when Marlee got up to bat. Jeri would try to steal second base, but Lisa would snag Christy's pitch and rifle it down to throw her out.

"Out," the umpire would yell, and Jeri would slap the ground in frustration. The East Valley infield would hoop and holler, and then Sam would...

The imaginary events came to a screeching halt. Sam would have been her teammate. Lisa blew out a sigh and pulled out her phone. She scrolled down her contacts for William's phone number and hit the talk button. She desperately needed to change the subject in her mind.

"Hello?" a male voiced said.

"Hello? Is this William?" Lisa picked at the hem of her shorts.

"Yes. Who's calling?"

"Oh, it's your...it's Lisa." She wanted to say, "It's your daughter, Lisa," but that seemed like a betrayal to her real father.

They exchanged pleasantries for a few moments and then Lisa asked, "William, will everybody stare at me if I go to your wedding?"

"Well," he paused as if trying to figure out how to answer her question, "I think they might, but only out of curiosity, not judgment."

"Are you sure?"

"My closest friends and family know who you are, and so does Evelyn's family. Everybody else will just have to try and figure it out."

Lisa wanted to laugh, but she wasn't sure if she wanted to put herself through that scrutiny. "I'm not sure what I'll say if people ask me who I am."

"Well, I think honesty is the best policy. Why don't you say, 'I'm William's long lost daughter,' and then let them try and figure it out."

Lisa laughed. "What do I say when they look at me cross-eyed and ask me to explain that."

"Oh, that one's easy. Send them to me, and I'll explain it to them."

"You will?"

"Of course." He cleared his throat. "Once I got a chance to meet you, I've kind of been coming clean with everybody about it. Not that you were a secret to be kept hidden or anything, but I'm finally doing the right thing. Shoot, I'll be thirty-four next month, so it's about time I grew up and took responsibility for something."

He laughed, so Lisa did, too.

"And, Lisa?"

"Yeah?"

"You can bring your friend, Samantha Rose, to the wedding if you want."

"Okay. Thanks."

"I can't wait for you to meet my baby sister, Fran." He laughed into the phone, a bubbling carefree sound that made Lisa smile. "She and her wife, Margaret, have been married for three years now."

"Married?" Lisa wasn't sure she'd heard him correctly. Did he know? Did William know about her and Sam?

"Oh, yes. Fran and Margaret live in Boston and are legally married in Massachusetts."

"Oh."

"Lisa, it's okay. The way you talked about Sam when I took you to lunch clued me in, so don't be nervous about that, okay?"

"Okay." She swallowed hard in an attempt to disrupt the lump that had started forming. "I...thank you. Maybe I will come to your wedding after all."

"Hooray. Everyone is looking forward to meeting you, especially Fran and Margaret."

"They are?"

"Oh, yes. I told them all about you. My sister knew about your existence all along. She and Margaret are so excited to have a niece. See? You have two aunts already built in."

Lisa smiled at the prospect of having two aunts, and two gay aunts at that. "I'm looking forward to meeting them, too, then. Thanks for, um—" She wasn't sure how to thank someone for not freaking out over her being gay. She hadn't exactly come out to many people in her sixteen years of life. "Thanks for being cool about me and Sam."

He laughed. "Hey, my sister told me about herself when she was fifteen. And, you know what?"

"What?"

"You might get that little trait from my side of the family."

Lisa hadn't thought about it before. Maybe it was a genetic thing like hair and eye color. "Maybe you're right."

"Just don't tell your mother." He laughed, and she chuckled with him.

"Is Evelyn okay with me? You know, being one of her bridesmaids and all?"

"Evelyn's more than okay with it. The bridesmaid thing was her idea."

"It was?"

"Um hmm. Lisa, you're gonna love her. She knows the score about you and Sam, too. Oh, and, you know what?"

"What?"

"You're going to meet your grandparents."

Lisa inhaled sharply. She'd forgotten that she had another set of grandparents. "Are they—" The lump in her throat was back. "Are they okay with me, you know, popping up after sixteen years?"

"Yes, of course," he said softly. "They are very anxious to meet you. Like me, they thought about you all the time, especially on your birthday."

"They did?"

"Yup, we always wished the best for you, but like I told you at lunch, back when I was eighteen, I wasn't ready to be a dad. You and I were so lucky that your mother was ready to be a mom."

"Yeah." Lisa laughed. "And now she says she wants to be a grandmother."

"What?" He laughed into the phone. "Wait a few years, okay? You have some living to do first. Do you want kids?"

"Of course."

"Yes!" he said as if the Buffalo Bills had just scored a touchdown. "Listen, talk to my sister first. She and Margaret want to have kids, too and they've done a lot of research on the subject."

"Okay, I will. I can't wait to meet my new aunts and grandparents. This is going to be a little surreal. Instant family."

"Exactly. And if you bring Sam to the wedding, you'll have a support system built right in should the family get overwhelming."

"Thanks, William."

"No problem. Okay, listen, I've got to get back to work, but when you get back from camp—you're at softball camp now, right?"

"Yeah."

"Okay, when you get back from camp, give me a call, and we'll get you fitted for a bridesmaid dress. Evelyn will be so excited. She didn't give up hope and had the dress ordered for you anyway."

"She did?"

"Um hmm. We're very excited to have you in our lives, Lisa."

"Me, too."

"Okay, I've got to get going. You take care and call me whenever you want, okay?"

"I will. I'll talk to you next week."

After they hung up, Lisa closed her phone gently and grinned. Going to William's wedding might actually be fun. She was excited to meet his sister Fran and her life partner Margaret. And Evelyn, too. Lisa hadn't actually met William's fiancée yet, they had only waved to each other during the parade. And William wanted her to bring Sam. She took a deep breath for strength. Yeah, it was time. Time to call Sam and apologize for overreacting.

She stared at her phone for a moment. Asking Sam to go to the wedding with her would be like asking her on a date. Maybe it would be a way for them to start over.

Lisa kicked at a rock in the dirt and remembered Sam saying time and time again that she wanted Lisa to come to her house to meet her parents. She'd even said she wanted Lisa to meet Helene, the family nanny. *Yeah*, Lisa acquiesced, *I overreacted*. There was only one way to make it right.

Lisa slid her phone open and said, "Sam" into the mouthpiece. While the phone dialed the numbers, Lisa tapped her foot nervously on the dirt. She almost hoped Sam wouldn't pick up, so she could leave a voice mail message like a coward.

"Lisa?" Sam said in Lisa's ear.

"Hi!" Lisa said way too enthusiastically.

"Are you at camp?"

"Yeah. Are you at your summer house?" Lisa couldn't help the tingles that bubbled up as she talked to Sam.

"Yeah, we're getting ready to go sailing."

"Oh," Lisa sat up taller, "maybe I should let you go."

"No!" Sam blurted, and Lisa laughed.

"Okay. I'll stay."

"Okay."

The silence between them grew. Lisa spun around on the rock to face the shadowy forest as if talking to Sam would somehow seem less scary in comparison. She pulled her feet up on the rock and hugged her knees.

"Uh," Lisa stammered, "I just talked to William."

"Oh, you did? How is your old bio dad?"

"He's fine. I'm going to be in his wedding."

"Oh, you decided—"

"I want you to come with me," Lisa interrupted. *Oh, that was freakin' smooth.*

"You do?" Sam said. "When is it?"

"The Saturday after I get back from camp. Not this Saturday coming up, but the Saturday after that." Lisa knew she was babbling, but as she thought about possibly losing Sam, her heart couldn't bear it. She squeezed her eyes shut and hugged her knees tighter.

"I, uh, think maybe I could be available." Lisa detected a hint of teasing in Sam's voice.

Lisa's heart pounded. "You can? Are you sure?"

"Yeah. I'll just tell Coach Gellar I can't play that day."

"Oh, that's right. Summer ball started."

"Coach Gellar is over the moon about you and Marlee playing with us."

Lisa's heart smiled. It sounded like Sam maybe wanted to play ball with her. She looked at her soft cast. "Yeah, well, I'm not doing a lot of playing these days with my broken hand."

"Oh, she knows it'll be a few weeks more before you can actually play."

"At least." Lisa grinned sitting there all alone on a rock in the secluded woods. Sam wanted to play on the summer team with her.

"How is your hand, by the way?"

"Good, I think. The swelling has finally gone down completely, and it feels like it's healing."

"Oh, thank goodness."

Another awkward silence threatened, but Lisa stopped it by blurting, "Sam?"

"Yeah?"

Lisa felt her throat tighten again. "I miss you." She held her breath.

"Me, too. I miss you, too."

Lisa let out the breath. "I'm sorry. I should have trusted you."

"I'm sorry, too. I didn't know how to tell you. I mean, well, you'll see everything when you come out here. Well, not here at the summer house, although you can come here if you want, but I meant to East Valley. Where I live. Oh, God, I'm rambling." Sam laughed, and Lisa laughed with her.

"I don't know why I overreacted at D'Amico's that day," Lisa said. "I was kind of blindsided, you know? When Susie laughed at me, I kind of got my feelings hurt." She felt like a baby admitting that to Sam, but it was the truth.

"I don't think she meant to, but I'm sorry she hurt your feelings."

"That's okay. I like you so much, Sam. I just don't want to get run over again. Ever since Tara played me last summer, I'm a little shaky with trust. Once bitten, twice shy, you know?"

"Yeah," Sam said softly, "I get that. We can trust each other, can't we?"

"Yes." Lisa swallowed hard. She debated telling her that Tara was at camp, but decided to hold off for a little while. "Geez, I can't wait to see you again. Are we still, are we…"

"Yeah. Of course we are."

A hand touched her shoulder, and she jumped. She whipped around to see Tara standing right behind her, her head haloed by the noon sun overhead.

She held the phone to her chest. "You scared the crap out of me. What are you doing here?"

Tara leaned down and gestured toward the phone. "Is that Blondie?"

Lisa scowled. "Shut up." She pulled the phone back up to her ear.

"Who was that?" Sam demanded.

Tara leaned down and said, "Hey Blondie" into Lisa's phone.

Sam bellowed, "That's friggin' Tara, isn't it?"

"Sam, I didn't know she was coming to camp this summer. I swear."

Tara burst out laughing. Lisa stood up and stomped her way toward the path back to camp.

"Oh, sure, Lisa," Sam said. "You've got a lot of friggin' nerve talking about honesty and trust, and there you are at camp with that tramp."

"I'm not with her, Sam. She's just…she's just here," Lisa said weakly.

"Yeah, I'm sure she is. But, hey," Sam ranted, her voice getting louder, "since we're both being so completely honest and open now, remember my first girlfriend? Well, she wasn't that chick from Northwood. My first girlfriend was...Wait for it...Susie. Yeah, Susie Torres. Okay? Now we're both being completely honest!" Sam hung up, before Lisa could respond.

"Sam?" Lisa said weakly into the phone, even though she knew Sam was gone. She growled and whirled around to face Tara who had followed her. "You!" She stabbed a finger in Tara's direction. "Why did you have to do that?"

"What?" Tara shrugged innocently and stepped in front of Lisa.

Lisa took a step back. "You broke up with me, Tara. Why are you bothering me now?"

Tara took a step closer. "Oh, c'mon, baby." She reached out to touch Lisa's cheek.

Lisa swatted her hand away. "You stopped calling me this spring, even when I left messages for you. You didn't return any of my emails, either." She felt the white hot anger of rejection boiling in her gut. "So why, Tara, why are you so friggin' interested in me now?"

"Baby, c'mon. You live near Canada, don't you? How was I supposed to know we'd ever see each other again?"

Lisa controlled her anger, but with a lot of effort. What she really wanted to do was slap Tara across the face and storm back to the dorm. "Yeah, but you knew that last summer when we left camp. Why keep stringing me along?"

"Oh, c'mon, baby. Why so angry? It's just you and me now. We have a whole week to finish what we started. C'mon, let's go back to my room. Talk it out." Tara reached for Lisa's hand.

Lisa slapped Tara's hand away and growled, "Tara, you're sick. You *know* I've moved on. I love her." She held up her phone.

"Blondie?" Tara laughed.

"Her name is Samantha!" Lisa roared. "And she's nothing like you. She, at least, isn't shallow and transparent like you are. You never really cared about me at all, did you?" She didn't wait for Tara to answer. "No, you only cared about the conquest. We never did get all the way around those bases last summer, did we? And you can't stand that, can you?"

Tara smirked. "Yeah, whatever you say, Lisa." She dismissed her with a wave of her hand and slammed into Lisa's shoulder as she stormed down the trail toward camp.

"Oh, yeah," Lisa called after her, "that was mature, Tara."

Tara didn't turn around.

Lisa took a couple of deep breaths to calm her racing heart. She slid open her phone and hit the redial button.

Chapter Twenty Two

Have a Nice Life

IT WASN'T UNTIL Lisa had tromped all the way back to her dorm room that Sam's words sank in. "Susie was my first." Dazed, Lisa locked the door behind her and flopped onto the bed. Did Susie try to make Lisa look like an idiot at D'Amico's on purpose? Why? Was she jealous? Susie had Marlee now. It didn't make sense.

And geez, that time they all went to Northwood for dinner and then to the movies. After the movie, Susie drove them to Lake Birch. Lisa cringed when she remembered how hot and heavy she and Sam had gotten in the back seat. Susie must have heard everything. Lisa wondered if she might have taken it cooler if she'd known Susie was Sam's ex. Of course, Susie made out with Marlee in the front seat right in front of them, too, so what did it matter?

Lisa's eyes grew wider. Marlee didn't know that Susie and Sam used to go out. Did she? Lisa yanked the soft cast off her hand and flexed her cramped fingers. Her hand was healing, she could feel it, but she was getting dog tired of it. She was getting dog tired of trying to figure everybody else out, too.

With a sigh, she pulled out her phone and redialed Sam's number for the tenth time since her confrontation with Tara in the woods. The call went right to voicemail, so she left another message similar to the last nine. As calmly as she could, she said, "Sam, I'm sorry to blow up your phone like this, but I love you. Tara is nobody. I promise. You can trust me. I mean that. I don't even know what I ever saw in her. She's not the same person I thought she was, and there is no way in hell I would ever be with her again. Please, please, please believe me. I want you to come with me to William's wedding. I want..." She wasn't sure how to voice her feelings to Sam, so she took a moment to regroup. "I want us to be together, Sam. Now, next year, forever. I want—"

The phone beeped indicating that Lisa had filled up her allotted voicemail time. Lisa slid her phone closed and laughed. Maybe it was better that she had gotten cut off. She had been about to say, "I want us to have babies together and raise a family." That might have sent Sam running for the hills.

She sat up and checked her watch. She had fifteen minutes before she had to meet Coach Greer on the lower field. Thankfully Tara had been assigned to Coach Johnson, and they would be separated all afternoon.

By the time the afternoon session ended, Lisa was tired and her hand ached. Coach Greer dismissed the campers, but Lisa stayed behind to help her store the equipment in the shed behind first base. As they headed back toward the dorms, Coach Greer grumbled about somebody leaving a ball lying in left field.

"I'll get it, Coach," Lisa said and headed toward it.

"Thank you, Lisa. You're such a big help to me this summer."

"Thanks. I wish I could play, though." She held up her achy hand.

Coach Greer smiled sympathetically and gestured toward the dormitory. "Listen, I'm already late for the coaches' meeting, so I'm going to keep on going, okay?"

"Sure, Coach. I'll see you later."

Coach Greer nodded and headed toward the dorms by herself. Lisa sprinted to left field, snagged the yellow ball, and ran back with it to the equipment shed. She put the ball in the bucket and was just about to step out of the shed, when she heard Tara's voice. Panicked, she dove back behind the door praying Tara hadn't seen her. She peeked out of the crack of the slightly opened door.

Tara stood on the road talking with Brandy, the shortstop from Elmira.

"C'mon," Tara said to Brandy. "I want to show you something."

"Shouldn't we get those balls for Coach Johnson?" Brandy hesitated at the path into the woods.

"I want to show you something first. C'mon." Tara headed down the trail, and Lisa wanted to shout out to Brandy, "No, don't do it! Worst mistake of my life," but held her tongue. Brandy followed Tara like a puppy dog.

"God," Lisa mumbled, "is that what I looked like last summer? All innocent and gullible?" Lisa debated going out to spoil Tara's fun, but Brandy was a big girl and could take care of herself.

Lisa waited until they were well out of sight and then flew out of the shed and sprinted toward the dorms like she'd hit an in-the-park homerun. On the way, she decided she didn't want any part in finding out if her gaydar had been right about Brandy.

LISA SAT ON the curb waiting for her mother, her suitcases stacked behind her. A full week of camp had come and gone, and Tara had pretty much left her alone after their confrontation in the woods that Monday. The evening after the confrontation, it became painfully obvious that Tara and Brandy had hooked up. Lisa cringed watching Brandy follow Tara around. Lisa knew that she'd probably done the same thing the summer before.

Lisa thought it was ironic that Tara broke up with her because they lived too far apart. Tara must be geographically challenged because Elmira, where Brandy lived, was pretty far away from

Brookhaven, Long Island, too. And besides, Tara would be heading off to college in the fall. Lisa shook her head. What did she care what Tara did anyway? That was so past tense, it wasn't even funny. She was more concerned with her present tense, anyway. She pulled her phone out of her shirt pocket and slid it open.

"Sam," she said into the voice dial. Every day, three or four times a day, Lisa left Sam either a voicemail message or a text message. Her call went immediately to voicemail again, and she wasn't surprised.

"Hi, Sam. It's me. Again. It's noon on Saturday, and I'm sitting on the curb waiting for my mom to pick me up from camp. I think about you all the time, and I miss you. I'm sorry you don't trust me. Can we talk? Can I meet your family? Can I meet Helene? I want to know everything about you." She looked around to make sure she had privacy and said quietly, "I can't think about living my life without you, Sam." She hesitated and added, "Don't worry. I'm not suicidal or anything." She laughed softly into the phone for Sam's benefit, even though she wasn't sure if Sam still cared whether she lived or not. "And listen, I don't want to turn into a stalker chick or anything, so if you want me to stop calling you, I will. I won't like it, but I will." She hesitated for a moment and added, "I'll keep my phone on. Okay, bye."

She slid her phone shut with a sigh, and watched the other campers leaving. She rolled her eyes when she saw Tara shaking hands with Brandy's parents, just like she'd done with her own mother the summer before.

Tara headed toward Lisa as soon as Brandy's car was out of the parking lot.

"Hey, apple picker," Tara called. "You were right about her." She nodded her head in Brandy's direction.

"Are you going to dump her by letter, too?" Lisa stood up. At five foot nine, she had a three inch advantage over Tara, and she intended to wield it.

"Her? Nah. I'll text her in about a month." Tara looked Lisa up and down and then licked her lips suggestively.

"Oh, you are so gross."

Tara laughed.

In an attempt to derail Tara, Lisa said, "How'd you get my cell phone number anyway?"

"Oh, easy. Your little sister, Lynette is it?"

"Lynnie."

"Well, *Lynnie* gave me your number when I called your house Sunday. She gave it up right away. Nice kid. I like her."

Lisa nodded. She'd have to talk to Lynnie about that. "Hey, do me a favor."

"What's that?"

"Lose my number." Lisa turned away and looked for her family's van in the long line of cars.

"You're just jealous."

Lisa whipped her head around and laughed. "Of what? Brandy? You've got to be kidding. You're a predator prowling around for fresh meat. How old is Brandy anyway? Fifteen? And you're what? Eighteen?" Lisa's voice rose steadily. "You're going into college, and she just finished tenth grade for God's sake. Do you know how much trouble you could get in? You could get arrested. You want some friendly advice? Stay out of the nursery before you get yourself in trouble."

Tara smirked at Lisa as if she could care less. "I still think we'd be good together, you and me."

"Oh, please. Whatever." Lisa rolled her eyes. "You know what this is? The Rattle Syndrome."

"What are you talking about?" Tara narrowed her eyes.

"The Rattle Syndrome. A baby has a rattle, gets tired of it, and throws it away. Oh, wait, just like you threw me away. Then, someone else comes along and picks it up. When the baby sees someone else with it, she screams because she wants it back, even though she was the one who threw it away in the first place."

Tara seemed to consider it for a moment, but then said, "Oh, come on. You're telling me you weren't cheating with Blondie before we broke up?"

Lisa clamped her lips together and shook her head.

"Yeah, I doubt that," Tara said.

"Believe whatever you want." Lisa looked at the cars pulling in and was relieved to see her mother's minivan among them. She waved and grabbed the handle to one of her suitcases. She turned back to Tara. "As soon as I figure out how to do it, I'm going to block your number on my cell phone and on my home phone, too. And, if you try to contact me any other way, Tara, I'll sue you for harassment. I mean it."

Tara glared at Lisa as if trying to figure out if she was serious. Lisa glared back. The minivan pulled up to the curb in front of them. Lisa knew her mother was probably watching them, but she stood her ground.

Lisa's mother hopped out of the van and said, "Is everything okay here?" She looked from Lisa to Tara and back again.

"Yes, Mom, Tara was just leaving."

"Yeah, whatever." Tara turned on her heels. Without looking back, Tara said, "Have a nice life, Lisa. If you can find one."

"I plan to," Lisa shot back. She took a deep breath and plastered a smile on her face for her mother.

Chapter Twenty Three

Payton Valley

LISA COULDN'T MAKE sense of the dream she was having. A bird kept pecking at her shoulder. She groaned and swatted at it, but it pecked her again and then did something strange. It giggled. Slowly, Lisa rose out of the fog of sleep. She opened one eye and then the other and stared right into Bridget's face.

"Weesa, there you are. Mama said you have to get ready for church. She said, 'Now!'"

"Oh, you are so stern in the morning." Lisa, quick as lightning, picked up her little sister and pulled her onto the bed with her. A few well-placed tickles sent Bridget into a giggle storm.

"Lisa," her mother peeked into the room, "are you up yet?"

Lisa squeezed Bridget tight and yawned. "Yeah, my Bridget alarm woke me up."

Lisa tried to tickle her again, but Bridget squirmed out of her hold and ran out of the room.

"I called Revered Owens."

"You did?" Lisa sat up and stretched.

"You're meeting with him right after church."

"Today?"

"Mm hmm."

"I just got back from camp yesterday. I'm not ready."

Her mother sat on the bed beside her. "I don't think there's a way to get ready for this. Besides, you're just going to talk with him for half an hour."

Lisa sighed and willed herself not to roll her eyes. "Okay, fine." She stood up. "I have to get dressed."

Her mother headed toward the open door, but hesitated for a moment. "It'll be okay Lisa."

"I guess." Lisa was less than happy.

"Oh, I forgot to tell you. Sam called this morning." She turned away before Lisa could ask what Sam said.

Lisa leaped for her cell phone and powered it on. The chime of a text message sent her pulse racing. She took a deep breath to steel her nerves. She hoped it was a message from Sam, but then again it might be a message from Tara. She mentally crossed her fingers and looked.

"Yes!" She punched the air in victory.

She opened Sam's text message. "I'll pick u up @ ur house after church. 1:00. Ur mom ok'd it."

Lisa hit the talk button to call Sam, but it went right to voice mail. She wanted to say so much, but decided to use the KISS principle — Keep It Simple Stupid. "I'll be here waiting for you, Sam." She hesitated, not sure what else to say, so she simply added, "Okay, bye," and closed her phone.

Lisa put her phone on the bedside stand and headed for the bathroom. After that, a quick change from pajamas to church attire and a book stashed in her purse for Bridget, and she was ready for one of Reverend Owens's services. She hoped he wouldn't be long-winded during the service or when she met with him after, because all she wanted to do was hurry home, change into jeans and that red polo shirt Sam said was sexy, and pretend to wait patiently for her.

Lisa snapped Bridget in her car seat and then climbed in next to her. She wondered what she and Reverend Owens would talk about after church. Her love life was kind of private, wasn't it? Who she loved didn't seem to be anybody's business but her own. She hoped he didn't get all preachy on her. She chuckled under her breath because that's what reverends did — preach. But why worry about Reverend Owens? She was who she was, and nothing was going to change that. She'd much rather think about what Sam would say when they met later. Maybe they'd go to their usual spot at the Clarksonville Community College softball field to get reacquainted. Lisa squirmed in her seat. Three whole weeks was too long to be in a fight, too long not see each other. Sam had even missed defending her lawn darts title at their Fourth of July cookout. Lisa never wanted that much time to pass them by again.

Lisa listened half-heartedly to Lawrence Jr. babbling on about a cartoon he had watched that morning. She said, "That's awesome, Lawrence Jr." a few times, but she really wasn't listening because her brain started painting not so good scenarios about her reunion with Sam. Scenarios like Sam breaking up with her. Oh, geez, what if Sam wanted to do it in person the way Bobby broke up with Marlee? Sam would be the kind of person who would do it face to face, not over the phone. *Oh, God. Maybe that's why she didn't answer any of my calls.*

Lisa sighed and looked out the window, no longer pretending to listen to Lawrence Jr. The corn in the fields seemed to have grown two feet since the last time she'd noticed. That meant summer was well on its way. Summer was supposed to be about spending time with Sam, and it was already the middle of July. Lisa wanted a total do over.

"Lisa!" her mother said sternly.

"What?" Lisa snapped to attention.

"You're in space this morning."

"Sorry." She attempted a smile, but didn't really feel it.

Her mother sighed. "I asked if you wanted a quick bite to eat after church before having lunch at Sam's."

Lisa was confused. "Lunch at Sam's?"

Her mother's eyes softened. "Yes, honey. Sam's taking you to East Valley after your appointment with Reverend Owens."

Lisa's eyes flew open. "She is?" She sighed in relief. "Really?"

Her mother nodded.

"I guess I'll just wait for lunch at Sam's."

Her mother nodded and turned toward the front.

The church service was relatively quick, and her meeting with Reverend Owens was even quicker. While her family waited out front kicking a soccer ball around, Lisa followed the reverend to his office in the building behind the church. She wasn't sure what to expect as she sat down with him, but basically he told her that God loved all his children, and that love, in any form, was not a sin. He told her to pray for guidance and to make good choices. He said that her mother was concerned that she not make hasty decisions at age sixteen. Decisions that could affect the rest of her life. It was good advice, but did nothing to change what she already knew about herself. She was a lesbian, even though labeling herself with a much-hated word like that was difficult.

In the van on the way back home, Lisa bounced her leg up and down. Couldn't her father drive any faster? Once they got home, she flew into the house and changed her clothes. She brushed out her hair but wasn't sure if she should braid it. The doorbell rang, so the decision was made for her. She wanted to bolt to the front door and twirl Sam in her arms but forced herself to slow down and take a deep breath. She had three weeks of stupidity to undo and couldn't risk rushing it.

With a deep breath she took one last look in the mirror and was satisfied with the way her tight red polo shirt hugged her. Sam would have to be blind not to notice.

Lisa headed to the living room and stopped dead in her tracks. Sam's blond hair was pulled back into a loose ponytail, her three-quarter sleeve oxford shirt hugged her trim figure. Gold hoop earrings dangled tantalizingly near her bare neck. Lisa felt weak in the knees as she fought for composure.

Lynnie was thanking Sam again for the Harry Potter books. "You're so very welcome, Lynnie. I'll bring you some more books about magic when I bring Lisa back home later, okay?"

"Okay." The smile on Lynnie's face melted Lisa's heart.

Sam looked up and her face softened when she saw Lisa. Her lips parted slightly. "Hi," she said simply.

"Hi."

"Ready to go?"

Lisa nodded. She hugged her parents, said goodbye to Lynnie, and gently explained to Bridget and Lawrence Jr. why they couldn't go with her. On their way to the car her mother called after them. "Back by midnight, okay, girls?"

"Okay, Mom."

"Will do, Mrs. Brown."

Lisa walked up to the red Sebring, and was surprised at how nervous she was. Now that Sam was actually there, she couldn't think of a single thing to say.

Sam opened the passenger door, and Lisa got in. Sam walked behind the car and got in the driver's side. Once she was seated in the driver's seat and started the engine, Lisa's hands began to sweat.

Sam said, "So, we'll head back to East Valley, okay? Helene is making lunch for us." She smiled at Lisa, but the smile didn't quite reach her eyes as if she wasn't so sure how much to commit.

"Okay. I'm, I'm looking forward to meeting her," Lisa stammered.

Sam nodded and headed out to C.R. 62 toward East Valley. They passed the McDonald's billboard just outside of Clarksonville, and Lisa pointed. "Is that the one?"

Sam nodded, but didn't elaborate.

After a few awkward minutes of silence, Sam cleared her throat and said she'd gone to Christy's graduation ceremony and party afterward. "It was weird seeing Christy's parents at a party in their own house."

Lisa laughed. "Yeah, I bet. Jeri's graduation party was fun. We went to D'Amico's, of course."

"Of course."

Lisa patted her stomach. "I've been eating way too much Italian food lately. I'm going to have to go on the grapefruit diet soon."

Sam looked her over appreciatively. "You? No, not you."

Lisa blushed and looked down at her hands in her lap. "Thanks for picking me up. I didn't know how to get you to call me back. Sam, I honestly didn't know Tara—"

"I know," Sam interrupted quietly, "but I don't want to talk about any of that. Not yet. Let's just enjoy the ride for now, okay?"

Lisa nodded. "Okay."

The rest of the forty-five minute drive to East Valley was filled with small talk. Lisa desperately wanted to reach for Sam's hand, but didn't want to push things. Sam told her about the summer team she, Susie, and Marlee were playing on in East Valley. The coach, Coach Gellar, hoped Lisa would come out to the games to watch, so she could be part of the team while her hand healed. Other than that, they didn't discuss anything important. Lisa was with Sam, and that's all that really mattered. They drove through the town of East Valley, and just when it looked like they were heading back out into the wide open countryside, Sam put on her left blinker. Lisa hadn't even noticed the private driveway.

Sam drove up the narrow paved drive, through a thick stand of tall pines. A sturdy iron gate blocked the driveway and seemed impenetrable. She reached up to the visor and hit a button on a remote control. The gate swung open in front of them. She drove up the driveway slowly as if to give Lisa the full effect. A white mansion rose up in front of them, almost blocking out the sky.

Sam drove up the slight incline and pulled around the circular drive. "I usually park in my garage over there," she pointed to one of five garages they had passed, "but we won't be here that long. I want to drive you around East Valley and show you why people call it Payton Valley behind our backs."

"Okay." Lisa stepped out of the car and tried to steady her shaking hands. The front lawns rolled on and on as far as she could see. A large fountain surrounded by colorful flower gardens dominated the driveway. She recognized the tulips, daffodils, and roses, but not many of the other flowers. The garden was an obvious attempt to cheer up the yard, but with no sounds of children playing, dogs barking, motorcycles revving, it didn't seem like home. Even the crows cawing in the distant pines added to the loneliness.

Sam met her on the passenger side of the car. Lisa must have had a nervous look on her face because Sam said, "Don't worry. My parents are still at the vacation house in Watertown."

"Okay." Lisa hadn't even gotten that far in her thoughts. She was still trying to take in the mansion and lawns without gawking openly. Seven or eight stone steps led up to the front door. Four giant pillars, columns, or whatever they were called, made Sam's house look the Vanderbilt's house. *No, it's not a house, it's a freakin' mansion.*

"What?" Sam asked.

Oh, geez, she had said the last part out loud. "I said, 'your house is a mansion.' I've never seen one." She swallowed hard and knew that Sam saw her do it. She was so nervous that she couldn't think straight.

Sam laughed. "It's okay, Lisa," she said quietly. "This is hard for me to show you all this, too." Sam gestured up at the four columns. "That balcony is off my parents' bedroom."

Lisa couldn't help seeing that the balcony alone was wider than her entire house. The outdoor chandelier and elegant furniture looked expensive. She couldn't begin to imagine what kind of furniture was inside the house.

"And that section of the house," Sam gestured toward a one-story section to the left of the main building, "is Helene's quarters."

Helene's quarters are bigger than my house, too Lisa thought, but simply nodded.

"C'mon," Sam said, "let's go in so you can meet Helene."

Sam led the way up the stone steps, and Lisa tried to imagine Sam climbing them after school with a backpack slung over her shoulder. It was hard to picture. Sam held the front door open, and Lisa walked onto spotless marble floors. She couldn't help noticing the colossal gold chandelier overhead. Several glass tables held crystal vases of fresh flowers as if that was their only function. An antique-looking red velvet couch sat on one side. The bedroom she shared with Bridget was smaller than the entryway where they stood.

"This is the foyer," Sam said. She pointed to a room on the left. "That's the music room and Mom's sitting room where the *ladies* come for tea in the afternoon." She said the word 'ladies' with a hint of disdain. "That room further up the hall is Dad's study. To the right is the kitchen and dining room and way in the back," she pointed, "are the living room, TV room, recreation room, and fitness room. Oh, the pool is in the back with changing rooms and stuff. The tennis courts, maintenance shed, gardener's cottage—they're all out back." She swept her arm toward the back of the house.

Lisa nodded, but had gotten stuck on trying to figure out the differences between a living room, TV room, and recreation room.

"Helene?" Sam called. "I'm home."

A youngish middle-aged woman stepped out of what must have been the kitchen, and wiped her hands on a towel hanging off her apron. She was absolutely gorgeous with high cheek bones, silky blond hair piled in a bun on her head, and elegant clothes. She was *not* what Lisa had expected of a nanny.

Helene smiled. "Ah, you must be Lisa." She held Lisa at arms' length. "You are a gorgeous young lady."

Lisa felt her face get hot. "Thank you." What else was she supposed to say to that?

Helene let her go, looked at Sam, and said, "You were right. She's stunning." Helene smiled at Lisa.

"Thanks, Helene. I know."

Lisa almost choked. She put a hand up to her mouth to hide her embarrassment.

Sam smiled at Lisa and said, "C'mon, let me show you my room."

"Lunch will be ready in twenty minutes, girls." Helene headed back toward the kitchen, but then called after Sam. "Door open, Samantha Rose."

"Okay, okay." She put both hands out as if to keep Helene back. "It'll be fine, Helene."

"Nothing like the last time, okay?"

Lisa had no idea what they were talking about, but the crimson shade of Sam's cheeks told her she probably didn't want to know.

At the top of the stairs, Sam turned and pointed toward the front of the house. "That's my parents' suite, like I showed you out front. My room's in the back."

They turned right at the top of the stairs into what could only be called a wing. Sam led the way past several closed doors, but Lisa was afraid to ask what was behind them, afraid another wing of the mansion would appear. The plush red carpeted hallway seemed to go on for miles until Sam paused in front of the last doorway on the left. She gestured for Lisa to go in first.

Lisa walked in and found herself in a living room complete with floor-to-ceiling bookshelves overflowing with books. On one side of the room, a couch and two love seats formed a U in front of a wall-mounted flat screen television, DVD player, stereo, and various gaming equipment. More book shelves, a built-in desk, and two computer systems with several printers and scanners filled the other side. The room seriously looked like a room on a designer show, the kind her mother watched on HGTV.

"Where are we?" Lisa asked.

"My room."

"This is your room?"

Sam nodded. "I do my homework and stuff there," she pointed toward the desk area, "and I entertain friends in the TV area here."

"Where do you sleep?"

"Oh, in here." Sam walked over to a closed door at the far end of the room past the desk. Sam opened the door, but stood in the doorway. Lisa looked past her into a bedroom easily three times the size of her parents' master bedroom. "I can't—I'm not—" Sam sighed. "I'm not allowed to have friends in my actual bedroom, um, where my bed is." Sam's face turned a deep shade of red.

"Okay. No bedroom. Check." Lisa smiled to try to put Sam at ease, but felt her own cheeks get warm and doubted she was helping.

"It's Helene's rule. My parents don't know about the rule." Sam bit her lip and looked at Lisa for a long while, searching her eyes for something, but before she had a chance to say anything, Helene's voice shattered the quiet. Lisa jumped.

"Is your front door still open?"

Sam sighed and went to her desk. She hit a button on an intercom device. "Yes, Helene. It's fine. I promise, promise, promise. Okay?"

"Okay, I'll be in the kitchen if you need me."

Sam looked back at Lisa and rolled her eyes. "She's a little over protective." She went back and re-closed the door to the off-limits bedroom "Let's go sit, and I'll tell you everything, okay?"

"Okay." Lisa wasn't sure she wanted to hear the details, but if she and Sam were going to clear the air, it would have to be okay.

They headed toward the couch and Sam sat on one end while Lisa sat on the other. Sam kicked off her sandals and put her feet on the couch in between them. Lisa did the same, except she kicked off her sneakers.

"I've missed you, Lisa."

"Oh, God, me too." They both chuckled.

"I'm sorry I got jealous."

Lisa smiled. "I think we were both afraid of getting hurt."

Sam nodded. "You I trust. Tara not so much."

Lisa waved her off. "Oh, believe me. I handled her." Lisa told her about the Rattle Syndrome and how she called Tara a predator scouring the nursery for jailbait.

Sam put a hand to her mouth in disbelief. "And she didn't rip your head off?"

"Hey, I could have taken her, even with my bad hand." She held up the hand with the soft cast.

Sam leaned forward and reached for Lisa's hand. "How is it? Can I see?"

Lisa gestured for Sam to undo it.

"You sure?"

Lisa nodded, and Sam gently undid the Velcro straps.

"Oh, Lisa. This looks so much better." She rubbed it gently. "The bruising is all gone."

"It's so weak though. I haven't used it in three weeks."

"That's how long we've been..." Sam looked down at the hand she held in her own.

Lisa scooted closer. "We can't do that stupidity anymore, okay? I'm sorry I knee-jerked when Susie made fun of me."

Sam smiled with sad eyes. "I should have told you sooner."

Lisa started to protest, but Sam interrupted, "No, I held that back from you on purpose. Susie wasn't trying to make fun of you, either. She was trying to get me to do the right thing. She'd been on me for weeks to tell you, but I was being stubborn."

"You mean she wasn't laughing at me?"

Sam shook her head and grinned. "Uh, that's a big no there. She was laughing at me."

"Okay. I thought maybe she was jealous of me or something."

"Susie? No, when we broke up, we parted amicably. I mean, it was my idea, but later on she agreed that we make better friends. And then she met Marlee, and I met you, and that's all there is."

Lisa looked at the hand that Sam still held. "Are you ever going to let that go?"

Sam shook her head. She lifted Lisa's hand to her lips and gently kissed each knuckle. She turned the hand over, and kissed the palm. Lisa let out a sigh, it felt so good.

Sam said, "I know we're being truthful and honest with each other, so I need to tell you what happened." She gestured to her closed bedroom door.

Lisa wrapped her weak fingers around Sam's hand and kissed the palm in answer. "Not right this second, okay. I just want to be close to you for a few minutes."

"Okay, but no more secrets. I promise." Sam's eyes were vulnerable.

"Me, too. And no more knee-jerk spaz attacks for me."

"Me, either. And no more hanging up on you and not returning your calls. I'm sorry." Sam stood up, gave Lisa's hand a gentle squeeze, and let go. She ran to her front door, and swung it closed to within one inch. At Lisa's raised eyebrows, Sam said, "Hey, it's still open, isn't it?"

Lisa nodded and opened her arms. Sam filled them willingly.

Chapter Twenty Four

Kissing Girls

LISA WOKE TO the gentle sounds of her family getting ready for their day. Bridget and Lawrence Jr. loudly helped their mother in the kitchen. She couldn't hear Lynnie, but guessed she was probably in one of two places—reading in her bedroom or reading in the living room. Her father would be gone already. Summer was roofing season and the busiest time of year for him.

"Mama," Bridget whined, "I want pancakes."

"Sweetpea, all this restaurant has right now is Cheerios. Maybe your big sister will make pancakes for lunch."

"Weesa!" Bridget yelled on the run.

Lisa sat up and stretched to get ready for the three-year torpedo heading her way. Bridget threw open their bedroom door. "Weesa!"

"Bridget," Lisa admonished, "inside voice please."

Bridget threw herself on Lisa's lap and whispered, "Could we have pancakes for wunch?"

Lisa chuckled. "Sure, why not? Sam can help us make them, okay?"

"Yea." Bridget leaped up and bounced out of the room. "Mama, Weesa said we could have pancakes."

Lawrence Jr. started a chant of "Pancakes, pancakes, pancakes," to which Bridget joined in with gusto. Lynnie added her voice to the chant, and Lisa laughed. Lynnie, apparently, had been reading in the living room.

Lisa threw on her robe and headed toward the bathroom. Her mother intercepted her and pulled her into a quick hug. "The natives are restless," she whispered into Lisa's ear.

Lisa laughed. "No kidding. Are you sure you want to start work today?" Lisa hoped her cheesy grin would at least make her mother laugh. "Maybe the Split Endz Hair Salon doesn't need you for another week, maybe two."

Her mother did her best to look serious. "Not a chance." She couldn't hold the pose and laughed. "You're on your own today, Lisa Bear. Call me if you need me, but Lisa?"

"Eh?"

"Don't need me."

Lisa chuckled. "Okay." She stepped into the bathroom, but her mother lingered. "Was there something else, Mom?"

"Are you calling in reinforcements today?" Her mother's

expression grew serious.

"Yeah. Sam'll be here in about an hour. Around nine." Lisa pulled her robe tighter because she knew what her mother was going to say next.

"Just remember what we talked about."

"I know, Mom." Lisa nodded. "When you get home, Sam's going to take me to meet William and Evelyn in East Valley to get fitted for my bridesmaid dress, and after that we're going to her softball game, okay?"

"That's the summer team in East Valley you want to play on when your hand is healed up?"

Lisa nodded. "Yeah, I'm going to meet the coach and the players tonight."

"Okay." Her mother smiled. "I'm glad you and Sam patched things up. It's nice to see you happy again."

Lisa felt her cheeks heat up. "Me, too."

"Okay, go on and get your shower. I have to leave in fifteen."

"I'll be quick." Lisa closed the bathroom door.

After her shower and a power bar for breakfast, Lisa walked the kids to the playground while she waited for Sam. Bridget and Lawrence Jr. happily played Tonka trucks in the sandbox. Lynnie, of course, sat on her usual bench reading one of the Harry Potter books. Lisa lay down on the bench nearest the sandbox. She squinted into the mid-morning sun and put a hand over her eyes. She pulled her braid out from underneath her and twirled the end thinking about her reconciliation with Sam the day before, her brother and sisters faded from her consciousness.

LESS THAN TWENTY four hours before, Sam had closed the door to her front room to within an inch, technically within Helene's guidelines, and then flew back to the couch into Lisa's waiting arms. The warmth of Sam's body pressed against hers felt like home. Lisa started shaking, wanting the moment to last forever, knowing it might not, but hoping beyond hope anyway. She sought out Sam's lips and the connection between them intensified like a nor'easter slamming into the North Country. Hungrily Lisa ran her hands up and down Sam's back while they kissed. They reluctantly broke off, and Lisa blinked back tears as she opened her eyes to look into Sam's.

Sam said, "Are you okay?" She pulled Lisa's bad hand into both of her own.

Lisa nodded, not trusting her voice. The things she felt with Sam were so intense, it scared her a little.

"I love you, Lisa Anne Brown."

Lisa murmured, "Same," and pulled Sam back into another heated kiss. Sam ran a finger lightly over the palm of Lisa's hand.

Lisa's pulse raced. "Oh," she moaned, "keep that up and we're going to violate that no bedroom rule."

Sam's eyes grew wide. "Oh, sorry." She let go and scrambled to the opposite end of the couch. "Better?"

Lisa laughed. "No, but it's probably safest."

Sam smiled. "In the name of honesty," she motioned toward her bedroom, "I must now disclose what happened."

"Oh, God. Do I want to hear this?"

Sam shrugged. "I don't know, but I'm going to tell you anyway."

"Okay, if it'll make you feel better." Lisa took a deep breath.

"Honesty is our new policy, so I have to." Sam cleared her throat. "I never had any close friends growing up. I know, I know. Poor little rich girl, but believe me, I thought I did have friends. Little by little I realized that my *friends* didn't want me, they wanted Samantha Rose Payton who lived in the mansion with a swimming pool and servants and tennis courts. They wanted Samantha Rose Payton who gave kids presents on her birthday instead of the other way around. After a while I stopped trying to make friends because I didn't know if they wanted to be friends with me or with the money and the stuff." She looked up and the sheen of tears in her eyes almost broke Lisa's heart.

"But then I discovered softball," Sam continued. "I'd finally found something I was good at and didn't have to be Samantha Rose to do it. I mean some of the people were still leeches. My teammates' parents were the worst actually, but that's a tale for another day." Sam smiled. "So, anyway, Susie and Christy became my first real friends. They didn't care who my family was. Well, more Susie actually. Susie didn't care about the mansion or my convertible. She cared about me. Do you notice that we usually come over in her beat up Toyota?"

"Yeah, I was wondering about that."

"Susie is a really giving person, and I think she knew I needed someone to like me for just me and nothing else."

"She sounds like a good friend."

"She is. I'm so glad she and Marlee found each other."

"Me, too."

Sam looked down and scratched at the inside of her knee as if the next part was going to be difficult. "Anyway, last summer Susie and I realized we were both attracted to girls and we, uh..." Her cheeks turned pink. "Well, one time she dropped me off at home after one of our summer league games, and I couldn't stand being all alone in this big house, so I invited her in. I don't know where Mom and Dad were that day. Off somewhere as usual, but we went up to my room, and I kissed her for the first time. I don't think she was expecting it, but she didn't protest. So, anyway. Susie and I would steal moments away from our friends and family and, you know, we'd get closer. We'd sneak away whenever we could without Christy getting mad. Susie and Christy were so tight then, just friends of course, but tight, you know?"

Lisa sensed that Sam needed a breather so she asked, "How is Christy these days?"

"She decided on UCLA."

Lisa sat up taller. "In California?"

"Yeah, she wants to get as far away from home as possible."

"Is she gonna play ball?"

"Yeah. Well, maybe. She's going to try to walk on the team."

"That's going to be tough."

"I know, but even if she doesn't make the team, I think she'll make some new friends and be much happier."

"I hope so." Lisa nodded.

"Well, one day," Sam blew out a sigh, "Susie and I decided to hang out in there." She pointed to her bedroom door, but didn't look at it. "We had just kissed before." She looked up at Lisa and said, "Okay, I know you don't want details, so I'll just say that we were on the bed kind of fumbling around half-dressed when Helene walked in."

"Oh, geez." Lisa cringed.

"I know. We never even heard her."

"You were a little preoccupied, I guess."

"Uh, yeah." Sam pulled her knees up to her chest and hugged them. "Susie jumped off the bed and hid, but we were totally snagged. Helene turned her back, but stood right there in the doorway. She told us both to get dressed, and for Susie to go home. She said it so calmly and quietly that I thought it was the calm before the storm or something."

"You must have been scared to death."

"I was. I didn't know what Helene was going to do. After Susie left, this was in early September by the way, Helene made me sit down right here on this couch, but I couldn't look at her. I mean, come on, my nanny caught me half-naked with a girl."

Lisa shook her head in sympathy.

"Oh, I know this is weird for me to tell you this, but I keep holding things back and that's not cool. It's not fair to you. Okay, so me and Susie, well, we weren't really right for each other, you know? I broke it off with her soon after that. She wasn't happy at first, but we both agree now that we make much better friends."

A weight lifted off Lisa's shoulders, one of the weights she'd been carrying since softball camp.

Sam smiled as if she'd witnessed Lisa's weight evaporate. "Helene laid down the ground rules. No friends in the bedroom. Ever. The front room is okay if the door stays open. She said under no circumstances were my parents to find out."

"Your parents don't know about you?"

"Hell no." Sam shook her head.

Lisa felt the weight return as she realized something. "So they don't know who I am." It wasn't a question.

"No. I mean, they know I have a friend named Lisa, but that's about it."

"Does Helene know that we're more than friends?"

"Helene?" Sam nodded. "Oh, yeah. Helene knows everything. She's the one that told me to stop being an idiot and call you back."

"She did?"

"Oh, yeah. She's rooting for us, and I can tell that she likes you already, but we have to be discrete around here because Samantha Rose Payton has to be the perfect heiress to the fortune." Sam rolled her eyes and laughed.

"So are you keeping me hidden?" Lisa asked, not sure she wanted to hear the answer.

Sam got serious. "No, no way. Even though Helene wants me to keep this part of my life hidden, I have to come out to my parents one of these days. I want them to know that you're important to me. I don't want them to miss the fact that I've fallen in love for the first time in my life."

BRIDGET'S SQUEAL BROUGHT Lisa hurtling back to the present. She bolted upright on the playground bench.

"What's the matter, Sweetpea?"

Bridget pointed. The morning sun glinted off the hood of Sam's red convertible. One look at Sam behind the wheel was enough to give Lisa the courage to face anything, and that included helping Sam come out to her parents.

Sam pulled up to the playground and got out of the car. The kids ran over and hugged her tightly. She had her very own private fan club. Once Sam extracted herself from her fans, she pointed to some grocery bags in the backseat. "Guess what I brought, guys."

"What?" Lawrence Jr. reached into the backseat and reached for the bags without success.

Sam smiled. "I heard we're having pancakes for lunch, so I brought the fixings for Sam's Supersonic Strawberry Supreme Pancakes."

"You did?" Lisa raised an eyebrow. "It looks like it involves a lot of whipped cream."

Sam nodded once. "C'mon, everybody, hop in. Let's drive home and unpack this stuff." She patted Lynnie on the back. "I forgot to give Lisa some books for you yesterday, but I brought them today. They're in the trunk. They're by an author named Anne McCaffrey, and they're all about dragons and dragonriders."

"Really?" Lynnie's eyes grew wide. "Thanks, Sam." She hopped in the backseat.

Lisa's heart wrapped itself around Sam when she saw Lynnie's grin.

Once they drove home and put Sam's groceries away, they settled themselves at the kitchen table to play Candy Land.

"Lynnie," Lisa said, "can you go get a pen so I can keep track of who wins?"

"Okay." Lynnie got up and looked in the usual spots for a pen, but when she couldn't find one, ended up going to her bedroom for one. She handed Lisa a blue pen.

Lisa took it without thinking, but then realized it was her favorite blue extra fine gel pen. "Hey, this is—" Lisa cut herself short when Lynnie avoided her glance. "Lynnie, where did you get this pen?" She glared at her sister.

Out of the corner of her eye, she saw Sam shoot her a look of concern, but Lisa didn't take her eyes off her sister. "Lynnie, look at me."

Reluctantly, Lynnie looked up. Her cheeks were bright red as if she knew she had been caught red-handed.

Lisa held up the pen. "Where did you get this?"

"Sorry." She lowered her head.

"Oh, you'll be sorry when we talk about this tomorrow." Lisa threw the pen on the table in disgust. Lynnie jumped at the suddenness of it. The pen was proof enough for Lisa that her sister had been reading her journal, but Lynnie's quick apology sealed the suspicion. Lisa could only imagine how much the nine-year old understood from the things she'd written in there. She hoped Lynnie hadn't read anything about William or about kissing Sam. Oh, God, she prayed Lynnie didn't know what 'getting to second or third base' meant. She groaned under her breath.

The Candy Land game finally got underway, with Sam keeping track of the score with the discarded blue pen. After several games, the team of Bridget and Sam were declared the Candy Land champions with full bragging rights until the next Candy Land rematch. After a short trip to the playground, Lisa popped a Transformers DVD into the machine and turned it on. Bridget crawled into Sam's lap on the couch and started petting Sam's hair. "Wet's wash your hair."

"What?" Sam looked at Lisa.

"Oh, my mom has a haircutting studio." Lisa pointed toward the back of the house. "My dad remodeled the back porch for her."

"Let's do it." Sam stood up.

"No, Sam, c'mon. We don't have to wash your hair." Lisa laughed.

"No, c'mon. Let's go for it." She took the band off of her ponytail. She looked at Lynnie with a gleam in her eye. "Show me where it is."

Lynnie leaped off the floor and headed toward the back. "It's in here." She led the way and then sat down in the hair washing chair. "You sit like this and then, oh, we have to get a towel for your neck first, but then you lean back and put your neck on the edge of the sink." Lynnie demonstrated as if Sam had never been to a hair salon and had never had her hair washed before.

"Okay, I get it."

Lisa wrapped a towel around Sam's neck. "You're crazy, you know."

"I know, but it's all in fun." Sam sat down in the chair. "This is comfortable."

Bridget stood next to her and patted her arm. "Okay, wean back and put your hair in the sink."

Sam did as instructed, and Lisa turned on the sprayer.

Lawrence Jr. grabbed for the sprayer. "Me first."

Lisa pulled it back. "Hang on, let's make sure it's the right temperature. We don't want to freeze Sam on her first day here, right guys?"

"Oh, yeah." Lawrence Jr. put his hand down.

Once the water was of adequate temperature, Lisa handed the sprayer to her brother. "Don't get water in her eyes now." To Sam she said, "You'd better close them."

"Okay."

"I want to shampoo." Bridget gestured at the shampoo bottle.

Lisa pushed a squirt of shampoo into her good hand and then scooped some into Bridget's. "Be gentle. Work it in, like this." Lisa massaged the shampoo into Sam's scalp with one hand. Bridget did the same, but with both hands.

"Mmm," Sam said. "That feels nice, Bridget. Like a free massage."

Bridget giggled.

"Do you want to help, Lynnie?" Lisa asked.

Lynnie shook her head.

"Tell you what. You can rinse the rest of the soap out once Lawrence Jr. thinks he's done." Lisa reached down to wash the long length of Sam's hair. She had shampooed a lot of her mom's customers, so she was used to the task.

Lawrence Jr. checked the temperature before using the sprayer to rinse out the shampoo. "Here Lynnie." He handed the sprayer to his sister when he was done.

"Thanks." Lynnie meticulously rinsed the rest of the soap out properly.

"Do you want conditioner?" Lisa asked Sam. "This is a full-service salon."

"Sure," Sam said and dared to open one eye.

Lisa took off her soft cast and flexed her hand. It felt good. She pumped some conditioner into it and began massaging Sam's head with both hands.

"Mmm," Sam said. "That feels good."

A tingle ran up Lisa's spine. It did feel good. Too bad the kids were around, because she needed to kiss Sam. She'd have to wait until they could steal a moment alone.

The Transformers video they'd left playing in the living room grew louder as the action intensified. Lawrence Jr. bolted out of room toward the television with Bridget scampering right behind him.

"Oh, shoot," Lisa said. "Lynnie, can you go watch them while I finish this?"

"Okay." Lynnie skipped after her brother and sister.

"Are they gone?" Sam snuck a peek out of one eye.

Lisa slowed her massage. "Yup."

"Good, I want the *full*-service in this full-service salon. Kiss me."

"Oh, I see how you are." Lisa looked over her shoulder to make sure none of the kids had come back and straddled Sam on the seat.

Sam grabbed Lisa's hips, pulled her down, and held her tight. Lisa braced herself on the edge of the sink with both hands, so she wouldn't fall, and leaned down to touch her lips to Sam's. Sam moaned, so Lisa kissed her harder.

"Why do you always have to be kissing girls?" Lynnie stamped her foot.

Lisa jumped off of Sam just as Lynnie punched a stack of clean towels to the floor and ran out of the room.

"Lynnie, wait," Lisa called after her sister.

"Here," Sam said, "rinse me out quick, and I'll go talk to her, okay?"

"Okay." Lisa turned the water back on and rinsed out the conditioner. "Geez, I am in so much trouble. My mom told me specifically not to let the kids see."

"It's not your fault, Lisa."

Lisa knew it was, though. "Okay, you're good." She handed Sam a clean dry towel.

Sam wrapped her hair in the towel and dried it as she left the porch. Lisa cleaned up and then headed back to the living room.

Sam stood just outside of Lynnie's closed bedroom door. Lisa sat down on the couch with Bridget and Lawrence Jr. who were mesmerized by the Transformers movie.

"Lynnie, it's me, Sam."

"Go away." Her voice sounded far away. She was probably on her bed.

"Oh, c'mon. Don't do me like that. It's just me."

There was no answer, so Sam persevered. "Listen, Lynnie. I love your sister, and when people love each other, sometimes they kiss." Sam turned to look at Lisa and shrugged.

Lisa motioned for her to continue.

"Sometimes girls like to kiss other girls."

"Does that mean I have to kiss girls, too?" Lynnie's voice sounded closer as if she had moved closer to the bedroom door.

Sam laughed. "No, honey, it doesn't mean you have to kiss girls, too, but if you ever wanted to, it would be okay."

"I don't want to."

"Then you don't have to. Do you want to kiss boys then?"

"Eww, no way."

Sam laughed. "So, you have a few years to figure it out, right?"

Lynnie opened the door and must have nodded because Sam said, "I love your sister, and I think she loves me, too. I hope she does, anyway, so kissing her is no biggie, really. It's natural."

"Okay." Lynnie took a tentative step out of the room. "I guess."

"Hey, your mom and dad kiss each other sometimes, right?"

Lynnie nodded.

"See? It's natural." Sam smiled and then flashed Lisa a quick grin. She turned back to Lynnie. "Hey, I think it's time for pancakes. Do you want to help?"

Lynnie's face lit up. "Yeah."

"Okay, c'mon everybody," Sam announced. "It's time to make Sam's Supersonic Strawberry Supreme Pancakes."

A cheer went up in the Brown house, and they raced to the small kitchen.

Chapter Twenty Five

Weddings

LISA'S MOTHER ADJUSTED a spray of white baby's breath in Lisa's hair. Tendrils of black curls bounced in front of Lisa's shoulders.

"C'mon, Mama," Lisa's father said. "Stop fussing, so I can take a picture of the girls."

"Okay, Papa." Lisa's mother stepped back and looked at Lisa and Sam standing on the front stoop under the archway. "You girls look so beautiful."

"Mom," Lisa said, "don't start crying again, okay? We're just going to William's wedding."

"I know." Her mother smiled at them and sniffled.

Sam chuckled and looked up at Lisa standing by her side.

Lisa smiled back admiring the smooth lines of Sam's blue sundress. The color complemented her own strapless silk chiffon bridesmaid's dress perfectly. She reached up and rubbed her fingers on the new gold necklace that Sam had slipped around her neck when they were getting ready earlier.

"Smile, you two. This one's for the family album." Lisa's father pointed his digital camera at them.

Lisa smiled as her father snapped the picture and couldn't help the smile in her heart. She hadn't yet spoken to her father about being gay, but she knew that he would be okay with it, at least she hoped so.

"Okay, little ones," her father said to Lisa's sisters and brother, "go ahead and get in the picture, but do not, I repeat, do not get Lisa or Sam dirty."

"Okay, Papa." Lynnie reached for Bridget's and Lawrence Jr.'s hands. They crept up slowly as if Lisa and Sam would shatter if they got too close.

Sam put a hand over her mouth to hide her laughter, and Lisa clamped her lips shut as her siblings stood quietly in front of them. Lisa put a hand on Lawrence Jr.'s shoulder, but didn't dare look at Sam, because that would send her into a fit of giggles. They didn't have much time to spare since they had to head out for East Valley pretty soon. William and Evelyn wanted her at the church by one o'clock for the two o'clock ceremony, and they still had to drive all the way back to East Valley.

Her father lifted the camera. "Ready, everybody? Say 'hot dogs and mashed potatoes.'"

He snapped several pictures while everybody laughed, and then handed the camera to Lynnie to take a few pictures of her parents with Lisa and Sam. Sam then reached for the camera and insisted on taking some pictures of the entire Brown clan.

"Okay, guys," Lisa grabbed her clutch purse and white wrap, "we really have to go now."

"Oh, Lisa." Her mother gave her a quick hug. "Have a wonderful time." She turned and hugged Sam, too. "Take care of my baby."

Sam looked surprised by the request, but said, "I will."

Lisa hugged her mother and then hugged her father tightly. She whispered in his ear, "Papa? You know you're my number one, right?"

He nodded.

"And when it's my turn for a wedding, you'll be the one walking me down the aisle."

He cleared his throat and said, "Thank you, Lisa Bear." He nudged her toward the car. "You two had better get going." He backed up toward her mother.

"Okay. I love you guys."

They drove off in Sam's car, and Lisa looked back to see her mother lean her head on her father's shoulder. "Geez, you'd think we were eloping, the way my parents are carrying on."

"This is emotional for them. You're becoming part of your bio dad's life now. I don't think they were quite ready for that."

"I know." Lisa fanned herself. "I wish we could put the top down."

"Oh, hell no," Sam said with a laugh. "And ruin all that work your mother put into doing your hair? Not on my watch." She turned the air conditioning on in the Sebring. "So," Sam glanced at Lisa, "you never told me how the talk went with Lynnie this week."

"Oh, the talk about her reading my journal?" Lisa grunted. "It went okay, I guess. At first she didn't want to admit she'd read it, but we stared each other down for a while, and she cracked under the pressure."

"Yeah, I know that Lisa Brown glare. Especially when I'm trying to steal second base on you."

"Shut up." Lisa stuck out her tongue.

"Now that's mature."

"I know." Lisa sighed. "Anyway, Lynnie finally admitted that she'd taken my journal to her a room a couple of times."

"Just a couple?"

Lisa shrugged. "Probably more than that, but at least she admitted it. She apologized, and I think she was genuinely sorry. I've found a new hiding spot, though, just in case."

"Are you gonna let me read it?"

"My journal? No way!" Lisa grinned. "There's private stuff in there."

"About kissing girls?"

"Yeah. About kissing you."

"Ooh," Sam said suggestively, "I may have to pull the car over so I can get a better idea what you mean."

Lisa laughed and pointed toward the road straight ahead. "Keep driving, missy. No way you're messing up my makeup."

"Yes, ma'am." Sam saluted.

Lisa reached for Sam's hand and settled back for the forty-five minute drive to East Valley.

Several hours later, Lisa sat alone at her assigned table in the reception hall. She and Sam had just danced together to a fast Beatles song. Afterward, Sam escorted her back to the table, and then went up to the bar to get them some sparkling grape juice. Meeting William's family, the wedding itself, the photographs with the wedding party, and the reception afterward were becoming a blur in Lisa's mind. She was exhausted.

She smiled as she watched her new family on the dance floor. Her new instant grandparents insisted she call them by their first names, but Lisa still wasn't sure if she could call them Shirley and Manny. Manny was tall with brown hair, and had a pot belly that he couldn't quite hide behind his tuxedo jacket. Shirley, slim and tall, had a touch of gray in her deep black hair. Manny told Lisa she probably got her dark hair from Shirley. Lisa felt her cheeks get warm and then warmer still when Shirley told her she was their only grandchild. Oh, no pressure there. It was very confusing trying to figure out how these strangers fit into her life.

Lisa wished Sam would hurry back to the table. She was on information overload and needed her support system. She turned to see what was keeping her, and wasn't surprised to see her talking to an older woman at a table near the bar. Earlier that day, when they first walked into the church, Lisa got a taste of what it meant to be Samantha Rose Payton. Everybody seemed to know who she was and wanted to say hello, get a quick hug, or talk to her about something. It was like being with a celebrity. Lisa knew she was being given the rare privilege to see the other side of Sam's life. No, not Sam, but Samantha Rose Payton, and part of being Samantha Rose Payton meant being gracious and charming and talking to everyone and anyone who wanted a piece of her.

Lisa looked back at the dance floor and watched her new aunt Fran, and Fran's wife Margaret slow dance together. Fran was the spitting image of William. She was tall with short black hair, minus the mustache. Margaret's light brown hair was even shorter, almost boyish like Marlee's. They seemed to fit together perfectly in each other's arms. They looked just like every other couple slow dancing on the hardwood dance floor, except that they were two women. Lisa sighed. She wished she could slow dance with Sam, right there in front of everybody. William and his family would have been okay with it, and even Evelyn's family seemed pretty liberal about William's gay sister and her partner. No, not partner, Lisa admonished herself. Wife. Fran and Margaret were legally married. The tiniest of black clouds swarmed around her heart, and she tried hard not to let the fact that if she wanted to live in New York State when she got older, she wouldn't have the legal right to get married. It was so unfair. She didn't want to have to move away to Massachusetts or Canada. She wanted to live near her mother and father. She wanted to watch Lynnie, Lawrence Jr., and Bridget grow up. She wanted to see them go to high school, fall in love, and get married.

"Hey, brand new niece," Lisa's aunt Fran said as she sat down. "You look like you just lost your best friend."

Lisa forced herself to chuckle. "Oh, no, I'm fine. I'm just a little overwhelmed with all of this." She whirled her hand to encircle the whole room.

Aunt Margaret sat down at the table. "Breathe, Lisa, breathe," she teased. "I can only imagine what all of this is like for you."

Lisa chuckled genuinely that time. "I'm okay, really."

Once Aunt Fran and Aunt Margaret seemed satisfied that Lisa was comfortable, Aunt Fran gestured toward Sam who held the interest of the entire table of guests. "Sam is absolutely beautiful, Lisa."

"Thank you. I think so, too."

Her aunts laughed, and Aunt Fran added, "We'll keep her secret like you asked."

Lisa sighed in relief. "Thank you so much. She's not out to her parents yet, and she wants to be the one to tell them, not, you know, the whole town."

"Yeah, coming out is always a tough gig." Aunt Margaret nodded.

"Hey," Aunt Fran said, "you're lucky I broke William in for you."

"Oh, yeah, thanks for that, too. I'm glad he wanted me to be part of his life and his wedding."

"You're family, Lisa." Aunt Fran smiled and then, as if to lighten the mood, said, "Who else but family would make you wear powder blue silk chiffon?" She tugged at the hem of her bridesmaid's dress.

Aunt Margaret rolled her eyes. "Fran's not a dress person. She can't wait to get back into jeans and T-shirt."

Lisa laughed, but didn't want to say that she absolutely loved her dress and doing her hair and putting on the makeup.

"Oh," Aunt Fran gestured toward William and Evelyn who were making their rounds to various tables, "speaking of family, and the things that they do—I, for one, am really proud of my big brother for sending you money every month for all those years."

Lisa didn't know what her aunt was talking about. It must have shown on her face because Aunt Fran said, "Oh, honey, didn't you know? He never missed a month."

Lisa shook her head in confusion. As if called by Lisa's distress, Sam came back to the table and handed her a glass of sparkling white grape juice. "It's so hard to break away sometimes." She sat down, but took one look at Lisa's face and said, "Baby, are you okay?"

Lisa nodded, but didn't have a chance to tell Sam what she'd just learned from her aunt, because William and Evelyn walked up to their table.

William pulled out a chair for his new bride, and Lisa couldn't help seeing how giddy they both were about being married. She hoped one day to capture that feeling for herself.

"You're positively glowing, Evelyn," Lisa said.

Evelyn blushed and squealed, "Thanks" in a high tight voice that made everybody laugh.

Lisa turned toward William, "And you." She poked him in the arm. "You are the luckiest man alive today."

When his cheeks turned scarlet, everyone laughed again. He said, "I am, and I know it." He smiled at his new bride. Aunt Fran tapped her wine glass insistently with the edge of a knife. Soon dozens of wine glasses tapped out their frantic demand. William shrugged for the crowd and then leaned over to kiss his new bride. A cheer went up in the reception hall.

Aunt Fran leaned in front of Lisa to get her brother's attention. "William, she doesn't know about your monthly checks."

"I know." He looked at Lisa and took a deep breath. "Your mother didn't tell you, but I sent her money for you every month. Sometimes more, sometimes less, but I always sent something. She said she put every single cent into a college investment fund for you."

"She did?" Lisa asked. "I didn't know."

William smiled. "Hey, I didn't know she was doing that either until I called her a few months ago. She told me that you probably have about three full years of college already paid for."

A cheer went up at their table.

"I do?" Lisa was overwhelmed.

William nodded, and Evelyn reached up and squeezed his hand.

William laughed and added, "Well, you do if you go to a state school. If you want to go to Cornell or something then you probably have half a year paid for."

Lisa laughed, and then threw her arms around her bio dad. "Thank you, William." She pulled away and blinked back a haze of tears. "You're the luckiest guy today, but I think I'm the luckiest girl."

"We'll share him," Evelyn said.

"Okay." Lisa grinned.

Evelyn grinned, too. "Thank you so much for being in our wedding, Lisa. We're so happy to have you in our lives."

"Thanks." Lisa knew her face must be turning fifteen shades of purple over the attention. A few people that day had stared, mostly out of curiosity, and a few others had pointed, but for the most part, she'd felt accepted.

"With that," William stood up, "we must leave this pleasant company and keep circulating." He put his hand out. Evelyn placed her smaller hand in his and stood up. William turned to Lisa. "You are a beautiful young lady, Lisa."

She smiled. "Thank you. Good genes."

He started laughing. "Thank goodness you got your mom's looks." Everyone at the table laughed, but then a serious demeanor took over his face, and he looked from Lisa to Sam and back to Lisa. "Promise me you'll take care of each other."

Lisa felt her face get warm. "I promise. For the rest of my life. If she'll have me."

"Same." Sam's smoldering gaze made Lisa melt.

"Hey, girls!" William wagged a finger at them. "One wedding at a time."

More Barbara L. Clanton titles to enjoy:

Out of Left Field:
Marlee's Story
Book One in the Clarksonville Series

High school junior Marlee McAllister lives and breathes softball. She's the pitcher for the Clarksonville Cougars in the North Country of upstate New York. With the season opener approaching, Marlee and her best friend, Jeri D'Amico, go to scout their rivals, the East Valley Panthers. The Panthers star pitcher, Christy Loveland, took the All County pitching title the preceding year. It is a title Marlee covets. Marlee and Jeri settle in for the game but as the Panthers take the field, Marlee finds herself staring at Susie Torres, the Panther left fielder.

For reasons Marlee doesn't understand, she's drawn to Susie. Over the course of the next few weeks, Marlee and Susie will slowly act on their mutual attraction. But suddenly Susie pulls away without explanation and Marlee realizes it has to do with Christy. Susie won't explain the bond she and Christy share but whatever it is threatens Marlee's burgeoning relationship with Susie.

Struggling to maintain her grades, dealing with the ever-increasing estrangement from her best friend Jeri, and handling the pressures of the All County Pitching competition, Marlee also has to confront the bittersweet realities of what it might mean to be gay.

ISBN 978-1-935053-08-8
1-935053-08-6

Art For Art's Sake: Meredith's Story

High school senior Meredith Bedford is a social outcast. Her family recently moved from the Catskill Mountains to the sprawling suburbs of Albany, the capital of New York State. Shy and self-conscious about her acne scars, she stays to herself and tries to remain invisible. Her twelve-year-old brother, Mikey, has Down Syndrome and she tries hard not to blame her troubles on him. Despite verbal and sometimes physical harassment, she survives because she has her art. She was selected to be part of the elite Advanced Placement art class and is quite good at capturing the emotions of her subjects in her portraits. Art is the one thing, besides her family, that helps her cope with her outcast status. One day, at a senior class meeting, she sees Dani Lassiter, president of the senior class, captain of the lacrosse team, and knows that she must paint this enigmatic young woman. One class period later, Dani manipulates things to have Meredith as her partner for a history project. Meredith is suspicious of Dani's motives, but takes a chance. And it pays off. Meredith slowly sheds her invisibility cloak and allows Dani in - a little at a time. They explore an old Victorian house for their history project and become close with Esther and Millie, the two older women who own the house and who've lived together for about forty years. But, when Dani reveals to Meredith that she is gay, Meredith simply can't deal with the news. How had she not known? What is it that won't allow her come to terms with this unexpected news? Will Meredith control her own homophobia or will she reject the one person who had taken a chance on her and made her feel human?

ISBN 978-1-935053-14-9
1-935053-14-0

Quite An Undertaking:
Devon's Story

Devon Raines, sixteen-year old journalism nerd, was happily minding her own business when wham, her life was turned upside down. She struggled with grief when her grandmother died from a sudden heart attack. But it was at her grandmother's wake that she locked eyes with the most beautiful black girl she'd ever seen. Rebecca Washington was the most beautiful girl she'd ever seen, period. Would this beautiful dancer freak out if she knew Devon was gay and attracted? Enter Jessie Crowler, Rebecca's basketball playing best friend. Or were they only friends? Devon tried to hide her attraction for the ebony dancer, but would fate allow Rebecca to look her way? Would Jessie get in the way? Would the difference in skin color keep them apart? All this adds up to quite an undertaking in Devon's formerly quiet existence.

ISBN 978-1-935053-021-7
1-935053-21-3

OTHER REGAL CREST TITLES

Brenda Adcock	Reiko's Garden	978-1-932300-77-2
Victor J. Banis	Come This Way	978-1-932300-82-6
S. Renée Bess	Breaking Jaie	978-1-932300-84-0
S. Renée Bess	Re: Building Sasha	978-1-935053-07-1
S. Renée Bess	The Butterfly Moments	978-1-935053-37-8
Q. Kelly	The Odd Couple	978-1-932300-99-4
Lori L. Lake	Different Dress	978-1-932300-08-6
Lori L. Lake	Shimmer & Other Stories	978-1-932300-95-6
Lori L. Lake	Snow Moon Rising	978-1-932300-50-5
Lori L. Lake	Stepping Out: Short Stories	978-1-932300-16-1
Lori L. Lake	The Milk of Human Kindness	978-1-932300-28-4
Greg Lilly	Fingering the Family Jewels	978-1-932300-22-2
Greg Lilly	Devil's Bridge	978-1-932300-78-9
Megan Magill	A Question of Integrity	978-1-935053-12-5
Megan Magill	A Question of Courage	978-1-935053-24-8
Linda Morganstein	My Life With Stella Kane	978-1-935053-13-2
Cate Swannell	Heart's Passage	978-1-932300-09-3

Be sure to check out our other imprints,
Yellow Rose Books and Quest Books.

About the Author:

Barbara L. Clanton is a native New Yorker who left those "New York minutes" for the slower-paced palm-tree-filled life in Orlando, Florida. She currently teaches mathematics at a college preparatory school in the Orlando area. When she's not teaching, playing softball, tiling her floors, or evicting possums from the engine block of her RV, "Dr. Barb" plays bass guitar in a local band called *The Flounders* with her partner who plays the drums. Her ultimate dream is to one day snowbird between upstate New York and central Florida.

VISIT US ONLINE AT
www.regalcrest.biz

At the Regal Crest Website You'll Find

- The latest news about forthcoming titles and new releases

- Our complete backlist of romance, mystery, thriller and adventure titles

- Information about your favorite authors

- Current bestsellers

- Media tearsheets to print and take with you when you shop

Regal Crest titles are available from all progressive booksellers including numerous sources online. Our distributors are Bella Distribution and Ingram.

CPSIA information can be obtained at www.ICGtesting.com
Printed in the USA
LVOW080343201211